"Lucy,"

Mike said hoarsely, reaching for her hand. But she stood up abruptly, and he only caught the bottom edge of her robe.

"So," she said in a bright, false tone. "Now you know all about me." She looked down at him. Her lips trembled slightly, then tightened, and Mike could see the rest of her hidden pain in her dark, troubled eyes. *And I don't know a damned thing about* you, he knew she wanted to add.

His throat tightened with sympathy for her. How hard this must be for her. He wanted to tell Lucy the truth, tell her *something,* at least, but he didn't dare. If he told her anything, he would have to tell her everything. And how could he involve her in something that might put her in danger—might get her killed?

Dear Reader,

As always, it's difficult to know where to begin when talking about this month's Intimate Moments lineup. We've got so many wonderful books and authors that I guess the only place to start is at the beginning, with Kathleen Creighton's American Hero title, *A Wanted Man.* And I promise you'll want Mike Lanagan for yourself once you start reading this exciting story about reporter-on-the-run Mike and farmer Lucy Brown, the woman who thinks he's just a drifter but takes him in anyway. Like Lucy, you'll take him right into your heart and never let him go.

In *No Easy Way Out,* Paula Detmer Riggs gives us a hero with a dark secret and a heroine with a long memory. *Days Gone By* is the newest from Sally Tyler Hayes, a second-chance story with an irresistible six-year-old in the middle. Kim Cates makes her first appearance in the line with *Uncertain Angels,* the story of a right-side-of-the-tracks woman who finds herself challenged by a do-gooder in black leather. In *For the Love of a Child,* Catherine Palmer brings together a once-married couple and the voiceless boy whom heroine Lilia Eden hopes to adopt. When little Colin finally speaks, you'll have tears in your eyes. Finally, there's *Rancher's Choice,* by Kylie Brant, whom you met as our 1992 Premiere author. I think you'll agree that this book is a fitting follow-up to her smashing debut.

Enjoy!

Leslie Wainger
Senior Editor and Editorial Coordinator

AMERICAN HERO

A WANTED MAN

Kathleen Creighton

Published by Silhouette Books New York
America's Publisher of Contemporary Romance

ISBN 0-373-07547-2

A WANTED MAN

This edition published by arrangement with Harlequin Enterprises B. V.

Printed in U.S.A.

Books by Kathleen Creighton

Silhouette Intimate Moments

Demon Lover #84
Double Dealings #157
Gypsy Dancer #196
In Defense of Love #216
Rogue's Valley #240
Tiger Dawn #289
Love and Other Surprises #322
Wolf and the Angel #417
A Wanted Man #547

Silhouette Desire

The Heart Mender #584
In From the Cold #654

Silhouette Books

Silhouette Christmas Stories 1990
"The Mysterious Gift"

KATHLEEN CREIGHTON

has roots deep in the California soil, but has recently relocated to South Carolina. As a child, she enjoyed listening to old-timers' tales, and her fascination with the past only deepened as she grew older. Today, she says she is interested in everything—art, music, gardening, zoology, anthropology and history, but people are at the top of her list. She also has a lifelong passion for writing, and now combines her two loves in romance novels.

For two very special aunts:

My great-aunt Gwen, a truly unique and indomitable lady, who can always manage to make me laugh;

And for Mary, who is the closest thing to a sister I'll ever have, and as beloved as any sister could ever be.

ACKNOWLEDGMENTS

A special thank-you to Richard and Dawn Ellison of Lawton, Iowa, for answering all my questions and for "showing" me around their beautiful farm in words and photographs.

Thanks also to my cousin Nina and her husband, Reverend Steve Mueller, for introducing me to the Ellisons.

And to my mother, Winnie Henderson, for many things, of course, but in this case, for everything I know about pigs.

Prologue

The Chicagoan, April 29

"My Kind of Town" by Mike Lanagan

The other day one of those TV network newsmagazine shows called me the Crusading Columnist. I've been getting quite a bit of flak about that from the people I work with who know me for the craven coward I am, so I feel I should set the record straight.

I'm no crusader. It's just that I've always had a thing about bullies. There's something about big people picking on little people that makes me see red, and when that happens I have a tendency to go charging in where no sane person would.

The first time it happened I was about nine, maybe ten. It was recess time. I was out on the school playground, minding my own business, as usual, watching some little first-grade kid squirming in a headlock inflicted on him by our neighborhood bully. You know the type—he was in the same grade I was and had five-o'clock shadow. Hoxie was his name. I don't remember now whether that was his first or his last name—it didn't seem to matter. It was enough, like Rambo is enough. Or Hitler.

Normally, like everybody else of at least moderate intelligence, I steered clear of Hoxie. That day for some reason I walked over and spoke to him. I said, "Hey, why don'tcha pick on somebody your own size?"

I don't think I actually meant me—for one thing, Hoxie would have made two of me. Hoxie, however, took my suggestion to heart. He looked me up and down, shrugged and said, "Okay," and punched me square in the mouth. He didn't even have to let go of the first grader to do it.

Though it came as a great surprise to me at the time, that was only the first of many fat lips, black eyes and bloody noses I received over the course of the next few years, delivered by Hoxie and others of his ilk, usually in response to those fateful words, "Pick on somebody your own size."

Then one day I wrote an article for my junior high school newspaper describing a thriving extortion ring operating out of the boys' bathroom, and thereby discovered that the pen is indeed mightier, not to mention safer, than the sword.

I am reminded of poor old Hoxie—I wonder what penitentiary he wound up in, anyhow—because of something somebody said to me today. Cora is her name. She's black and she's poor and she's old, and she's about to lose the only home she's ever known, through no fault whatsoever of her own.

Cora made me think of that first grader on the playground, all those years ago, the way she looked at me with tears on her face and asked me, "Why? How can they get away with doing something like this? Isn't there anybody who can stop these bullies? Where's the law? Where are the people who are s'posed to protect people like me?"

Where, indeed? Trouble is, the guys who have Cora and her neighbors in a headlock aren't your ordinary playground and garden-variety bullies. Uh-uh. We're talkin' BIG. And tough. Ruthless. Mean. If these guys have hearts, they're made of stainless steel. I know their names, as well as I knew Hoxie's, and so do you. They're called Corporate Greed, Corrupt Government—oh, yeah, and Organized Crime. They're all in this together, and the game they've got going this time is called the Westside Highrise Development Project.

Now, who in his right mind, you ask, is going to step up to these guys and say, "Pick on somebody your own size"? Man, there isn't anybody their size. Not even the law.

That's what most people think. I know that's what Cora thinks. And they're wrong.

Oh, don't look at me. I'm not stupid, and I'm certainly no hero. No, the hero here is something called Truth, and it's bigger than Organized Crime, bigger than Corrupt Government, even bigger than Corporate Greed.

Now, the way I see it, a newspaper's job is to print the truth. A journalist's job is to write it, and a reporter's job is to find out what the truth is. And that, Cora, is where I come in, see, because before I got paid to write this column I was a reporter, and that's what I'll always be, in my heart of hearts. A street-pounding, door-knocking, poke-your-nose-into-everybody's-business newspaper reporter.

So my job—and I'm damn good at it—is going to be to find out all there is to know about Westside Highrise, and the development corporation that's building it—where the money came from and where it's going, who okayed the project and who's going to benefit from it. Because I know one thing. It sure isn't Cora and the other good people of Chicago.

And when I do find out, the newspaper I work for, the *Chicagoan*, is going to print it.

That's a promise. You can count on it.

So, Cora, that's why I'm saying to those bullies of yours right now, this minute, today, in front of you, Chicago and God, "Hey, pick on somebody your own size!"

Maybe I'm crazy, but I happen to believe Truth is plenty big enough, powerful enough, brave enough to take on even that ugly threesome, Organized Crime, Corrupt Government and Corporate Greed. And win.

Truth always wins, in the end.

Chapter 1

The fire was out, finally. The sirens were silent, except for one far away and safely anonymous. Hoses lay slack in the oily sludge like drowned worms after a cloudburst.

Beyond the police barricades Lanagan could see his neighbors standing around in clusters, hugging themselves and talking in hushed voices, their faces reflecting the slightly guilty mix of horror, sympathy and relief typical of witnesses to someone else's disaster. As near as he could tell it was still an hour or two until dawn. Without the orange-red glow of the flames and the opacity of smoke, the sky had returned to the milky ambiguity of big-city night. Only the smell lingered, that indescribably awful odor of house fire, made up of all the modern substances that convert to poisonous gases when they burn, and kill by what the news reports euphemistically refer to as "smoke inhalation." In his lifetime as a street reporter Lanagan had smelled that smell more times and written more of those reports than he had any wish to count or recall, but this time he had a feeling the stench was going to stay in his nostrils and in his memory for a long, long time.

"Mr. Lanagan?"

A fireman materialized before him, fine droplets of water shimmering on his slicker like sequins. Lanagan noted them with faint surprise, only then aware that it had begun to rain. He took his hand from the pocket of his trench coat and tilted the brim of his hat forward a little bit more, then straightened and pushed away from the cold, comforting support of the fire engine at his back. "Yeah."

The fireman gestured and spoke with the careful deference reserved for those recently bereaved and possibly still in shock. "You want to come with me, please? There's something over here you might want to take a look at."

Lanagan didn't want to do either of those things, if the truth were told, but before he could make any decision on the matter one way or the other, a TV news reporter trailing cables and cameraman like a large, docile dog on a leash pushed his way through the barricades and shoved a microphone into his face.

"Mr. Lanagan—Mr. Lanagan, do you think this had anything to do with your column yesterday? What's the story on Westside Development Corporation? Is it true you have documented proof of mob connections? Mr. Lanagan—"

A uniformed cop straight-armed the reporter out of Lanagan's way, another one grabbed the cameraman's arm and together they hustled the trespassing news team back across the police barricade. Lanagan hunched his shoulders, stuck his hands into his pockets and followed the fireman through the oily maze of hoses and puddles toward what had once been his town house.

A little knot of men gathered near the front of the house loosened as he approached and made room for him. His escort murmured, "Watch your step," and stood aside.

At the group's center a man wearing a dark raincoat was crouched, balanced on the ball of one foot, one forearm resting across his drawn-up knee. He extended the hand to Lanagan, who took it with a mute nod, catching a glimpse as he did so of a rawboned wrist and an inch or two of striped flannel pajama sleeve.

"Wilson—arson squad."

"Arson," Lanagan repeated without real comprehension.

Wilson regarded him for a moment with a cop's unreadable gaze. "You want to see what caused your fire? Look here." He took something—a pen—from his coat pocket and poked at the soggy ashes with it. "This here is what we call an incendiary device." He squinted up at Lanagan through the mist. Lanagan shook his head in the manner of a dazed prizefighter. "Firebomb," the arson investigator clarified patiently, almost gently.

He stood, fastidiously wiped the pen on his pants and put it back in his pocket. "Mr. Lanagan, I'm sorry to have to bother you at a time like this, but I'm going to have to ask you a few questions."

Lanagan shrugged and opened his mouth, but before he could say anything a uniformed cop he didn't recognize came shouldering in next to the guy in the raincoat, tucking away his notebook with an air of accomplishment. "Well, that checks with what the neighbors say. Couple of 'em say they heard glass breaking—little after midnight, they think—then a car apparently left in a hurry, tires squealing, etcetera. Looked out and saw the flames through the front window, here, and put in the call. Said the place went up in seconds. They were lucky just to keep it from spreading." He nodded at Lanagan, then glanced significantly upward. "Lucky you weren't in there, pal, or you'd have been a goner for sure. Guess that woulda been your bedroom, huh? Right above here?"

"Yeah," said Lanagan, automatically looking up, too. A cool spring mist sifted down onto his face from where his bed should have been. "Lucky."

Wilson gave a soft grunt that could have been sympathy. Or maybe skepticism. In Lanagan's experience, people in Wilson's line of work rarely believed in luck.

The arson investigator took out a pack of cigarettes and offered one to Lanagan, who took it gratefully. "Why weren't you in there, Mr. Lanagan?" He struck a match and lit his own cigarette, then held it out for Lanagan.

Lanagan bent to the tiny flame, wincing slightly as its heat briefly touched his face, then straightened and drew calming smoke deep into his lungs. After a moment he huffed it out in soft, ironic laughter. "I went for a walk."

Wilson's eyebrows went up. "Kind of late for a walk, wasn't it?"

"Yeah, well, I didn't feel much like sleeping." Lanagan pulled thoughtfully on his cigarette, weighing his pride, then, with a sense of utter bewilderment, added the reason. "My girlfriend had just left me." That was what he felt more than anything about all of this. Dazed disbelief. None of it could possibly be happening.

The uniformed cop gave a whistle of cheerful sympathy. "Hasn't been your night, has it?"

Lanagan's dry snort of laughter was more pain than mirth. His mind was betraying him, filling with images of Monica, whose sleek, golden body should have been naked in his bed right now, almost certainly in his arms. And who suddenly and inexplicably had packed up and *left,* left him with nothing but the note he'd crumpled and tossed on the hall table.

The note was ashes now, and so was the hall and the table. So was his bed. And so, too, would Monica have been if she hadn't picked tonight, of all nights, to walk out on him. And if he hadn't gone for a walk to try to figure out what in the hell it was he'd done wrong this time...

"Not my night," he agreed, drawing a shaken breath. It was time to pull himself together. "Let's see." He polished off the cigarette, then tossed it down in the sludge and ground it carefully out with the toe of his shoe, reflecting briefly on the small irony of that act even while he frowned with the effort it took to concentrate on the facts of the matter at hand. The cop needed answers. So did he—answers that made some kind of sense. "I got home about ten o'clock, I guess," he began, working into it slowly. "I was working late—"

He broke off suddenly as a much-delayed double take hit him, feeling as if somebody had just punched him in the belly. He rounded incredulously on the uniformed cop. "Are you telling me that somebody did this? It was a *firebomb?*"

"Looks that way," said the cop as only a cop can, utterly without inflection. Lanagan just stood there and swore, softly and with feeling.

Wilson tossed his cigarette after Lanagan's, but didn't bother to step on it. "Worked late, huh? Whereabouts was that?"

Lanagan responded vaguely, "Uh, the *Chicagoan* Tower." *Impossible. This is all impossible.* "I was doing some work on my column for day after tomorrow—"

The cop snapped his fingers and suddenly became human. "Hey, you're *Mike* Lanagan, the columnist, right? Oh, man, I read you all the time. Hey, that one yesterday was really something. You got guts, you know that? I mean, taking on city hall *and* the mob—"

Wilson, obviously less impressed, or less easily distracted, interrupted patiently, "And what time would you say you left for this walk of yours?"

"I don't know..." Lanagan swore again under his breath and rubbed at his temples. "Maybe eleven, eleven-thirty."

"You have a car?"

"Yeah, sure."

"Where is it?"

"Now? It's right there, across the street, where I always park. These row houses don't have garages."

"So anybody might have pretty good reason to think you were at home." Wilson's voice was silky casual. He took out his cigarettes and again offered them politely to Lanagan. "You leave a light on when you went out?"

Lanagan took a second cigarette with a steady hand, then just held it, ignoring Wilson's proffered match. Both his fingers and his lips had gone numb. "Yeah," he mumbled, "I did."

Nobody said anything. Lanagan stood rock still with the unlighted cigarette halfway to his mouth, listening to everything they weren't saying, while around him the fire fighters went about their business of mopping and packing up, and the mist dampened his hat and the shoulders of his trench coat. He didn't feel the mist at all, but suddenly he felt cold clear through to his insides.

"You appear to have made a serious enemy, Mr. Lanagan." Wilson's soft voice was matter-of-fact, but not without concern. He eyed him sideways, eyes narrowed behind a curl of smoke. "Any idea who that might be?"

Lanagan shook his head; his mind was blank. The uniformed cop snorted. "You kiddin' me? Want a list? After that stuff you been writing, threatening to blow the whistle on everybody from the mayor to the Mafia? Hey, man, if I had enemies like you've got enemies, I think I'd be making serious plans to leave town. Maybe for good."

"I didn't expect this," Lanagan muttered, half to himself. "Geez, not so soon." He'd only gotten the files in his hands today, just this afternoon. They were still in his briefcase. He hadn't even—

He hardly heard the arson investigator's flat, practical voice telling him what he was supposed to do next, barely felt the hand on his elbow, guiding him back through the rubble, out onto the wet, soot-gritty sidewalk. The reporters had gone to file their stories, probably too late for the morning edition. His neighbors had gone home to bed. The fire trucks were coming to life one by one and roaring away down the silent street between rows of glistening cars and the gently dripping canopy of new-leafed trees. It seemed very quiet all of a sudden.

"You have your car keys?" It was Wilson again, blunt and businesslike, watching him with narrow-eyed concern over his dangling cigarette. "Or did you leave them in there?" He jerked his head backward, toward the gaping hole in the row of town houses. Like a missing tooth, thought Lanagan.

He felt a moment's panic as he clutched at his pockets, then a wash of relief. "Nope," he mumbled. "Got 'em."

"Wallet? Credit cards?"

Lanagan patted his hip. "Right here." His voice was hoarse, gritty as the sidewalk under his feet. It had suddenly hit him that all he had left in the world was what he had in his pockets, and on his back. And in his car. That was something, at least. He still had his car, and his briefcase safely locked in the trunk.

"You're in great shape," Wilson said comfortingly, clapping him on the shoulder. "Go check into a hotel—get some sleep. Come see me tomorrow, make your statement and we'll see what we can do to catch the ones who did this."

"Right," said Lanagan. He was standing beside his car, looking without recognition at the keys in his hand. With careful concentration he inserted them into the lock and opened the door. He took off his hat and tossed it on the back seat, settled himself behind the wheel and inserted the keys into the ignition. Turned the key and listened to the engine fire. He drew a long, steadying breath.

Yes. At least he still had his car. And his briefcase, his precious briefcase, which he'd brought home optimistically thinking he'd get into those files tonight, but had left locked in the trunk because on the way home he'd started thinking about Monica, and how he'd been neglecting her lately, and how long it had been since they'd made love. Getting his hands on those files from the city planning commission had been a major triumph, and the success, the heady sense of power had put him in an amorous mood. It seemed a long time ago, now.

Wilson leaned down to him, one hand on the top of the car, the other on the open door. "Take care now, you hear?"

Lanagan looked up in surprise, but the door had slammed shut and all he saw of the arson investigator was a retreating figure hunched in a black raincoat, with the pale edge of pajama bottoms showing between the cuffs of his trousers and the tops of his shoes.

He sat for a few moments with the steering wheel cold in his hands, then carefully, as if he'd had a little too much to drink, put the car in Drive and pulled away from the curb. It was a few more moments before he remembered to turn on the headlights and windshield wipers.

For a while he drove on automatic pilot, following well-worn paths, the traffic light enough, the streets empty enough at that hour to allow him that dangerous lapse. Eventually he found himself on Michigan Avenue, heading north into the skyscraper canyons of downtown, where traffic was never still and the streets never empty. It was one of the things he'd loved about Chicago from the first, he remembered, that vitality, that pulse of life that never quit, day or night, no matter what the season.

Chicago—my kind of town.

Across the river and there it was on his right, the Gothic tower of the *Chicagoan* building, dwarfed by taller skyscrapers, and yet he remembered how it had loomed larger and grander than all of them the day he'd arrived, fresh out of the university of Southern California's School of Journalism, with an internship at the L.A.-by-God *Times* under his belt, ready to take on the world.

Chicago. Grimy, contentious, *alive*—his kind of town. It had been love at first sight, and she'd been a demanding mistress all those years. Come to think of it, he wondered now if that was why his girlfriends—Monica had by no means been the first—always ended up leaving him. Women liked, and had a right to expect, to be someone's first priority. With him, no matter how fond he'd been of them, they'd always come second, maybe third, after his job and his city. His town.

Only now, it seemed, that mistress, too, had deserted him. Her streets felt alien to him. Aloof and cold.

He turned onto Lakeshore Drive, thinking about all the times he'd watched the sun come up across the water, more often than not at the end of a long night rather than the beginning of a new day, and of the way it always made him feel energized and renewed. He hadn't seemed to need sleep in those days. A Chicago sunrise and a cup of coffee and he was ready to hit the streets again.

Only this morning there wouldn't be a sunrise. Drizzle was blowing in ragged sheets across the lakefront walk, and the sky was a surly and unforgiving gray only a shade or two lighter than the water.

This morning someone had tried to kill him. This morning, in the wee small hours, someone had thrown a bomb through his front window, someone with every reason to think he'd be sound asleep and all unsuspecting in the room just above. Someone ruthless enough, determined enough, not to care who else died along with him, whether it was one innocent woman or a whole row of town houses.

If I had enemies like you've got enemies...

Maybe the cop was right; he shouldn't have been surprised. But he was. Shocked, in fact, just as it had been a shock to him each and every time a playground bully had taken him seriously enough to rearrange his face. This, though, he really could not understand. For God's sake, why would anyone want to kill him? Not that he'd never pissed anyone off before, even received a few threatening phone calls and an anonymous letter or two. Certainly nothing he'd ever taken seriously. But this? The cop couldn't be right—it couldn't possibly be that column. Not yet, not so soon. Hell, he'd barely started digging. All he'd done so far was blow a lot of hot air. Threats, that was all.

But the fact remained that two days ago he'd threatened to expose some very big crooks indeed, and this morning somebody had tried to kill him. Good God—*would* have killed him if his girlfriend hadn't picked the same night to walk out on him. Ironic, wasn't it?

I'd think about leaving town.

What the hell was he going to do? The arson cop—what was his name, Wilson?—had told him to go to a hotel. Yeah, he could do that. He didn't have much cash, but he had his credit cards. He could find a nice hotel, buy himself a toothbrush and some underwear and hole up and wait to see what the cops came up with. And what else? Wait for whoever it was who wanted him dead to try again?

He was surprised at that point to find himself on the expressway, apparently heading west, against the flow of rush-hour traffic. He had no clear recollection of how he'd gotten there, but his mind was clear enough now, and scurrying around and over his present situation like a bunch of berserk mice.

What was he going to do?

If it was that damned column, and there was a contract on him, then he was a marked man—some might say a walking dead one.

"God, I don't believe this." His voice sounded hollow and tinny in his ears; his hands on the steering wheel were cold, slippery with sweat. He thought he knew how a hunted animal feels, doggedly keeping one step ahead of pursuit, hanging on to the hope of life for as long as he could...

He uttered a single swearword, sharp and sibilant and replete with self-disgust. What he needed right now was a place to hide, someplace safe, where he could rest, catch his breath and figure out what to do next.

But where in this world could he go? If he checked in to a hotel—hell, if he so much as bought breakfast—using his credit cards, he'd leave a paper trail a green intern could follow. He didn't have much cash on him. If he went to his bank... And that was when it dawned on him that if these guys knew where he lived they could also know everything else about him. That meant where he banked, where he ate, where he shopped, who his friends were. The truth hit him like only the latest in a series of numbing blows. He wasn't safe anywhere. And neither would his friends be, if he was anywhere near them. There wasn't any place he could go. Not in this town, anyway.

So it looked as if the cop was right. First thing he had to do was get as far away from Chicago as he could. After that? After that... he'd think of something.

But he couldn't think. Once more, his mind seemed to have shut down. When he looked back on it he couldn't remember that he ever did make a conscious decision. So it could have been that Aunt Gwen was right, and it was Providence's fault he wound up where he did, out in the cornfields somewhere in Iowa, in a blinding rainstorm, utterly and completely lost.

Lucinda Rosewood Brown stood with her thumbs hooked in the side pockets of her overalls and watched the battered gray pickup bounce away down the gravel lane, kicking up a spiteful little dust cloud just before it turned onto the paved road. She gave her head a shake, inviting the wind to do whatever it wanted to with her hair, and muttered, "Good riddance."

The back porch screen door slammed. Her great-aunt Gwen came down the steps with a pan full of kitchen garbage for the chickens and inquired in her voice that always seemed to teeter on the brink of laughter, "Where's Herb off to so early?"

"He quit," said Lucy disgustedly.

Her aunt's eyebrows shot up, pushing pleats into her forehead. "He did! What did you do?"

Lucy's chin edged self-righteously upward. "I didn't do a thing. The man's so thin-skinned he can't even take a little constructive criticism."

"Uh-huh. What was it you said to him this time?"

"All I said was any idiot ought to be able to figure out how to arrange hay bales in a stack. He said in that case I was welcome to hire one." She paused, chewing on her lip and frowning. "I suppose he'll be wanting his pay."

"Where are you going to find another hired man?" Gwen asked, sounding as if the prospect was both remote and mildly funny. "You must be about out of possibilities, at least from around here."

"Hey," cried Lucy, stung to defensiveness, "if these guys' precious egos are too delicate to handle working for a woman, I'd just as soon not be bothered. If I have to, I'll do without."

Gwen shook her head and went off to the chicken yard, smiling, with the pot full of garbage propped on one hip.

"Who needs an old hired man, anyway?" Lucy muttered to the dog, Dodger, who'd come trotting alertly up to report for duty. She fondled his ears and ruffled his fur, then bent to encircle his neck in an impulsive, one-armed hug. "Yeah, who needs 'em? Right, ol' Dodger? It's just you and me. We can handle it. Can't we? Just you and me. . . ."

The little Border collie wagged his cropped tail in enthusiastic agreement, then went off to see if Gwen needed any help herding chickens.

Lucy straightened abruptly and turned her face westward into the wind, shutting her eyes against the brightness of the afternoon sun and the sting of unexpected and inexplicable emotions. It's the season, she told herself, breathing deeply of the warm, sweet-smelling wind. Spring fever...

The wind freshened suddenly, tugging at her hair. She felt the change in light and temperature on her eyelids and skin, and opened her eyes, frowning, to find that building thunderheads had swallowed up the sun. Below the advancing clouds, near the western horizon, the sky was the sullen blue-gray of gunmetal. Her heart quickened, and for a moment she stood absolutely still, sniffing the wind like a wild animal.

Lucy didn't mind the wind—liked it, in fact—which was a good thing since there was seldom a time out here on the plains when it didn't blow. But storm winds were different. Lucy hated storms, especially thunderstorms. To her, a storm's gale bore as much similarity to the usual prairie breezes as the Big Bad Wolf did to... well, to Dodger. They were the stuff of which nightmares are made.

They were also a fact of life in Iowa in the spring and summer months. And Lucy couldn't afford to give in to the nightmares; there was too much to do. So as usual she didn't acknowledge fear at all, only a vague tension and uneasiness. Adrenaline flooded her system. She felt keyed up, energized, shutting out all thought of the approaching menace, concentrating only on what needed to be done. The chores would have to be done early, the animals fed, the chickens and baby pigs shut up in their houses. There was seed to be covered. She had to get the tarp back on the haystack and securely tied down, and, of course, there was still half a load left on the truck, thanks to that idiot, Herb. It would have to be covered as well. Wet hay would mildew and rot, and could even spontaneously combust and burn up the whole stack. Then there was that sow that was getting close to farrowing. If there was time before the storm hit she probably should put her inside, just in case. So much to do.

Deliberately averting her eyes from the deepening darkness on the horizon, Lucy started down the slope toward the livestock yards. From far off in the distance came the first grumbles of thunder.

The thing was, Lanagan wasn't the sort of person who got lost. Put him in a city, any city, and he could generally wander around until he got himself straightened out, and enjoy the heck out of himself while he was doing it. But one cornfield looked pretty much like another cornfield to him, especially in the dark. And Lord, it was *dark.* Used to the perpetual twilight of the city, he'd never known or even imagined such darkness—or rain, either. He'd lived in the Midwest long enough that he wasn't awed by violent weather anymore. As a matter of fact, he really liked thunderstorms, for a lot of the same reasons he liked Chicago. The noise and electricity, tension and excitement made him feel exhilarated, in a very literal sense *turned on.* But out here in the cornfields, with nothing between him and the sky but all that blackness, the lightning came with shocking violence, the thunder had weight and substance, and the rain seemed a solid obstacle, something he had constantly to steel himself against, all his instincts expecting and braced for impact.

It didn't help matters, either, that he was exhausted. He'd gotten off the interstate in the first place because common sense and instincts of self-preservation had told him he'd reached the end of his rope. He'd just passed a crossroads with a couple of motels and truck-stop restaurants when the storm hit, and he'd made up his mind he'd pull off at the next one that came along. Except that the mile markers kept rolling by and the rain kept getting worse and the darkness thicker, and finally he'd made the fateful decision to get off the freeway at the next exit, turn around and double back to the oasis he was sure of. He wasn't quite certain where he'd gone wrong after that.

Damn, he'd never *seen* such rain—couldn't see three feet in front of his car's bumper. At first he'd doggedly followed the white line down the middle of the pavement, trusting that to keep him on the road, but eventually he'd lost even that. He had to get himself turned around, that's what he had to do, get back on that highway and hope it would take him to a town. They did have towns out here, didn't they? So far all he'd passed were looming hulks of barns and silos, just indistinct shapes in the darkness and rain, and the pale, blurred blots of farmhouses.

A flash of lightning suddenly illuminated a bank of wind-whipped trees close to the road on his right, as unexpected and startling as turning and discovering someone hovering silently at your shoulder.

He slowed reflexively, peering through the side window. The same flash had revealed what looked like—yes, there it was—a road, just a short stretch, like a driveway, leading up a short incline to what must be a bridge. Finally, a place to turn around where he wouldn't have to worry about getting stuck in the mud! He nosed cautiously into the driveway and continued forward onto the bridge so as to allow himself plenty of room to back around.

It came as a most unpleasant shock when the front end of his car suddenly dropped out from under him.

He probably said "Whoa!" or some such thing, out of pure astonishment. After that he simply held on to the steering wheel as best he could while his car jounced nose-first down a steep embankment and came, after a reassuringly short journey, to a bone-crunching, teeth-snapping stop. Then for a moment or two he sat very still, in utter darkness, arms and legs braced and shaking, listening to the rush of wind and rain, and swearing in heartfelt thanksgiving.

Oh, boy, he was alive. But what in the hell had happened? Where in the hell was he?

An obliging flash of lightning gave him answers he didn't care for. Foamy water was swirling across the hood of his car, gray and opaque in that blue-white light, like molten lead. The bridge had apparently been washed out in the storm, and he'd driven into the ditch. Or creek—whatever it was.

He didn't seem to be in any immediate danger of being washed away, but neither was there any possibility he could extricate his car from the stream, and he didn't have any idea how much higher the water was apt to rise. So the first thing he had to do was get out of the car while he still could.

The engine had died—drowned, certainly—so he turned off the ignition, put the car in Park and set the emergency brake. Somewhere under that leaden water the headlights were presumably still shining, so he shut them off, too. Then he grabbed his raincoat, opened the door and stepped cautiously out onto the steep, pebbly bank. Thank God, at least that part of it was still above water.

The rain had slackened considerably, the lightning came fitfully now and thunder grumbled off in the distance. So at least the storm had passed, which struck Lanagan as more ironic than comforting. By the time he'd managed to claw his way back to the road he was soaked anyway, from the sodden grass and creek mud, and the trees dripping remorselessly onto his head and down the back of his neck. He longed for his hat, but wasn't about to go back for it. Who would have thought it could be so cold in May?

He had blacktop under his feet again and was standing in shivering indecision when a distant flicker of lightning briefly brightened the sky, showing him the tantalizing silhouette of a farmhouse on a little rise beyond the trees. For a moment longer he hesitated, then hunched his shoulders inside his trench coat and set out walking toward it. Several more times the dying storm lit the way for him, almost, he thought, as if it were a will-o'-the-wisp, beckoning him on.

But when he reached the gate at the foot of the lane that led up to the farmhouse he began to have serious reservations about trying to rouse its occupants. There wasn't any sign of a light showing in any of the windows, and from somewhere up there in the general vicinity of the front porch a dog had begun to bark. There was no telling what time it was, and people weren't likely to welcome a sodden stranger on their doorstep in broad daylight, let alone the middle of the night, asking to use the telephone. Certainly not in Chicago or L.A.

The dog's barking suddenly seemed to him more insistent and ominously nearer. On his right he could make out the looming bulk of a building—a barn, undoubtedly, its partially open door a blacker rectangle in the thinning darkness. Hide in a barn? It was a cliché that appealed to Lanagan, for some reason. Probably his mind had passed the point of exhaustion and was now on a downward spiral into giddiness. *Under the haystack, fast asleep...*

He slipped through the dark rectangle of the barn door and was instantly engulfed in the humid smells of fresh hay, old wood and leather, decaying straw and manure. Alien smells to him, but oddly comforting. Feeling his way through the utter blackness with both hands and feet, he made his way to what seemed to be an open stall and, after listening long and intently, concluded that it was probably unoccupied. Its concrete floor was covered with a thick layer of straw, which, when he knelt and investigated with his bare hands, seemed to be both clean and dry. His lying down was more a collapse than anything willed by his tired mind.

Just before sleep overwhelmed him it occurred to him, with a faint sense of surprise, that for the past several hours he hadn't thought once about his ruined town house, or the fact that someone was bent on killing him.

The Chicagoan, May 1

Section A, Page 2
Late-Breaking News Roundup:

CHICAGO—Chicago police are investigating an arson fire which completely destroyed the residence of

Chicagoan columnist Mike Lanagan early this morning. The blaze, which police say appears to have been started by an incendiary device, had completely engulfed the structure by the time fire fighters arrived. Fortunately, although there was minor damage to several adjoining buildings, no injuries were reported. Mr. Lanagan was not home at the time of the incident, and as of press time, still could not be reached for comment.

Chapter 2

The fact that someone was bent on killing Lanagan was the first thing that came to his mind when he woke up, partly because something sharp and unidentifiable was poking him in the chest, something cold and hard and indisputably made of steel.

And partly because an unidentifiable voice, raspy with tension and hoarse with menace, was saying to him, "Hey—hey *you*—wake up! And don't make a move. . . ."

Moving was the last thing Lanagan had any plans to do. However, since he'd been given conflicting orders in that regard, he thought it might be a good idea if he took a chance and at least opened his eyes. Maybe find out where he was, and what the hell was going on.

He did, then quickly shut them again and uttered a soft, heartfelt oath. The sun was hitting him right in the face, and its assault felt like hammer blows on his unsuspecting retinas.

The voice—the owner of which he'd had time to identify only as a looming silhouette—spoke again, accompaniment to a marked increase in the pressure of cold steel on his chest.

"Okay, mister, now you better tell me who you are and what you think you're doing in my barn."

Before the events of the past twenty-four hours had shaken the very foundations of his soul and self-confidence, Lanagan had considered his wits sharpest and quickest in times of crisis. It went a long way toward restoring his battered spirits to find that they hadn't permanently deserted him, after all. Because he'd been able to ascertain two important things from the voice's second utterance. One, it didn't seem nearly as menacing now as it did apprehensive; and two, and definitely most importantly, it had asked him *who he was*. Clearly, then, this was not one of the parties who wanted him dead. At least, not yet.

"Come on..." The hard thing prodded him again, but not with any great force or deliberate cruelty. "I know you can talk, I heard you cuss. Open up your eyes and tell me who the hell you are, or I'm going to—"

"I've got the sun in my eyes," Lanagan protested in a croak, "and you won't let me move."

"Oh." There was a faint rustling, and the pressure against his chest came from a new angle. A shadow settled like a cool compress on his eyelids. "That better?"

"Thanks," said Lanagan, and opened his eyes a second time. The silhouette now stood between him and the wide-open barn door, and was no longer a silhouette. What it was, he saw to his surprise and immense relief, was a girl. Not a very big one, either, even from his perspective—kind of scrawny and scruffy-looking, in fact. Wearing a pair of farmer's overalls several sizes too big for her.

Utter astonishment made him start to get up, an impulse he immediately regretted. He glanced down at the pitchfork braced against his chest, its steel tines looming before his face like the bars of a cage, and muttered dryly, "I think."

"Don't get up," the girl warned in her crusty rasp of a voice. "Not until I know I can trust you. First thing I want's your name."

"Cage," said Lanagan readily, inspired by the view through those immutable steel bars.

"Cage? That's all?"

"Uh, it's Mike. Mike...Cage." That seemed safe enough. Mike was a common name, and it would be too much trouble trying to remember to answer to something else.

The girl chewed on her lip, considering the information. "Got any ID?"

Damn. "Uh, sure." Again Lanagan started to rise, and again thought better of it. He'd about had enough of that damned pitchfork. "Do you mind?" he said coldly, looking up at the girl through its tines, then took one gingerly and deliberately between a thumb and forefinger and moved it to one side, off his chest.

He held the girl's narrow-eyed gaze long enough to be sure she was going to accept that without mayhem, then raised himself up on one elbow and shifted so he could reach his hip pocket. After reassuring himself that his wallet was where it should be, he carefully twitched his coat around to cover it up and said with what he hoped was convincing dismay, "*Damn.* Guess I must have lost it when I was climbing out of the creek." He shrugged and grinned, trying out some dormant charm. "Sorry, I guess you'll just have to trust me."

Lucy stood with the pitchfork in her hand and chewed on her lip while she thought over that possibility. Trust him? Funny thing was, up until he'd said that, she'd been just about ready to do so. For one thing, he just looked too scared and sleepy and bedraggled to be dangerous. And for another... but it was too hard to put into words what kind of things had gone through her mind all the while she'd stood there watching him sleep.

Well, of course, the first thing he'd done was scare the living daylights out of her. She'd nearly had a heart attack, coming into the barn with a box full of baby pigs under her arm, to get a handful of straw for their bedding, and the first thing she'd seen was a pair of legs sticking out of an empty stall. First she'd thought he was dead. Then she'd found out he wasn't, which was probably worse. Her heart hadn't stopped pounding yet.

But besides that, she'd gotten a certain amount of simple enjoyment out of the experience. It wasn't every day she went out in the morning and found a good-looking man in her barn, sound asleep on a pile of nice clean straw. Wasn't every day she found one this good-looking in *any* condition. It had been quite a few years since she'd seen one that might tempt her to lie down and share that straw with him, but as she'd stood there listening to this one snoring like a buzz saw, the thought actually did flit across her mind.

It never occurred to Lucy that what she ought to have done was turn around and go straight back to the house and call the police. She was used to dealing with things herself, as they happened to come her way. So what she did first was put the pigs down in the next stall where they'd be out of the way in case she'd misjudged the situation. And then, since the pitchfork was right there handy anyway, it seemed like it wouldn't hurt to have it, just in case. Not that she was likely to have to use it; she'd been known to get the better of both of her brothers, and they'd been bigger and in a whole lot better shape than this guy appeared to be.

What he looked like to her was City. Not a bum or homeless person, although he was certainly a muddy, wrinkled mess at the moment. Just because Lucy preferred not to wear them herself most of the time didn't mean she didn't know nice clothes when she saw them, and this man's clothes were definitely nice, and they weren't particularly old, either. He was wearing city shoes and a city raincoat and city slacks, and at one point she thought he'd probably had on a tie; he just looked like the type who'd wear one. Although he also looked like the type who'd yank it off without thinking about it—sort of careless about his appearance. His socks didn't quite match, he looked as if he hadn't shaved in at least a couple of days and his hair was too long. Not stylishly long, though—kind of the way Clark Gable might look if he needed a haircut. There was one little piece of it that had hung down across his forehead and over his eyebrow while he was sleeping, and she'd had the strangest urge to reach out and touch it away with her finger.

It was that thought that had shaken her up as much as anything, and probably made her a little rougher than she really needed to be with the pitchfork. The man definitely had something.

"Why should I trust you?" she asked him flatly now, standing her ground while he worked his way to a standing position in painful stages. "I never saw you before in my life, and you still haven't explained to me what you're doing in my barn."

"*Your* barn?" Lanagan broke off a groan with a soft huff of surprise. Not a girl, after all, he could see now. Most certainly a woman, although he hadn't been mistaken about the rest. She was still small and scrawny, even smaller now that he was standing and she wasn't towering over him with that pitchfork. And she was certainly wearing farmer's overalls several sizes too big for her. The T-shirt she had on under the overalls fit her better but didn't reveal much more, except for a long neck and slender arms that had definite muscles in them, and skin that was freckled and weathered from too much exposure to the sun. Her face was freckled, too, and there were tiny sun lines at the corners of her eyes. Keen, intelligent eyes, he thought—and dark, like her straight, chin-length hair.

Yes, she was definitely a grown woman, although she still didn't look much like his idea of somebody who'd own a barn, much less everything that undoubtedly went with it. He hadn't met very many farmers in his life—none at all, in fact, which came as somewhat of a surprise to him—but he had a clear picture in his mind of what farmers were supposed to look like. A good bit bigger than this, for one thing. And although, having been raised in a household of very vocal and opinionated women, he would never be so foolish as to label any occupation gender specific, in this case he would have thought, almost certainly *male*.

"Listen, I'm sorry about trespassing," he said, exhaling audible chagrin and dropping the charm, which he was pretty sure was wasted on her, anyway. He told himself he'd have to be careful what lies he told, too; he had a feeling she'd see right through him. "The truth is, I lost my way in that storm last night. I was trying to get myself turned around, and I, uh..." He coughed and concluded lamely, "I think I must have driven my car into a ditch."

Being a man, he found it embarrassing, to say the least, to have to admit to a woman, especially one this feisty and self-reliant, that he'd done something so stupid. Very early he'd learned two basic rules of manhood. First, you never admitted to being lost, and second, you never, never, under any circumstances, let on that you couldn't handle a car. So he was surprised to see the sharp lines of the woman's face relax, her mouth curve and soften, and an expression that was surely sympathy come into her eyes.

"That storm..." She said it softly, under her breath, then turned with one abrupt, decisive movement and stood the pitchfork up against the side of the stall. "Well, you'd better come on up to the house. You'll probably want to use the phone. You might as well have some breakfast and dry off while you wait."

The last part of that came distant and muffled, because while she was talking she'd already ducked out of his stall and into the one next to it. By the time he'd recovered from his surprise at the unexpected turnaround in his immediate fortunes, gathered his wits enough to stick his incriminating wallet way back under the straw, and followed her, she was down on one knee beside a cardboard box, doing something with what was inside. Whatever was in there was making some strange and alarming sounds. Scuffles, mixed with grunts and an occasional squeal.

"What's that you've got there?" Lanagan asked curiously, coming up behind her to look over her shoulder. And then, jumping back in surprise, "My God, they're *pigs*."

"Very good." Her voice was scratchy soft, and from the sound of it, though he couldn't actually see her eyes, he'd have been willing to bet they were laughing at him.

To his own disgust he heard himself harrumphing and blustering in an attempt to salvage his masculine pride. "No, I just mean—I've never seen any that...small." Fascinated, he watched her scoop up a wad of straw from the floor of the stall and scatter it in the open box. Then, putting it down to a reporter's need to know, he ventured another cautious look over her shoulder. Several rubbery pink noses came pushing and poking through the straw, emitting little woofing noises. "I take it these were just born, uh, recently?"

Her head was lowered, her gaze intently focused on her own strong brown hand as it efficiently rearranged straw between squirmy pink-and-white bodies, at the same time dodging those busy noses and some wicked-looking teeth.

After a moment she nodded and said without looking up, "Yeah, last night, during the storm. Darned stupid sow farrowed in the mud—my best one, too. I knew I should have put her in, but I...didn't. Just plain ran out of time." She gave a soft huff of vexation and her head a quick little shake that dislodged a strand of hair from where she'd tucked it behind her ear to slither errantly across one cheek. "Lost three, drowned or laid on. And these four are pretty weak. Serves me right." Her tone was dry and matter-of-fact, but Lanagan could see angry tension in the set of her shoulders and the back of her neck. It gave him an odd feeling of kinship with her to know that she didn't like admitting her mistakes any more than he did.

She stood and gave the knees of her overalls one cursory brush, then used both hands to put her hair back where it belonged and said briskly, "The sow's got nine healthy ones with her, but she won't have for long if I don't get her into a farrowing shed pretty quick. So if you don't mind, I'll take you and these pigs on up to the house now."

When she bent to pick up the box, Lanagan noticed that her hair slithered right out from behind her ears and across her cheeks again. He found himself becoming sort of fascinated by that hair of hers. He thought it must be really silky and soft to keep doing that. Must have a mind of its own, too.

"Need any help?" he heard himself say, too preoccupied with watching her to know he was going to.

She threw him a sharp, amused look. "What, with the sow? Mister, if you don't mind me saying so, right now you look in worse shape than she does. I think I'd better just clean you up and feed you some breakfast. And anyway, seems to me you'd better worry about how you're going to get that car of yours out of the creek." A smile was playing around the corners of her mouth as she hefted the box and started to edge past him.

"Let me take that for you," Lanagan said, again before he knew he would.

She checked and gave him another amused, considering look, but it was tight quarters in the stall and the box was right there between them, sort of brushing both their fronts, and it only seemed natural for him to intercept it. She shrugged and said, "Okay," and let him have it, but in a way that made it plain she was just humoring him.

The box made furtive woofing, scuffling noises, and its weight rolled and shifted in his arms as he followed the woman out of the barn and into the sunshine.

Once free of the barn's shade he paused to turn in a slow, dazzled circle, overwhelmed by the intensity of the light and the sheer volume of sky. Last night in the storm the sky had seemed to him like a solid thing, like a great, suffocating blanket, but this morning—Lord, this morning it went on forever, three hundred and sixty degrees of it, shimmering white-gold infinity.

He wished for his hat, remembered where it was and wished instead for sunglasses, trying to think where they'd be, and it crossed his mind that he might not even own a pair of sunglasses anymore. That thought made his throat catch and his stomach feel queasy, and he pushed it out of his mind and stared hard at the horizon until the feeling went away.

Even though the horizon seemed a perfect, unbroken circle, the land wasn't really flat, but undulated away in wave after wave of variegated hills, like a rumpled quilt, some patches the rich black corduroy of fresh-plowed soil, others showing the yellow-green velvet of new growth, still others the vivid emerald sheen of pasture grass, swiss-dotted with white cattle. The trees, which last night had seemed to press ominously in on his flanks, had retreated in the sunlight to innocent clusters well back from the road. Great oaks and elms hovered like gossipy matrons around pristine white farmhouses, windbreaks of poplar and evergreens stood in stately formation along fencerows, and in the low places between hills, thickets of cottonwoods and willows tamed last night's torrents into playful trickles.

There was something disorienting about it all, like waking from a nightmare in an unfamiliar room—although last night was beginning to seem unreal to him, too, the way a nightmare grows hazy as soon as you open your eyes. It couldn't all have happened, his home wasn't gone, he couldn't possibly be here, in the middle of a bunch of cornfields in—what state was he in, anyway?

But it had, and he was. And the only thing that hadn't changed from the incredible night just past was that all those hills and cornfields and farmhouses still looked alike to him.

Up ahead the brown-haired woman was stopping to pet a dog that had come running out to meet her, with its head down and cropped tail wagging. It was a medium-sized black, white and tan dog, long-haired but not shaggy, with alert-looking ears and freckles on his muzzle. Having assured himself of his master's affections, he now came loping with ebullient curiosity to greet Lanagan.

"Nice dog," said Lanagan hopefully, but the dog was as benign in daylight as everything else that had seemed so menacing to him in the night.

"That's Dodger," the woman said when they caught up with her, nodding at the dog, who'd already lost interest in the newcomer and gone running on ahead.

"Oh, you a baseball fan?" Lanagan asked carefully, trying not to show the effects the uphill climb was having on his breathing.

"What?" She threw him a quick, sideways glance, then grinned with understanding and shook her head. "The Cards are my team. No, that's his talent. He's a Border collie. You'd understand if you saw him work."

"Work?"

"Cattle."

"Ah." He was truly impressed. Pigs *and* cattle—it seemed like a lot for one person to handle, big or small, male or female. In fact, surely she didn't, not all alone. He began to wonder whether in fact she was alone, and other things about her—the reporter in him, struggling to life in spite of everything. "Now I know your dog's name," he said pointedly, shifting the box to one side to make it easier to keep up with her.

She gave him another of those quick, appraising glances—everything she did seemed to be like that, quick, efficient, decisive—and said simply, "Lucy Brown."

He repeated it thoughtfully under his breath, but something in his tone made her raise her head and inquire with a sharp note of suspicion, "*What?*"

There was challenge in the lift of her chin, which Lanagan had an idea was her usual, almost automatic response. But strangely, although her gaze was steady enough, he couldn't find the same belligerence in her eyes. He thought her eyes seemed . . . not defensive, not even puzzled, exactly. But as if something had taken her by surprise, and she hadn't quite got it figured out yet.

In any case, the pause was long enough for him to study her eyes, certainly a lot longer than he meant to. Out here in the sunlight he could see that they were brown. Just . . . brown, like her name. Nothing remarkable about them, except maybe the fact that it was so hard to let go of them.

"Nothing," he said finally. "It's a nice name. I like it." But for some reason it didn't seem like enough, not for someone with so much energy and self-confidence. Walking along beside her, he could feel the vitality radiating from her body in waves, like heat from the hood of a car. She seemed almost to glow with it, as if, he thought, she collected the heat and light from that enormous sky and distilled it into one tight beam of energy, the way a magnifying glass turns ordinary light into fire. It began to seem not so difficult after all to believe such a person could singlehandedly manage this farm and any number of cows and pigs and who knew what else besides.

The gravel road they were walking on went curving past the white frame farmhouse toward a cluster of buildings of various shapes and sizes, at whose function Lanagan couldn't begin to guess. At least one, though, had open sides, its corrugated metal roof providing shelter for an assortment of machinery painted in glowing primary colors—red and yellow and green, like children's toys. In fact, hadn't he played with one just like that when he was a boy?

A very little boy...trouser knees worn thin from the hard-baked dirt, the sun burning hot on the back of his neck, industriously making brrrmm-brrrmm noises as he pushed a small green-and-yellow tractor around his mother's backyard. Amazing, he thought, that a memory so long dormant could seem so vivid....

From there his imagination leapt to picture the woman at his side, a tiny woman whose head barely topped his shoulder, in command of one of those real-life, mammoth machines. He found the idea mind-boggling, but also somewhat exciting. Meaning erotic.

"This way," she said, jerking her head as an indication that he was to follow, and angled off across a wide, oak-shaded lawn toward the back of the farmhouse. He noticed in passing that the lawn was lush but in need of mowing, and that the house could have used a coat of paint.

A rope swing was hanging from a gnarled limb of one of the largest oaks. Lanagan gave it a thoughtful tug with his free hand as he passed, wondering for a moment if he'd misread the situation completely. But the rope was stiff and crusty with disuse, and in any case the place seemed too tidy—and too quiet—for there to have been children currently in residence.

"My dad put that up," Lucy offered, noticing his brief pause. Apparently those sharp brown eyes of hers didn't miss much. "Years ago, when us kids were small."

He ventured, "Us kids?"

"Brothers—I have two. One older, one younger."

"I see." That explained it. "So," he pressed, "they farm here with you?"

She gave a dry little laugh and shook her head. "Everett—Rhett—lives in Des Moines. We don't see too much of him, which is just fine with me. He's a lawyer and a stuffed shirt and I expect he'd like to go into politics and be governor some day. With a social-climbing wife and two perfectly awful children, he'll probably get his wish. As for my little brother, Earl. . . ." She put her hand on the rope swing and watched it drift slowly back and forth, a slight, probably unconscious smile on her lips. After a moment she twitched back one side of her hair and stilled the swing. The smile faded. "Well, he gave it a try, right after my folks died." She angled a glance his way. "That was six years ago. But he was always a restless soul, and after a couple of months he took off and joined the Marines—served in the Persian Gulf. Somalia, too." Her voice had grown soft, but she'd started off walking again, and he couldn't be sure whether it was with pride or irony. "Earl always did want to see the world, and I guess he got his wish, too."

Lanagan lengthened his stride in order to catch up with her, reawakening the baby pigs, who scrabbled and woofed indignantly inside their box. "You've lived here all your life, then?"

"Yep, all my life." She twitched her hair back behind her ear just in time for him to watch a dimple come and go.

It struck him, then, that for someone who'd just given him a wake-up call with the business end of a pitchfork, she was being remarkably friendly and forthcoming. When he played his conversations with her over in his mind—something he was still pretty good at, from his years as a street reporter—he realized that her whole attitude toward him seemed to have turned around the minute he'd mentioned getting lost in that storm.

He was thinking about that, bemused by the irony in it—the fact that her sympathies should have been won by the very thing that caused him the most embarrassment—when she suddenly turned those eyes, and the tables, on him and asked point-blank, "Where're *you* from?"

Caught off guard like that, he said what came naturally to him, which was the truth. "Los Angeles."

She accepted it with a nod, eyes twinkling with revelation, and mouthed the word *Dodgers*. He laughed and didn't deny it—old loyalties had proven hard to break. She persisted, "So, you're heading east?"

"No, actually..." He stopped and gave a little huff of wonder, because until that moment he hadn't known it himself. "Actually, I've...been away for a while. Right now I'm heading back there. I'm going home."

She nodded as if that was entirely understandable to her. She didn't have a chance to say so, however, because at that moment a screen door banged and a different voice spoke instead, a voice higher pitched than Lucy's scratchy alto, rich with laughter and melodious as a flute.

"Lucinda, what in the world have you got there?"

So there *is* more, thought Lanagan, enlightened. *Lucinda*. Yes, that was more like it.

"This is my aunt Gwen," said Lucy. "Great-aunt, actually."

Lucy's aunt had to be near eighty, he estimated, but tall, rail thin and ramrod straight, with silvering hair braided and wound into a knot at the nape of her neck—all the pioneer woman clichés, straight out of American Gothic. Except that there was nothing stern or severe about this particular woman, far from it. The hair around her face was cut short and whimsically curled, and under her bibbed gingham apron she wore blue jeans and a man's work shirt with the sleeves rolled up to the elbows. She had a magnificent hawk's beak of a nose, a family trait which was shared in a slightly more delicate version by Lucy, Lanagan now realized. He wondered how he'd missed it before. But where the rest of Lucy's face was all sharp points and constantly changing angles, this woman's face—every line, every wrinkle—appeared to have been shaped and molded by irony and laughter. Her mouth seemed to quiver with it, poorly suppressed; it lurked behind her shrewd blue eyes, as if she were privy to some hilarious secret. Although the lines etched deep in her forehead made it clear she carried no false illusions about life and the human condition, obviously here was one who believed it was better to laugh about them than cry.

Lanagan went up the steps to meet Lucy's aunt Gwen as if he were being pulled along and lifted up by an unknown buoyancy. In his mind he was already composing columns about her.

Lucy closed the washroom door behind her with a faint and furtive click and tiptoed across the hallway and into the kitchen where Gwen was fixing breakfast.

"Well," she said in a hoarse whisper, "what do you think of him?"

Gwen went on deftly turning pancakes. "Did you tell him to leave his muddy things in the washtub? What did you find for him to put on?"

"Some of Earl's things. Underwear and socks, sweatshirt and jeans. I think they ought to fit him okay. Except Earl's shoes were going to be way too big. I found him a pair of Dad's old loafers. He's taller than Dad, but Dad was broader, bigger boned. So they should be about right."

They'd given her pause, those shoes—scuffed and well-worn and even still smelling a little like Dad's feet. And she'd gotten a lump in her throat, too, remembering how he'd always liked to slip into those comfortable old loafers when he came into the house, leaving his barnyard shoes out on the back porch.

"You certainly noticed a lot about the man," Gwen observed without turning around.

"I studied him some," Lucy admitted. "I wasn't going to invite him up to the house for breakfast without sizing him up first. Anyhow, tell me what you think."

"He's a nice-looking young man," said Gwen, and turned to give Lucy one of her very best Looks, as if she knew something Lucy didn't. And since Lucy was willing to allow that Gwen knew a lot of things she didn't, she waited eagerly for the rest. It was delivered on a lilting note of amusement. "Sort of Cary Grant, gone to seed."

"No, not Cary Grant," said Lucy, grinning. She'd been thinking more in terms of Harrison Ford, actually, but she stopped there, hoarding that particular thought to herself.

Instead she straddled a chair, hitched it close to the table and picked up her fork. A moment later around a mouthful of pancakes she remarked, "I think he's on the lam."

"Lam?" repeated Gwen, rippling the word with laughter.

"Running. From the law, or who knows what."

"What makes you think so?"

"Wouldn't let me see his ID when I asked him. Said he lost it climbing out of the creek." She washed down pancakes with a swig of hot coffee. "And you saw what happened when he went to use the phone, and then changed his mind and asked if I had a tractor instead. Why didn't he use a credit card, or call triple A, like anybody else?"

"He couldn't very well if he's lost his wallet," Gwen pointed out.

"Yeah, but he hasn't," said Lucy flatly. "I saw it. He tried to hide it from me, but I know it was there in his hip pocket. I'll bet a dollar he hasn't got it now, though. I'll bet he hid it in that stall." She chewed for a moment, then added, "I gave him every opportunity, anyway. It's probably there under the straw right this minute."

"Well, are you going to go and see?"

Lucy shook her head and swallowed more coffee. "None of my business."

Gwen gave a melodious chirp of laughter and turned to lean against the counter, regarding Lucy with fond amusement. "You mean you sized him up, decided he's a dangerous wanted criminal and invited him up to the house for breakfast anyway?"

"Uh-uh," said Lucy, mopping syrup with the last bite of pancake. "I never said criminal, and I never said dangerous. Anyway, if he'd wanted to rob and murder us, he could have done it a lot easier last night when we were both asleep in our beds. The house wasn't locked."

"Dodger was out."

"Hah. Any self-respecting ax murderer'd take one look at Dodger and fall down laughing." She considered for a moment with her head to one side and amended, "Then I suppose Dodger might lick 'im to death."

Gwen turned back to the stove, still shaking with silent laughter, while Lucy went on gazing into the distance over the rim of her coffee cup, thinking hard. After a while she shifted her chair back just a little, cleared her throat and said very casually, "I thought I might offer to pull that car of his out of the creek for him."

"Well," said Gwen, considering that with a straight face, "that'd be nice. I'm sure he'd appreciate it."

"Of course," Lucy went on, "it's going to be hard to find the time to do it, since I don't have a hired man anymore." Renewed indignation suddenly bubbled up inside her like milk coming to a boil, and carried her to her feet. "Damn that Herb, anyway! I know good and well I wouldn't have lost those pigs if he hadn't quit on me like that. How could he do that to me? Right out of the blue, with a storm coming in—and for no good reason!"

"No reason? You called him an idiot," Gwen placidly reminded her. "More than once."

"He *is* an idiot."

"Most men are. They don't like to be reminded of it so often."

"Hmm," said Lucy vaguely. Though unconvinced, she let her mind go on to other matters. "I was thinking I might ask him to help me get that sow in."

"Who, *Herb?*"

"If Herb ever sets foot on my place again, I'll run him off with Dad's shotgun. No, I mean this guy, of course. Two or three others are getting close to farrowing—wouldn't hurt to put them in at the same time. Then there's that hay that got left when Herb walked off in a huff. If it's not already ruined, we could get that stacked up—"

"Lucinda Rosewood Brown," said Gwen, amid wondering ripples of mirth, "are you thinking what I think you're thinking?"

"Don't be ridiculous," said Lucy.

"On the other hand," said Gwen as she turned to scoop pancakes off the griddle, "it does seem a little bit like fate, doesn't it, for a man on the lam from the law to pick your barn to hide out in, on the very same night your hired hand quit?"

"A city man," scoffed Lucy. "Fate must have a weird sense of humor."

"Providence, then."

"Same thing."

"Not so," said Gwen softly as the man in question came into the room. Her eyes twinkled with her private thoughts and secret wisdoms. "Not so."

Lanagan had come out of the washroom and into the hallway in time to hear the last part of the conversation taking place in the kitchen, and as he sat down at the big oak table in the spot Lucy indicated and accepted the plateful of pancakes Gwen brought him, he was smiling a secret smile of his own.

Lucinda Rosewood Brown. Now *there* was a name. A name worthy of the little brown-eyed dynamo sitting across the table from him, sipping coffee and regarding him, demeanor as innocent as a Dickens pickpocket, while she plotted his future for him. He'd like to ask her where she'd come by such a name, but he doubted he'd ever have the chance. She could plot and manipulate all she wanted to, but just as soon as he could get his car out of that creek he was heading on to California.

Actually, he'd come to that decision while he was washing his face in the laundry tub in Lucy's washroom. He'd caught a glimpse of himself in the blotched and wavy glass of a very old mirror that was hanging from a nail above the tub, and the idea that had come to him as a revelation out on the front lawn had solidified into a definite goal. More than a goal, almost a yearning. How long had it been since he'd seen his mother, anyway? Much too long, he knew that. Not since her wedding—what had it been, two years ago February? Yeah, Valentine's Day, that was it. He'd been a little surprised by the romantic notion, and it had come as a shock to him to see his mother looking so flushed and starry-eyed. So pretty. So *young*. Well, what the hell, he thought, she was young, not even sixty. And he was happy for her, too, just sorry she'd waited so long. Too long.

He'd thought of all the times he should have called her, and his sisters, too. But he'd been busy and so had they, caught up in their own lives, their own families. Then he'd thought about someone else, a stranger, calling his mother to tell her that her son was dead, and a wave of loneliness had swept him, so deep it was almost desolation. He had thrust his cupped hands under the faucet and buried his face in the cold, clear water until the feeling had passed, but when he'd found his reflection in the mirror again he had known what he was going to do. It would be all right, he told himself. No one knew where his mother lived. Her name wasn't even Lanagan anymore. It would be all right.

Beyond that, Lanagan couldn't think at all. He only knew that he wanted to go home.

The Chicagoan, May 2
Metro Section, Front Page
by Ralph Buncomb, staff writer

CHICAGO—Chicago police still have no leads and no suspects in yesterday's firebombing of a southside town house belonging to *Chicagoan* columnist Mike Lanagan. According to chief arson investigator Lieutenant Charles Wilson, neighbors reported hearing glass breaking shortly after midnight, followed immediately by the sounds of a car leaving in a hurry. One neighbor, who wished to remain anonymous, apparently then looked out and saw flames through the front window of the Lanagan residence and immediately called 911. Fire fighters were on the scene within minutes, but found the structure already fully involved, and the fire threatening to spread to nearby buildings. Fire fighters credit the neighbor's quick response for preventing the entire block of recently renovated row houses, located in a newly popular yuppie enclave on the near south side, from going up in flames.

Police also credit a stroke of fortune for the fact that there were no casualties in the fire. According to Lieutenant Wilson, Lanagan had left his home only moments before the incident to go for a walk. He returned to find police and fire fighters on the scene and his home totally destroyed.

(Continued on page 3—see FIRE)

* * * * * * * *

"My Kind of Town" by Mike Lanagan

Mike Lanagan has the day off.

Chapter 3

Lanagan stood on the front porch overlooking the lane and the barn and the cornfields beyond, marveling at the difference a full stomach could make on a person's general outlook and attitude.

Almost nothing was left of last night's storm. With the sun at his back and still low behind the house and its canopy of oak trees, the sky once again seemed like a solid thing, and almost touchable. But not a smothering blanket now, more like a lovely blue porcelain bowl turned upside down, with a few fuzzy white clouds clinging to the far side of it, like cotton balls put there by a sticky-fingered child. The gravel driveway, grassy verges and thirsty black soil had soaked up the rain like a sponge, leaving only a few small puddles scattered here and there, reflecting the sky like tiny chips of the same blue porcelain.

He took a deep breath, hauling in a chestful of air laced with unfamiliar smells, then remembered his cigarettes, which, lacking pockets in his borrowed clothes, he'd tucked into the sleeve of his sweatshirt. He took one out and lit it, his first of the day, exhaling luxuriously into the fresh, clean morning. A gust of warm wind came bustling up the hill like a fussy housewife, blew away his smoke and replaced it with the scent of manure and freshly turned earth and all manner of growing things—cattle and pigs, budding roses and wildflowers, and sprigs of sprouting corn. Alien smells, but Lanagan didn't mind. What he felt was content, and that was remarkable, considering.

Considering... But he didn't want to think about that right now, and in fact couldn't think of any reason he needed to. Chicago seemed far, far away, and everything that had happened to him there a half-remembered dream.

Lucy came around from the back of the house looking for him, her arrival blowing away the last remnants of the dream just as the wind had blown away his smoke.

"There you are," she said when she saw him, faintly accusing, as if he'd been a truant schoolboy. She dumped a pair of tall rubber boots on the bottom step, then nodded toward the cigarette in his hand and muttered, "Didn't know you smoked."

Lanagan murmured automatic apologies and looked guiltily around for a place to dispose of the incriminating evidence.

"Hey, it's all right with me," said Lucy with a shrug, "as long as you don't do it indoors. Or throw your butts on the ground."

Lanagan, who'd been about to do just that, hastily palmed it instead.

Lucy nudged the boots closer to him with her toe. "Here, you'll need these. They go on *over* your shoes."

Lanagan, who'd already started to slip out of the loafers she'd given him, hastily stepped back into them, then into the boots. They fit him fine but felt clumsy, and he said so to Lucy.

"You'll get used to them," she said with airy confidence, and headed off across the lawn.

The hell I will, thought Lanagan, smiling darkly to himself as he set off after her, clumping along like Frankenstein, with a live cigarette cupped in his palm. But he was feeling good-natured about it. He didn't plan on being around long enough to get used to those boots.

Still, since he knew very well what she was up to, he thought it wouldn't hurt to have a little bit of fun with her in the meantime. He thought he might play along with her just enough to let her think she was playing him, which would at least keep his mind busy and off his own troubles. Plus, he might even learn something.

He was beginning to get a better idea of the layout of Lucy's farm now, and he had to admit that he was impressed by what he'd seen so far. The farmhouse and its guardian oaks capped a little hill set well back from the main road, surrounded by lawn and beds of newly set out pink and red and white petunias, and the gray-green spikes of iris already past their spring flowering. There were clumps of lilacs, also past blooming, and roses just getting ready to do so. He'd especially noticed one enormous climber that nearly covered the porch of a tiny white cottage just across the driveway from the swing tree. A cozy-looking little place, he thought, wondering what it was for and whether anyone actually lived there.

Next to the cottage, separated from it by a bank of shrubbery and a low picket fence, was a chicken house, with its yard all enclosed and roofed over with wire mesh—to keep the hawks out, Lucy told him when he asked. Behind the cottage and chicken yard there was a thick evergreen windbreak, and beyond that a maze of livestock yards that zigzagged all the way down the gentle slope to the barn at the bottom of the hill.

The graveled driveway, after slipping between the swing tree and the rose-covered cottage and skirting the back porch door, suddenly spilled out into a wide circle of hard-packed earth, surrounded by a sweep of garages and sheds and shop buildings, some of them with tin roofs and open sides, others white-painted wood, like the house. And like the house, Lanagan noted, they all could have used a fresh coat of paint. It wouldn't take much, he thought. A few nice dry days like this, and he could—

Hey, Lanagan! Don't be crazy. Lucinda Rosewood Brown was even more devious than he'd thought. But, dammit, the fact was, he *needed* to get to California, where he had family, at least, and hopefully a few old friends who might be willing to let him hide out for a while and maybe even help him solve his immediate cash problem. And of course the best thing about California was that it was a hell of a long way from Chicago, where people were trying to do away with him.

Remembering that particular fact gave him a feeling as if someone had drawn a cold finger right down his spine. Repressing a shiver, he carefully nudged the glowing end off his cigarette and stepped on it, put what was left in his pocket, then gave the side of the first structure they came to a robust slap and inquired, "What's this for?"

"Garage," said Lucy, giving him an amused look.

"Ah. And that?"

"Shed."

"Uh-huh," said Lanagan. "And those, I suppose, are..."

"Bins," said Lucy. "For grain."

"Ah," said Lanagan.

The great round steel bins seemed to be here, there and everywhere, conveniently located next to fields and pens and livestock yards. They mostly held corn, Lucy told him, and soybeans. They sold the soybeans for cash and kept the corn to feed the livestock, she explained, unless they had a good year, with a surplus. Then there was corn to sell, too.

"Last year we had a huge corn crop. Maybe you read about it in the newspapers?" Lucy, looking over at him questioningly, didn't seem to notice that he winced a little when she said "newspapers." "Broke all records," she went on in a dry tone of voice. "I heard they even had corn piled up in the streets in some towns, because they couldn't move it out fast enough and the elevators were full."

"Well, that's good," said Lanagan, his city-bred mind boggling even as his writer's imagination delighted in the images she painted of small-town streets buried beneath golden drifts of corn. "Isn't it?"

Lucy shot him a wry grin and paused to look out across the fields that fell gently away in freshly plowed ripples, following the contours of the land, around that hill and onto the next, and the next, and the next, and on as far as he could see.

"Farming's never that simple," she said, walking on again. "If the crop's too good, the price goes down. There's always something. If it isn't the weather..." She shook her head and her voice trailed off.

Lanagan made interested and enlightened murmurs, then stuck his hands into his hip pockets and crunched along beside her in silence for a while just to see what would happen. After a few moments of that, Lucy looked over at him and said with a hint of sarcasm, "Aren't you going to ask me what *that* is?" She jerked her head toward the equipment barn.

"What?" said Lanagan. "You mean that? Anybody knows that's a tractor." He squinted thoughtfully and managed to dredge the name up from the dusty files of facts in his mind. "John Deere, isn't it? I think I had one just like it when I was a kid."

To his complete enjoyment she gave a lusty bark of laughter. And though she lowered her head quickly and tried to hide it from him, the wind lifted up the sides of her hair like wings and let him see her dimple again. He found that he was smiling himself, walking along beside her in those ridiculous boots, soft-scented wind in his face, sun warming the borrowed sweatshirt between his shoulder blades, and he shook his head in amazement, wondering why it all felt so good to him.

Maybe, he thought, it was just good to be alive.

Lucy stopped at the gate to the hog run and waited for her new temporary hired hand to catch up with her. Dodger came ambling out to see if there was anything for him to do, accepted a pat and a scratch and went off on some quest of his own, leaving her free to study the man all she wanted to. And she was surprised how much she did want to. No way around it, he was good to look at.

She *was* sorry about saddling him with those great big old boots, but there was no way she was going to let him tromp around in the hog pens in Dad's favorite pair of loafers. But even with the boots, it was amazing how good he looked in Earl's old clothes. Of course, the jeans were left over from high school, so they were a little more snug than he'd probably have liked, but it did make it easy to see there wasn't much wrong with him that a little exercise, good wholesome food and sunshine wouldn't fix.

"What," she sang out when he got close, "no more questions?" Lucy was proud of her hog production system, most of which she'd designed. Of course, Earl had helped with the building, but she'd come up with the idea of connecting the farrowing sheds and the hog yards with a system of runways so she could manage the sows by herself if she had to.

"Uh, can't think of a one," he said, frowning dazedly. Then he contradicted himself and asked, "So, you drive the pigs down here, I guess?"

Lucy snorted and shook her head. "You can't drive a pig. They're smart, not like cattle. What you do is, you convince a pig she wants to go where you want her to go. Then you get out of her way. Here, let me show you how it works." She led the way down the runway to the hog yards, raising her voice so Mike could hear her over the racket the sows were making. They all knew her and were lined up at the fence squealing their heads off to be fed, even though the automatic feeders were full.

"See," she yelled back over her shoulder, explaining as she worked, "when you open the gate to the hog yard, it blocks off the runway so she can only go one way—that way, toward the farrowing sheds. Then you open the door to the farrowing shed, it blocks off that end of the runway, so she's got no choice but to go in. And the runway's too narrow for her to turn around in, in case she thinks she'd like to change her mind in the middle."

Of course, she was showing off wholeheartedly and enjoying every minute of it, especially the look of admiration on Mike's face, but the truth was, it was an easy job to separate out the two sows she wanted and get them headed down the runway. They'd done it enough times before and knew the routine as well as she did. She slammed the gate of the farrowing shed shut against the last sow's twitching tail, gave her rump a slap and said smugly, "See? That's all there is to it."

"The only thing I don't understand," said Mike in an awed tone, "is what you need me for."

She was inexpressibly pleased, but hid it from him and lifted a shoulder modestly. "I don't—not for this. The hard part is going to be that sow that farrowed outside last night. She won't be so easy. What we're going to have to do is get her babies away from her."

Mike nodded, game and trusting. "Uh-huh. How do we do that?"

Lucy grinned. "Carefully."

The sow was in the yard closest to the barn, which, since it was the lowest one, was also the muddiest. She'd found herself a fairly dry spot, at least, and was sprawled out on her side in the sunshine with her nine muddy babies lined up at her udder, contentedly nursing away. Lucy stopped to count them, relieved to see that they'd all found places and seemed healthy and strong in spite of their rocky beginnings.

She left Mike leaning on the fence studying the nursing piglets with a faraway look in his eyes. He got that look every now and then, she'd noticed, and it made her think hard about the fact that she didn't know anything about him, not who he was, or what the business was that had brought him to her barn, or why he'd lied about it. When she went into the barn to get a box for the pigs she glanced reflexively over toward the stall from which she'd discovered a strange pair of legs protruding only a few short hours ago, remembering the awful turn they'd given her, and thought about checking to see if the "missing" wallet was there now, under the straw as she suspected. She knew she ought to, but decided against it. She wasn't sure why.

When she went back outside with the box she found Mike where she'd left him, still squinting into the sunshine, still apparently daydreaming. She nudged him with her elbow. "Here, take this."

He came to, blinking. "What do I do with it?"

"Bring it," she said, pausing astride the fence to give him a look of patience sorely tried, "and come with me.

"What we're going to do" she murmured as they crept up on the sleeping sow like a pair of burglars, "is take the baby pigs off her and put them in the box."

"Right," whispered Mike, sounding doubtful but game.

"It'll be all right," Lucy assured him. "Just don't let them get to squalling. If they squall, the mother'll think they're in trouble."

"Uh-huh," said Mike. "And if they do, and she does, what do I do?"

Lucy gave him a look. "Run like hell for that fence over there. Ready?"

He huffed in a breath and said, "Sure, why not?" Lucy picked up two baby pigs and handed them to him. Laughter spread through her chest like warm cocoa as she watched an expression of pure astonishment come over his face. "My God..." he choked as the piglets began to squirm and huff.

"Quick, put 'em in the box," she rasped, trying desperately not to laugh. "They're going to cut loose in a minute."

He dropped the pigs into the box as if they'd been a couple of hot potatoes, but recovered his composure in time to take two more when she passed them to him. This time all he said was, "Wiry little devils, aren't they?" and popped them into the box.

Lucy hid her smile and handed him the next two.

"Box is getting full," Mike reported in a hoarse whisper.

"Never mind, it's okay. Here, take these so I can get the last—"

"Ouch!" He reared back in astonishment, staring at the tiny red bead on the ball of his thumb. "He *bit* me!" Apparently he was so surprised he'd pretty much forgotten about the baby pig he was still holding in his other hand. The pig was squirming like crazy and beginning to make angry noises.

"Yeah, I know, I have to clip their milk teeth," Lucy told him hurriedly. "Never mind it now, it won't kill you. You better let go of that pig, it's going to—"

Too late. The pig Mike was holding cut loose with all the noise a baby pig can make when he doesn't like the situation he's in, which is a considerable amount. The somnolent sow twitched, then came to life with a long, questioning rumble.

"Uh-oh," said Lucy. She stuffed the last two piglets into the box and shut the flaps. "Time to go."

"What—what—" Mike was still holding on to the squalling pig with both hands, looking both bewildered and horrified.

"Run," yelled Lucy, and scooped up the box just as the sow erupted out of the damp black earth with a bellow of maternal outrage.

She didn't wait to see if Mike took her advice, but as she was making for the fence she could hear him clumping along behind her as fast as he could, with the baby pig clutched in his hands and squealing his head off, and the angry sow hot on his heels. At the fence she balanced the box of pigs on the top rail while she scrambled over into the runway, then pulled the box to safety after her.

She was just turning to see whether there was anything she could do to help Mike out when she heard some wild swearing. The fence shook and quivered. There wasn't anything she could do but watch wide-eyed and openmouthed as Mike came lurching over the fence backward, still clutching that baby pig to his chest and yelling and kicking at the charging sow with his big rubber boots. In that position there was only one way he was going to land, and he did—flat on his back in the runway, with most of the wind knocked out of him. While he was lying there making small, helpless whooping noises, the baby pig went uff-uffing indignantly down his chest and over his belly, tromped right on down the button fly of those tight jeans to topple nose-first into the V of his legs.

Lucy dropped to her knees beside him, started to reach out her hands to touch him to see if he was injured or not, then changed her mind. She finally managed to gasp, "Oh, God, are you all right?"

Lanagan rolled his eyes in her direction. She was making strangled sounds, her face was puffed up and there were tears running down her cheeks. He felt fairly safe in assuming she wasn't weeping over him. "It isn't funny," he wheezed.

Lucy's response to that was to explode with laughter. She sort of collapsed back against the fence with her legs stuck straight out in front of her and doubled over with it, howling and whooping. Lanagan tried hard to stay sore and grumpy, but the truth was, he wasn't really hurt at all, and that laugh was as infectious as a yawn in a board meeting.

Before he knew it his chest had started to shake, and then pretty soon he was whooping and wheezing right along with her.

"Oh, man," Lucy said presently with a sigh, amidst subsiding chortles. She shook her hair back and leaned her head against the fence, gazing up at the sky. "You know, if it hadn't been for those damn boots, I think you might have made it."

Lanagan sat up slowly and draped his arms across his drawn-up knees. "If it hadn't been for these damn boots," he said wryly, searching for and then showing her the ragged tear in the back of one, "that mother would have taken a chunk out of me. Geez, I never knew pigs had teeth like that. Speaking of teeth—" He reached around behind him to retrieve the baby pig, who was rooting energetically at his hip pocket. "Are all baby pigs this ornery?"

"They're born fightin'," Lucy said fondly, taking the pig from him and popping it into the box with its brothers and sisters. "Survival of the fittest. That's what those teeth are for—fighting for a spot at the lunch counter. Nature gives them the tools, and after that they're on their own. They can cut up the sow pretty badly, though. That's why I clip 'em off. Which I need to do right now." She was already on her feet, brushing at the seat of her overalls; Lanagan was beginning to realize she never stayed still for very long.

He stayed where he was for a few moments longer, though, watching her and wondering. He couldn't quite figure out what had just happened to him, and getting chased by a large pig and bitten by a small one and falling off a fence were probably the least of it. He thought he should be feeling a whole lot worse than he was. At the very least, his pride should have been bruised. He probably should feel like a complete fool, but he didn't. What he felt was relaxed, even exhilarated. Little bubbles of laughter kept trickling up inside him, like the lingering effervescence in a bottle of soda pop. And where had that laughter come from, anyway? He couldn't remember the last time he'd laughed like that—probably not since he was a kid. He'd forgotten it could feel so good.

"Come on, Cage, off your butt. There's work to be done." Lucy was standing over him holding the box, a gleam of challenge in her eyes.

"Shh..." he muttered disgustedly under his breath, "you're as ornery as those damn pigs, you know that?" But he was smiling as he got to his feet. He brushed himself off as well as he could and started after her, chewing thoughtfully on his bitten thumb and wondering why, since she was so ornery, he was beginning to like her so much.

During the next hour or so he had a lot of time to watch Lucy and wonder about her, since there wasn't much he could do to help her except stay out of her way. And she wasn't big on conversation, either, although she didn't seem to mind his questions. It was just that she answered them the way she did everything else—with economy and efficiency, straight to the point and nothing wasted. As a reporter he should have loved her; she'd have made a great interview, if all he wanted were facts. He wasn't sure why her answers left him feeling vaguely frustrated, as if there was something more he wanted from her, and didn't quite know what it was, or how to go about getting it.

Between questions he watched her, fascinated by the wiry strength in her arms and hands as she clipped the baby pigs' needle-sharp milk teeth with a pair of stainless steel clippers, deftly examined them and painted their umbilical cords with disinfectant. When that had been accomplished to her satisfaction, she left them in their box and went to get their mother from the hog yard. Nothing but cooperation now, the sow trotted serenely down the runway and into the farrowing shed, grunted in ecstasy while Lucy hosed her off, snuffled happily over a panful of grain and didn't even notice when Lucy stuck a hypodermic needle full of antibiotics into her rump. All of this Lanagan watched, lurking like a craven coward behind the fence just in case the sow held grudges, and shook his head in fascination.

"What?" Lucy asked instantly in that suspicious way she had.

"Nothing," said Lanagan, smiling, and she just shook back her hair and went right back to work, completely unselfconscious, with no idea in her head that it was she who intrigued him so.

Breakfast over, the sow lay down with a groan and stretched out on her side on her bed of clean straw on the concrete floor of the stall just wide enough to allow her to get up and down, but not wide enough for her to turn around in, with a space at the bottom just big enough to allow the baby pigs to come and go. She then emitted a series of rapid grunts—calling her children to lunch, Lucy told him. Gingerly, but with a little more expertise now, Lanagan helped her take the babies out of the box and put them down in the clean straw beside the sow. There was a lot of pushing and shoving, and a racket of squeals and answering grunts while the sow got comfortable and the babies sorted themselves out. Lucy watched critically, making sure each piglet had found a place at the bar and was nursing strongly.

"She's got plenty of room," she said presently, with satisfaction. "I'll bring the other four down later on, after they've gotten warmed up and their bellies full." She looked up at Lanagan with mischief playing around her mouth and asked, right out of the blue and with unmistakable pride, "Well, what do you think of all this?"

He blinked and said, "What do I think?" But it didn't seem possible to tell her he'd never met anyone like her before, or that in his entire life it had never occurred to him that he could be where he was right now—on a hog farm in Iowa, for God's sake. Standing in a pig's stall, elbow-to-elbow with a woman in farmer's overalls, watching a litter of baby pigs nurse. Of all the impossible things that had happened to him recently, this took the prize. He felt as if he'd fallen down a rabbit hole.

Lucy laughed, that lusty chortle he found so infectious, and said, "Well, come on, we have to move some hay first, and then I'll fire up the John Deere and we'll go and see what we can do about your car. Feel like a little exercise?"

Lanagan figured he'd already had more exercise than he generally got in the average week, but he didn't say so. She had that familiar gleam of challenge in her eyes, and he was looking forward to a chance to redeem his masculine pride. Moving hay sounded like a job where brawn might have an edge over brains. At least, he hoped so.

Half an hour later he'd decided pride was pretty much overrated, and certainly not worth what he was going through. He had alfalfa hay dust in his throat, sweat was running down his back in rivers, his muscles were quivering with fatigue, and in spite—or perhaps because—of a pair of stiff leather gloves, he was developing blisters on his hands the size of Kansas. And while he sweated and grunted and manhandled heavy bales with iron hayhooks, Lucy was busy scampering all over the haystack, vaulting on and off the back of a flatbed truck, skillfully maneuvering those same bales with a block and tackle arrangement suspended from the top of the hay shed, all with the swashbuckling grace of Errol Flynn scaling the rigging of a pirate ship. And she still had breath left to shout orders at him.

"Heads up, Cage, quit daydreaming!"

He jumped back just in time to avoid getting flattened by the bale she'd swung his way. As she lowered it onto the stack, he grabbed it with the hayhooks and hoisted it into place, then paused to wipe sweat out of his eyes with his shirt sleeve. Lucy jumped nimbly down from the truck and came to join him, and it made him feel a little better to see that she was sweating, too. He noticed that the tips of her hair were damp where they touched her neck, and that her skin had a rosy sheen under her tan. She looked healthy and vibrant and full of energy. He didn't need a mirror to know *he* didn't look like that.

"Warm?" she asked him, with that teasing dimple in her smile.

"Dying," he admitted, grinning back. "You mind if I take this sweatshirt off?"

"Hey." She shrugged with elaborate unconcern. "Doesn't bother me. I've seen naked men before. Do what makes you feel comfortable."

It was strange, but the minute she said that he didn't feel comfortable anymore. He went ahead and took off the shirt because he figured he was probably going to die of heat stroke if he didn't, but for some reason, once she made that crack about naked men, he *felt* naked. He started to worry about things he'd never worried about before, like whether he was maybe getting a little soft around the middle, and the fact that last summer's tan was long gone and he hadn't had time to get this year's started yet. And it occurred to him that the last time he'd had a shower was when he'd still *had* a shower.

He sneaked a look at Lucy, wondering what it was about her that made him so self-conscious—something she'd said, or the way she'd looked at him. But she was already back on the truck, whistling away and ignoring him completely. He just couldn't figure it out.

Damn, thought Lucy. The way her heart was pounding, you'd think Harrison Ford had just stripped naked right there in front of her. She couldn't figure out what was the matter with her—she'd seen better-looking bodies all her life. Handsomer men, too. Well, a few. She just couldn't remember any of them ever affecting her like this. She thought maybe it was because it had been a long time since she'd seen a man she hadn't known when she was in pig-tails. Most of the men she knew she'd wrestled with in grade school, and had bested quite a few, too. They were as familiar to her as her brothers. On the other hand Mike

Cage—or whatever his name really was—was a stranger, and somewhat of a mystery, which she had to admit was no doubt what made him attractive to her. She wondered whether he really was on the lam, as she suspected. And if he was, who or what from?

And more importantly, what should she do about it?

"Okay, boss, what's next?"

She spun guiltily to find the stranger himself looking up at her, red faced and expectant, wiping sweat and hay from his bare chest with her brother's old high school sweatshirt. The stray lock of hair that fell across his forehead was spiky wet and dripping onto the bridge of his nose. His grin was wry, and so unexpectedly appealing that Lucy frowned at him and snapped peevishly, *"What?"*

He gestured with the sweatshirt. "Only thing left on that truck is you. You got some more hay somewhere you want unloaded?"

She jumped down off the truck, furious with herself and—for no better reason than the fact that he'd made her that way—with him. "Thought you were anxious to get that car of yours out of the creek."

"I am." He hurriedly pulled the sweatshirt over his head and had to run after her, since she was already heading for the machine shed at a brisk clip.

When he caught up with her she gave him a critical glance and muttered, "You're getting sunburned. Ought to have a hat."

"You don't wear one."

He was walking along beside her so his arm almost brushed her shoulder, and for some reason that bothered her. "I'm used to it," she snapped, walking faster, "and any fool can see you're not. Don't get out in the sun much, do you?"

"Not much," he admitted cheerfully.

Which, Lucy told herself, there could be all sorts of reasons for, not all of them seamy or sinister. He could just be a night person or have a desk job in an office somewhere, although neither of those would have made him any less alien to her than if he really was a denizen of the criminal underworld. For some reason that thought made her feel cranky and out of sorts.

"I have a hat," Mike said in a completely different voice, as if he'd just made a discovery that surprised and pleased him. "It's in my car."

Lucy threw him a puzzled glance, but he had the daydreaming look again and an odd tension in his body she couldn't define, but which, if she had been honest enough to admit it, scared her a little. Anyway, she decided not to ask him any more questions. None of my business, she'd said blithely to Gwen, but the truth was, she was beginning to realize there might be more to her mystery man than she'd first thought. The real reason she didn't ask him questions was that she wasn't at all sure she wanted to know the answers.

The Chicagoan, May 2

Metro Section, Page 3

FIRE: Continued from page 1

Asked whether police believe there could be any connection between the firebombing and a recent column of Lanagan's threatening an exposé of alleged ties between organized crime and the Westside Highrise Development Project, Lieutenant Wilson would say only that "all appropriate avenues of investigation are being pursued."

Meanwhile, Lanagan's whereabouts remain unknown.

Chapter 4

Lanagan stood back and watched while Lucy dug a key out of the pocket of her overalls and climbed onto one of the several tractors that were lined up side by side in the shed—the one he'd identified as a John Deere. She started it up and motioned to him, and he climbed up and settled himself on the high green fender. The tractor rolled out of the shed, across the hard-packed earth and onto the gravel driveway, Lucy's hands strong on the wheel, the sun strong and hot on her bare brown arms and the wind lifting the sides of her hair like shiny brown wings. The sun blew through his hair, too, and dried the sweat on his body. He felt his insides quiver with a giddy, almost childlike kind of eagerness.

He realized that he couldn't wait to see his car again. It was only a Dodge, several years old and of no particular distinction, and he liked it mainly because it seldom gave him any trouble and when it did he knew how to fix it. But it was his. *His.* And practically the only thing left that was, come to think of it.

Oh, he knew it hadn't really hit him yet, just how much he'd lost. As a reporter he'd seen a lot of people who'd just had their homes and everything they owned destroyed by fire. He'd seen their grief and heard it, too. He didn't want to face that kind of pain, and he meant to hold it off as long as he possibly could. But right then he felt like a kid coming home after a long trip—he wanted to hold his briefcase in his hands, put on his old brown fedora. He just wanted to touch something familiar, something that was *his*.

"There it is," Lucy yelled, turning to look back at him. "Boy, you did get it stuck in there good, didn't you?"

He didn't answer, and she must have seen something in his face, because she looked away again in a hurry and didn't rub it in. It had caught him by surprise, seeing his car like that, all forlorn, askew and abandoned. He felt ashamed of himself for having gotten it into that condition, embarrassed all over again at having to go ignominiously to a woman for help in getting it out. Worse, he was beginning to be very angry with the circumstances that had brought him to such a pass in the first place. And anger, he knew, was only the first step on the way to losing control.

He's upset, thought Lucy as she pulled the tractor up and backed it around, bringing the trailer hitch as close as she could get it to the car's jutting rear bumper. Not that she blamed him. She'd be pretty upset herself in the same situation, and she was glad she hadn't teased him about it. Beyond that first crack, anyway. Still, she couldn't get over the feeling there was more to it in his case than just being angry because he'd messed his car up and it was going to take some doing to fix it. Money, too, if she wasn't mistaken.

She threw the tractor into neutral and set the brake. "Might need the winch, but we'll give this a try first," she said as she hopped down, nimbly avoiding a puddle.

She went around to the back of the tractor. Mike was there before her, unwinding the chain in grim, rock-jawed silence, and with unaccustomed sensitivity she stood back and let him do it alone. She watched him wriggle under the car to secure the chain to the rear axle, then climbed back up on the tractor.

"Ready?" she asked when he'd emerged again, wearing a scowl as black as a thunderhead.

"In a minute. Let me get the brake."

She watched him pause a moment to light a cigarette, then go slipping and sliding down the creek bank until he could reach the car door. Saw him open it and lean inside to release the brake and put the car in neutral. When he withdrew his head and straightened up again, he was holding a hat in his hands. She smiled a little when she saw it.

"Okay," she yelled, "let's give it a try."

She turned to put the tractor in gear, then looked back. Mike was just reaching the top of the bank, hunched forward to give himself momentum, dark-stubbled jaws clenched hard with the effort of the climb. He'd put the hat on and tipped the brim low over his brow. The cigarette he'd just lit dangled casually from his lips.

Lucy's breath caught in her throat.

Then he straightened up suddenly, drew on his cigarette and looked right at her, and under the hat brim his eyes had a hard, angry glitter. Lucy's chest constricted and her breath rushed forth in a soft, involuntary gasp. Oh, boy, she knew exactly what he looked like. And even though she told herself it couldn't be, that she was being silly and melodramatic, and that there were a hundred innocent explanations for everything, something secret and shameful deep within her thrilled to the possibility that it might be true. Thrilled to the danger and excitement, to the very *wickedness* of the idea.

Because at that moment what Mike Cage looked like to her, more than anything else in this world, was a gangster. Straight out of "The Untouchables."

"*What?*" he demanded in a surly growl.

"Nothing," she muttered breathlessly, and turned with guilty haste to put the tractor in gear.

The John Deere roared and inched forward. The chain pulled tight with a heavy jingle, the crunch of steel meeting steel. Lanagan stood beside his car and stared at Lucy's back through narrowed eyes, tasting the metallic tang of anger. Not at her—God knows, she'd been nothing but kind to him, had put herself out for him above and beyond anything he could ever have expected, and he a total stranger, at that. In fact, he still couldn't quite believe it. Being a city boy born and raised, he wasn't used to that kind of neighborliness. The easy way Lucy and her aunt had accepted him, trusted him when he'd given them no real reason to think they should, both chastened and perplexed him, and in a strange way even contributed to his present state of nail-biting frustration. He wanted to be angry at the bastards who'd done this to him; since he wasn't exactly sure who that was, he wanted to be angry at the whole damn world. But how could he be, when there were people in it like Gwen and Lucy bent on proving to him that the world wasn't such a terrible place and that the sun really was going to come out tomorrow?

His car gave a loud groan of protest. "Whoa!" he yelled, throwing up a fist to signal Lucy to stop.

She nodded and hit the brakes. He glanced at her as he went to check the chain again, wondering why she seemed to be watching him with such intensity. She was sitting half-turned in her seat while the tractor idled lustily under her, with her teeth clamped down on her lower lip as if she were trying to suppress breathless laughter, and a bright gleam of excitement in her eyes, as if she found the whole enterprise thrilling, maybe even a little bit dangerous.

Well, hell, he thought, maybe she did. He hadn't known this Lucy Rose Brown very long, but he'd already figured out that she wasn't like any other woman he'd ever met. A woman who thought it was hilarious to get chased headfirst over a fence by an enraged sow was definitely one who marched to a different drummer.

He gave her a thumbs-up sign and the tractor edged forward. His car lurched and lumbered a foot or two backward before an ominous *crunch* made him once more throw up his hand and call a halt to the proceedings.

This time, though, Lucy had already hit the brakes. She put the tractor in neutral and came to join him where he was crouched on his hands and knees, peering under his car.

"It's hanging up on the edge of the bank," he reported pessimistically. "It's going to tear the hell out of the pan if we go any farther."

She nodded and murmured, "I was afraid of that." She still sounded slightly out of breath.

He eased back onto one knee, draped his arm across the other one, tipped his hat back and looked over at her. She had her thumbs hooked in the side loops of her overalls and she was stooping over to see what there was to see of the problem at hand, so as usual her hair had slithered forward to curtain her face. That is, until she reached up and with the already familiar gesture stroked it deftly behind her ear. Then he could see that she was wearing her dimple, along with that strange, shiny look of excitement poorly suppressed.

"What now?" he asked her. She turned to look at him. He suddenly found that she was very near, so near he could count every strand of that slippery, contrary hair of hers if he wanted to, so near he could see that the tips of her eyelashes were golden, and that her brown eyes had tiny gold flecks near the pupils, and that there was a fine, gold-dust sheen of perspiration across her cheeks and the high, proud bridge of her nose. So near he could hear the soft, barely audible break in her breathing.

She straightened up abruptly and headed back to the tractor with quick, purposeful strides, calling back to him over her shoulder, "Stay here. I'll go get the A-frame and the winch. That way we can just lift it straight up out of there. Only take a minute—be right back."

She eased the tractor backward to release the tension in the chain. Lanagan rose slowly and went to unhook it, then stood with the weight of it heavy in his hands and watched the John Deere go jouncing down the short, bumpy lane and onto the paved road.

Now, what the hell is she thinking? he wondered with the slightest twinge of unease. It almost seemed to him as if she'd had sudden—and in his opinion, rather belated—qualms about him. Second thoughts, perhaps, about trusting him? But he couldn't think of anything he might have done right then to change her mind about him, and besides, he'd never been good at interpreting the subtle nuances of a woman's expressions and moods. His memory did a quick flashback to the look he'd caught on her face just a little while before, when he was climbing out of the creek after checking out his car. That one had puzzled him, too, come to think of it. It had been there for only an instant—a look of surprise and wonder, almost, he thought now, as if she'd recognized him. Which he knew was impossible.

He was going to have to watch himself. A thing like this—somebody trying to kill him—could easily make a man paranoid. Before he knew it he'd be jumping at shadows.

He looked over at his car, still canted at an impossible angle, nosefirst into the creek with the trunk sticking up like the hind end of a stinkbug, and for a few moments he felt as if he were in shadows, felt the world turn darker and a chill breeze blow across the back of his neck, as if a cloud had drifted across the sun. He cast a furtive glance back over his shoulder, even though he knew Lucy and the tractor had already disappeared from sight, then slipped down the bank to retrieve his keys from the ignition. He unlocked the trunk with cold, stiff hands, took out his briefcase and closed it again, then put the keys back. By the time he'd finished with all of that he was sweating, and his muscles trembled as if he'd been trying to lift the front end of a truck. And his hands were still cold.

It was very quiet. He could hear no signs of Lucy returning with the flatbed truck, no tractors growling through distant fields, no barking dogs or lowing cattle. The only sounds were the lazy, vaguely reassuring voices of spring—birds and insects, chuckling water and new cottonwood leaves whispering in the ever-present wind. Lanagan sat on the creek bank with his briefcase on his lap and twirled the combination with his thumbs.

He felt the tiniest moment of hesitation. *Pandora's box,* he thought. Then he opened the lid.

His first thought was, God, they look so ordinary. Just plain old manila files, like the kind everybody uses to keep track of their income taxes and telephone bills. Hard to believe somebody would kill for what was in those cream-colored folders. Hard to believe he might have died for them.

And the amazing thing was, it was all there—the payoffs, the kickbacks, the skimming, the out-and-out bribes—all down in black and white, in memos, bank transactions, ledger entries, computer conversations. He hadn't believed it was real at first, hadn't believed anyone would be so stupid as to keep so much incriminating documentation, until it had occurred to him that with computerized record keeping, it was the *absence* of the information that would be most noticeable. In a way he had to admire both the boldness and the simplicity of it, like hiding something in plain sight. Only someone who knew exactly what to look for would ever find it. And Lanagan had known what to look for.

The call had come to the *Chicagoan*'s metro desk, anonymously, of course. Bunny—Ralph Buncomb, the senior staffer and Lanagan's close friend almost from day one—had taken it and passed it on to Lanagan. It was just another crackpot; let the columnist handle it, right? He might even get a piece or two out of it.

In an obviously disguised voice the caller had suggested that Lanagan ought to go down to the place where they were putting up the new Westside Highrise building and talk to some people. People who were going to be put out of their homes, the caller had said, to make room for the rest of the huge development project. Well, what the hell? It was a slow day and the weather was nice, so he'd driven out to the west side and talked to a lot of people. Including a woman named Cora. And when he'd gotten back to his desk there had been another call waiting for him.

This time the caller had suggested that if Lanagan was interested in knowing more, he ought to go to city hall. That had shocked him some, and he hadn't wanted to take it seriously, not until the caller had given him specifics—department, room number, the location of the files. Then he'd gotten *very* interested. But the caller was cautious—obviously he had known, as Lanagan hadn't, just what kind of people he was dealing with—and so it had taken a week or two and several more calls before arrangements could be made for him to have access to the files at a time when no one else did. And in the meantime, he'd written that column.

What in the world was I thinking of? Lucy wondered, shaking her head at the antics of her own imagination. *Gangsters.* Give me a break.

But she was just turning the tractor into the lane, and she couldn't help but frown as she passed the barn, regretting now the fact that she hadn't looked for that "missing" ID when she'd had the chance. What *was* she thinking of? The thing was, it wasn't like her to have these wild, fanciful ideas. Her brother Rhett—now *he* was the one, the dreamer, the one who could always come up with the wildest stories you ever heard, and sometimes even make you believe them. He was going to make a great politician, come to think of it.

But Lucy had been the practical one, the one who kept her wits about her at all times. Hadn't Dad always said she had good instincts? Which was why she couldn't just shake off the feeling she had about this guy—Mike, or whatever his name was. It wasn't just his hat, or the way he dressed, either. It was something in his eyes. She thought of the way her heart had nearly leaped through the wall of her chest just now when she'd found herself gazing into those eyes close up—which she had to admit hadn't been an entirely unpleasant sensation. No, gangster or not, there was something about him that wasn't right. She was absolutely certain the man was trouble. She just didn't know what kind yet.

"A gangster?" Gwen's eyebrows shot upward, pleating the furrows in her forehead. "What an idea. You've been watching too many old movies on cable TV."

"All right—*okay,*" said Lucy in an argumentative tone, and then added with some reluctance, "Not seriously."

She turned abruptly from her upstairs bedroom window and its view of the front yard, the cottage and the dark row of evergreens beyond. "I just wish you could have seen him in that hat. And don't forget, he does have a trench coat."

"There are other kinds of people who wear trench coats and fedoras besides gangsters," Gwen reminded her, regarding the socks she was sorting with amusement. "Spies, private eyes, FBI agents..."

Lucy considered, then snorted. "Definitely not FBI. He's too rumpled."

"I don't know. Seems to me driving into a creek and spending the night in a barn might even rumple an FBI agent some."

"His socks don't match."

Gwen looked up and uttered one short, melodious note of laughter before a faraway note crept into her voice and nudged it aside. "Edward's socks never matched, either—used to drive our mother crazy. Your mother, too, I imagine."

"Dad? You're kidding." Lucy stopped pacing to stare at her, but Gwen just averted her head to hide that maddening smile of hers and went back to folding the laundry. Lucy frowned and went back to pacing, knowing there wasn't any point in trying to figure out whether Gwen was teasing her or not. She could put more seriousness and truth in her teasing than most people did in sermons.

Her pacing had brought her inevitably back to the window. She leaned over and looked out, trying to be casual about it. "You go into town today?"

"I did," said Gwen.

"I didn't see you leave."

"I went while you two were unloading hay. When I got back, you were off pulling Mike's car out of the creek. Where is the car, by the way? I didn't see it out back."

"He asked me if he could put it in the barn," Lucy said without taking her eyes away from the window. "Doesn't that seem a little peculiar to you?"

"Depends," said Gwen. "Did he say why?"

Lucy made a soft sound of patent disbelief. "He said he didn't want to be in my way while he was fixing it. Gwen, he's hiding out from somebody, I *know* he is. And you know something else? I think he's broke, too. Flat broke." She lowered her voice to a raspy whisper. "He's got no luggage, not even a toothbrush. I had to lend him everything—comb, shaving stuff, *everything.*"

"You still thinking of offering him a job?" Gwen asked curiously.

"I wasn't..." Lucy half turned, then threw up her hands. No use trying to deny it; Gwen knew her too well. "Well, shoot, I thought about it. Why not? My hired man just quit, I'm two payments behind at the bank, not to mention the planting, and there's all the mess to clean up after that storm last night."

"You could use some help," Gwen agreed, nodding over a lace-edged pillowcase.

Lucy wriggled her shoulders. Those words always had an irritating effect on her. "It's not that I can't manage. But you said it yourself, it seemed like a gift from the Lord—an able-bodied man washing up on my doorstep like that, and one who looks like he might be down to his last dollar and could use a chance to earn a few more, to boot. Of course I thought about it."

"Thought. You haven't asked him if he's interested?"

"No," Lucy mumbled, gnawing on her lip. "I haven't."

"Why not?"

She didn't think she wanted to mention her instincts, or the uneasy feeling she got when she looked at him. Or the odd impression she'd gotten when she'd gone back with the flatbed and A-frame and found him sitting on the creek bank with his briefcase cradled in his arms. In that moment before he'd gotten to his feet and come to meet her, he'd seemed to her so *lost,* so terribly alone. As if, she thought—her second wild flight of fancy that day—he'd fallen through a crack into a strange and alien universe, and didn't know how to get back again.

"I want to see how he cleans up first," she said lightly, and idly nudged back the lace curtain with one finger. "I told him he could use the shower in the bunkhouse. I thought he might as well. Doesn't look like he's going to be going anywhere tonight, anyhow." Down below, half-screened by the rambling rosebush, the cottage door was opening. Her heart gave a queer little lurch. "Oops, here he comes now."

"Well," Gwen inquired after a moment, "what's the verdict?"

Lucy was silent, watching the man pause beneath the rose trellis to roll up the sleeves of the clean blue work shirt she'd lent him. He stepped unhurriedly down from the porch, and when he reached the gravel driveway paused again, took his cigarettes out of a shirt pocket and lit one, looking around him as he did so the way a tourist might survey a strange but interesting landscape. At one point he lifted his head and seemed to look right up at her, even though she knew that at that time of evening the west-facing window would be a mirror, reflecting nothing but sky. He'd shaved off the beard stubble, she noticed, and his hair was dampened down, not even lifting in the wind. Except for the one stray lock that still curved like a dark comma across his forehead...

She drew a slightly uneven breath and muttered, "It's an improvement, but he's still no Boy Scout."

"Thank goodness." Gwen's laughter touched lightly between her shoulder blades, and for some reason she shivered. "You know very well you wouldn't want him if he was."

"Have some more chicken, Mr. Cage."

Lanagan flashed a grateful glance upward, from the gnarled, blue-veined hands that held the proffered platter to Gwen's twinkling, youthful eyes. The casual, old-fashioned hospitality in the words and gesture struck chords of memory in him. His grandparents' house—or maybe even great-grandparents, he really couldn't remember—dim and cool on a warm Sunday afternoon... an upright piano, lace doilies on dark furniture, the lilt of an old-country accent. Long, long ago memories....

He coughed and said, "Thank you," helping himself to another drumstick while he struggled back to the present day. When he felt secure in his adulthood again he sought Lucy's eyes across the table. "I appreciate this, more than you can possibly imagine. For..." Unexpectedly overwhelmed, he stopped and made a helpless gesture with his hand. His last bite of fried chicken seemed to have parked in his throat, so he waited a moment or two before finishing lamely, "Everything."

And for not asking me any questions. He didn't ask himself why she hadn't. His battered mind was willing to accept any and all miracles.

"How's your car?" Lucy asked in so blunt and timely a contradiction of his thought that he had to smile. "Get it running yet?"

He snorted ruefully and shook his head. "The engine's pretty waterlogged. I'm going to have to change the oil, filter, spark plugs, air filter—pretty much everything. Dry it out. Then we'll see."

"Uh-huh. How long you figure that ought to take?"

Lanagan put down his fork and cleared his throat. This was the part he'd been thinking about all afternoon, and dreading. "Well, that's kind of a problem." He looked from Lucy, who was regarding him with a bland, interested gaze, to Gwen, who was rearranging dishes and carefully not looking at him at all, then back to Lucy again. "Uh, you see, I don't carry much cash, and without my wallet, credit cards..." Damn, this was hard. He could feel heat creeping up out of the collar of his shirt and into his face, and it wasn't the sunburn he'd gotten that day, either. He hadn't felt embarrassment like this since he was a teenager.

"That's right, you did lose your wallet." Lucy planted both forearms on the table and leaned toward him in earnest concern. "Have you reported that yet?"

"No," said Lanagan, grimly meeting her eyes, "I haven't. But I will. It's not as though it was stolen, and I can't do much about it, anyway, until I..." He paused, shrugged and left it unfinished.

"My," said Lucy in a fascinated tone, "you really are in a catch-22 kind of situation, aren't you? You can't fix your car without your credit cards, and you can't get your credit cards replaced until you get your car fixed." She "tsk'd" with what seemed to him to be undisguised relish. Her brown eyes danced.

"That about sums it up," said Lanagan heavily. He was thinking, You ornery little devil! She was contrary as a mule, or one of those pigs of hers. He knew he hadn't been mistaken about what he'd overheard, but of course she wasn't about to ask him to stay now, now that she knew he actually needed the job. She was going to bluff it out, make *him* do the asking. He'd never met a woman with so little regard for a man's pride.

The silence lengthened into a pause that could only be called pregnant. Lanagan's face felt stony; Lucy's looked as if she was enjoying herself tremendously. It began to feel like a poker game, everybody bluffing everybody else, except that Lanagan knew very well she held the aces, while all he had was a lousy pair of twos.

At last, on a resigned exhalation, he said, "I was thinking that...maybe you could use a hand around here." He waited. Lucy's eyebrows went up, but other than that her expression didn't change much. He coughed and went on. "On a temporary basis. I thought I could, uh, work for room and board, and a little extra, you know—for car parts."

"I don't know," said Lucy, chewing her lip.

Lanagan played his two deuces. "I understand your hired man quit."

It startled her a little bit, just enough to sharpen her. She sat up straight and shot back, "You don't have any farm experience."

"No, I don't," said Lanagan just as bluntly, "but I'm able-bodied and not too stupid. I think I could learn." Somehow their gazes had locked, their voices had become intense and quiet. Somehow the amusing little game had become a one-on-one contest of wills, more like arm wrestling than poker.

Lucy shook her head. "I don't know about this temporary bit. It's my busiest season. What I need—"

"I believe I could use a hand," said Gwen.

They both jerked and looked at her, pulling back from each other as if a string stretched tight between them had suddenly snapped.

She went on making her serene, unhurried way around the table, gathering up the empty plates. "My garden needs manure. And a good weeding." She paused beside Lanagan, beaming like a beneficent saint, put a bony hand on his shoulder—an acute reminder of his newly acquired sunburn—and said kindly, "Would you like some lemon meringue pie?"

"Thanks." His voice was an inexplicable croak. "Sounds great." He watched her purposeful march to the sink with the dirty dishes, then to the laundry room across the hall where he remembered seeing a second, very ancient refrigerator. When she was out of sight he shifted his bemused attention back to Lucy.

She popped up out of her chair as if his gaze had been a cattle prod. Swift, deft hands gathered up dishes and silverware; fierce, bright eyes steadfastly avoided his, until she whirled to glare at him, clutching the back of a chair in a way that reminded him of a little sparrow hawk. "Okay. Minimum wage on top of room and board. You sleep in the cottage. Take your meals in here with us."

For a moment he just looked at her. Then he cleared his throat and said softly, "Thanks. I appreciate it." He wanted to say more, but couldn't think what it would be.

She still wasn't willing to look his way. "I'll go get your bedding. And I guess you're going to need some more clothes." She dropped the load of dishes haphazardly onto the counter and went out of the kitchen as if she was angry about something, brushing by Gwen, who was just coming in with a meringue-heaped pie like an offering in her hands.

Gwen looked after her grand-niece with fond amusement, then lifted an eyebrow at Lanagan. "Where's she off to?"

He leaned back in his chair and let his breath out, unaware until then that he'd been holding it. Lucy had that kind of effect on him. "She's getting me some clothes and bedding. I guess that means I'm hired."

"Think you can handle it?" She was laughing silently at him; her voice had that strange and lovely musical lilt.

He grinned back at her, liking her more and more, drawn to her by threads he didn't entirely understand. "I think so, as long as I don't have to ride a horse."

"I didn't mean the work. I meant working for Lucy." She cut a huge piece of the pie and lifted it onto a plate. "She's no picnic."

He took a bite of the pie and savored it thoughtfully, in complete agreement, and wondering whether what he'd just done was a smart thing to do. He'd been having a hard time making decisions lately. It seemed easier, somehow, just to let his course be determined by fate, or forces of nature—which he was beginning to believe applied as well to Lucy as to thunderstorms.

He said, half to himself, half surprised, "I know, but I like her."

Gwen gave a low, melodious chuckle. "Well," she remarked as she whisked the pie pan away and started out of the room with it, "you don't have to worry about horses. We always had a few when Lucy's parents were alive, but..."

"She mentioned they'd died. How did it happen?" Lanagan asked, not even surprised that he felt comfortable enough to ask Gwen the question as a friend would, not a reporter, nor doubting for a moment that she'd answer him the same way.

"It was an automobile accident," she said gently, pausing with the pie in her hands to look into the past, not at him. "They'd gone to an awards banquet at the high school and were on their way home. Earl, Lucy's youngest brother, was in the back seat. There was a terrible thunderstorm—rain and hail so thick you couldn't see. They slid off the road and hit a tree."

She went out and left him sitting there, with sweet meringue dissolving on his tongue and his mind doing a slow dissolve to the scene in the barn, and Lucy saying softly, "That storm." Her attitude toward him had changed from that moment on, and he'd wondered why. Now he knew.

Only now it seemed to have done another about-face. He could hear her upstairs, thumping around, banging drawers, slamming doors. Familiar sounds to him. He'd had that effect on women before. But although he recognized the signs of an emotional storm when he heard one, he couldn't for the life of him figure out what this one could be about. Which, he reflected ruefully, was pretty much the story of his life—his love life, anyway. He could never understand what it was he did that frustrated his girlfriends so. He *liked* women. What was more important, he respected them as people and genuinely sympathized with their problems. Having helped his mother cope with an absentee husband and his younger sisters' adolescence had insured that. Also, he was reasonably neat and tried to be courteous, and he knew women found him fairly attractive. At least, he thought so, because he didn't have any trouble finding women eager to share his hearth and home. Or, at any rate, his bed. *Keeping* them—that was the problem.

At least, he thought, wincing at a thud that shook the ceiling above his head, whatever was bothering Lucy, it couldn't be anything he'd done. There wasn't anything even remotely sexual between them, either on her part—and he usually had pretty good instincts about those things—or his. All right, he liked her a lot, and there was definitely some chemistry there, but physically she wasn't his type. Not at all. And he hadn't known her long enough for her to be so aggravated with him on general principles. So it probably had something to do with the fact that she'd been overruled about hiring him. And yet, he could have sworn she was the one who'd had the idea in the first place. And now she'd changed her mind, or at least had some strong reservations about it. He wondered why.

He finished the pie to the last crumb of crust and carried his empty plate to the sink, and then, since he'd just reminded himself that he was both courteous and neat, he finished clearing off the table. After that, since neither Lucy nor Gwen had yet reappeared and the door was open, he wandered into the next room.

This was obviously the "front room," as his grandparents would have called it, or the parlor. And sure enough, there it was, the big upright piano—yes, and its top was crowded with framed family photographs, just like the one in his childhood memory. There were photographs on the old-fashioned fruitwood mantel above the fireplace, too, and on both the handsome hand-crank Victrola near the door and the big console television set in the far corner. Book-filled shelves lined the walls. Colorful crocheted afghans covered the backs of the sofa and chairs. The knickknacks on the tables and the pictures on the walls were the nondescript assortment that represents the accumulation of a lifetime, rather than any decorating scheme.

He went on into the room with no sense of trespass, pausing to pick up a magazine, tilting his head to read the spines of the books on the shelves, drawing his fingers soundlessly across the piano keys, bending to scrutinize the faces in shadowy photographs. Not all of the photos were shadowy. There were the usual graduation portraits, Lucy's with her hair parted in the middle and a stiff-looking smile, the kind that results when someone says "cheese"; a wedding picture with a beautiful blond bride and a handsome, solemn-looking groom; a formal portrait of a Marine in white hat and dress blues, American flag in the background; a studio portrait of a middle-aged but still attractive and youngish-looking couple.

"That's my mom and dad," said Lucy, stepping up beside him. He hadn't heard her come in.

"I figured." He put the picture back on the mantel where he found it. She reached instantly and possessively to adjust it to exactly the right angle.

"Ed and Ellen Brown," she said as if she were making a formal introduction. Her voice was raspier than usual. "That was their twenty-fifth wedding anniversary. We all pitched in and paid for the sitting. I'm glad we did, now. There aren't too many pictures of them around, especially Mom—she was always the one with the camera, and anyway, she hated to have her picture taken."

"I don't know why," Lanagan commented. "She's very attractive."

She nodded and said, "Yes, she was," with a slight emphasis on the last word. Then added as she picked up the portrait of the young Marine, "This is my youngest brother, Earl. Edward Earl, actually, after my dad. Mom insisted on it."

Lanagan touched the wedding portrait. "And this?"

"Everett, my older brother."

Good-looking, both of them, he thought. Tall and athletic, with dark hair and lean, strong features. He could see the family resemblance between them, but none at all to Lucy. He tapped the bride and said, "And this is the social-climbing wife?"

"Elaine..." She drew it out in a wry drawl, and laughed a little. "Yeah, that's her, my dear sister-in-law."

"She certainly is..."

"Yeah, she's gorgeous," said Lucy aloofly, "if you like the type." He caught an oblique glimpse of her impish dimple. "Tall, blond, boobs out to there and legs up to here...."

Since it was pretty much his type she'd just described and he had a feeling she knew it, Lanagan coughed and moved away from the mantel, strolling over to the piano instead. She followed him, obligingly identifying pictures when he asked, explaining relationships in the rapid, offhand way people do when they're afraid of boring you. But he wasn't bored—far from it. It was his nature to find most things about most people interesting, but beyond that there was a strange tension in him that he didn't understand, and a weight in his chest he couldn't identify.

One photo in particular had caught his attention when he'd first walked into the room, partly because it was bigger than most of the others and partly because is was obviously very old, but also because of an elusive sense of recognition, a resemblance he couldn't put his finger on. Now he lifted it down from its place on the piano in order to study it more closely—a woman in a plain, high-necked pioneer dress, hair pulled severely back from strong, sharp features, eyes staring into the camera with the fierce dark gaze of an embattled hawk. He looked up suddenly and encountered the same pair of eyes, alive and alight and regarding him with wry awareness.

The Chicagoan, May 3

Metro Section, Front page
by Ralph Buncomb, staff writer

CHICAGO—Two days after the firebombing of *Chicagoan* columnist Mike Lanagan's southside town house, authorities admit they still have more questions than answers regarding the incident. Just exactly who is responsible is of course among them; and whether the blatant attempt on Lanagan's life has anything to do with a recent column in which he openly threatened an exposé of corruption surrounding the construction of the huge and controversial Westside Highrise Project. But of increasing concern to police, as well as to the columnist's family, friends and associates is the question, *Where in the world is Mike Lanagan?*

According to chief arson investigator Lieutenant Charles Wilson, Lanagan left the scene the morning of the fire and has not been seen since. Police insist they have no cause to believe his continuing absence is attributable to foul play.

* * * * * * * *

The Chicagoan, May 3

Metro Section

"My Kind Of Town" by Mike Lanagan

Mike Lanagan is taking a vacation.

Chapter 5

"My great-great—I don't know how many greats—grandmother," said Lucy, shaking back the slippery wings of her hair and lifting her pointed chin in a way he recognized as both proud and defensive. "Lucinda Rosewood. I was named after her."

"That's quite a name," Lanagan said softly, not telling her he already knew it.

She grinned suddenly, thereby erasing most of the resemblance to the solemn portrait of her ancestor. "I asked my mom and dad once why they'd done such a thing to me. They told me it was because with a last name like Brown you need something special leading up to it. They did the same thing with my brothers, too—Edward Earl and Everett Charlton, for Heaven's sake."

She took the picture from him, gazing down at it as she fingered one side of her hair back behind her ear. He found himself following the gesture with his eyes, and from there the curving shape of her ear, the line of her neck, unexpectedly graceful....

"I suppose I do look like her—kind of a throwback, I guess you could call it." The edges of her mouth quirked slightly. She sighed, and he knew it was both an acknowledgment and acceptance of her own physical self and a purely feminine wistfulness for something she knew she could never be. He found it so unexpectedly poignant he wanted to protest aloud that physical beauty wasn't important, and somehow make her believe it.

"They told me she was small, too, like I am. You'd never know it to look at her here. Something about those pioneer women, they always look about eight feet tall. They say she once set her own barn and fields on fire to foil a Sioux raiding party. Then she tied her baby up in her apron and climbed down the well and hid there while the fire burned all the way to the river." She looked up, face solemn, eyes dancing. "My granddad used to tell me that story, over and over." She raised a finger in an oratorical pose and intoned, "'Lucinda,' he'd say, 'let that be a lesson to you. You keep your wits about you and you never need to be afraid of anything.' I heard that a lot when I was growing up."

She handed the picture of her great-grandma Rosewood back to him and made a quick, dismissive motion with her head, ending that chapter of family memoirs as firmly as if she'd closed a book.

The closure left Lanagan feeling vaguely disappointed. Staring down at the austere portrait in his hands, he had a sense of doors tantalizingly locked upon unexplored corridors and unsolved mysteries. He became aware, then, of the silence, aware that it had become awkward and uncomfortable. Glancing obliquely at Lucy, he was surprised to see that she was carefully not looking at him, studying the piano keyboard instead with the kind of fixed intensity that could only come from embarrassment. An acute awareness of confidences shared and, perhaps, regretted? But what confidences? he wondered. And why regretted?

To bridge both the silence and the awkwardness, which he found that *he* very much regretted, he restored Grandma Rosewood's portrait to its place on top of the piano and sat down on the bench. After another brief, sideways glance at Lucy, he slowly picked out the opening bars of "The Entertainer." When he looked up at her face again he was glad to see that the embarrassment was gone, and in its place a look both startled and pleased.

"You play the *piano?*" she asked in a tone that made it plain it was the last thing she would have thought him capable of.

Not for the first time, he wondered just what she did think of him, considering his circumstances and the way she'd found him. And considering how little he'd been able to tell her about himself, which was something else he regretted. When he'd first started lying to her he hadn't known he was going to have to sustain it for an indefinite period of time. It didn't come naturally to him. But since the truth was out of the question, and as long as Lucy and Gwen both seemed willing to accept him pretty much on faith, he couldn't see any help for it except to keep on as he'd started.

"Haven't in years," he said, answering Lucy's question with a rueful grin. "I took lessons when I was a kid. My mother insisted on it." He fiddled with the keys, trying out chords, testing his memory. "This is a nice old upright. Reminds me of one my grandparents had. Who plays? You?"

She gave a cracked little bark of laughter. "*Me?* Lord, no. My brothers—they're the musical ones. All comes from Mom's side of the family. Earl and Rhett can both play just about anything—guitar, piano...you name it. They can sing, too. When Mom was alive and the boys were both home, the three of them used to sing for weddings, church suppers, things like that."

She was silent again for a moment, but it was a friendly, remembering kind of silence. She still gazed intently at the piano keys, but now there was a soft sheen in her eyes, as if she saw her memories reflected in the polished ivory. Her hair swung gently across her cheeks. After a moment she gave a raspy chuckle, and Lanagan saw her dimple take shape behind the screen of her hair.

"I take after Dad's side, in that way as in everything else, I guess. Poor Dad didn't even know enough music to figure out he couldn't sing. Me, I pretty much stick to whistling, since my voice sounds like somebody sawing on a bucket with a rusty file. As for the piano, I can play 'Chopsticks,' maybe, but that's about it."

"'Chopsticks'? You know the top part?" He scooted over on the bench to make room for her. She shot him a look of uncharacteristic uncertainty. "Come on," he said, patting the bench, "give it a shot. It'll come back to you."

He saw her dimple flicker, then deepen. She tucked her hair behind her ear and sat down beside him, and he could feel the warmth of her body, hear her quick, suspenseful breathing. His own heartbeat shifted gears.

She laced her fingers together, turned them wrong side out and cracked them, like a concert pianist warming up, all the time watching him with laughter in her eyes. "Okay," she said breathlessly, "I'm ready."

"Like this." He showed her the sequence while she looked on avidly, fingers hovering over the keys, waiting her chance like a hawk poised to pounce. "Remember?"

"Yeah, yeah, I'm ready."

They ran through it slowly at first, after a couple of false starts, then later in double time, giggling like children. After that he showed her the top part of "Heart and Soul," and it turned out she knew that one, too. He did boogie-woogie variations on the bass until she got tangled up and lost her place in the melody, and in her frustration gave him a shove that pushed him clean off the bench. Then there they were again, laughing together as hard as they had that morning in the hog run.

When they could speak again, through wheezes and recurring chortles, each accused the other of sabotage and varying degrees of willful mischief, after which they eased gradually into hmms and sniffles and settling sighs, Lucy on the bench, elbows planted discordantly on the keyboard, Lanagan on the floor with his arms draped across his knees.

"Well, so much for the entertainment," said Lucy presently, sounding like herself again, if still a little out of breath. She bounced up off the bench and offered Lanagan her hand. "Come on, Cage, I'd better get you settled. I'm late for chores."

He accepted her help in getting to his feet, and once there asked dutifully if she needed any help. But the truth was, he'd have been glad to stay right where he was for a while, with the solid hardwood floor under his bottom and the sturdy leg of an upright piano against his back. The laughter had left him feeling strange—pensive and subdued, almost melancholy. And fragile, as if everything inside him had shaken loose. Suddenly he didn't quite trust his emotions. He knew he couldn't have said with any certainty, if such a thing had happened again right then at that moment, whether he'd have burst into laughter or tears.

Lucy rejected his offer to help with a quick shake of her head. "Tomorrow's soon enough," she said as she led the way into the kitchen. A large wicker laundry basket sat on the table, heaped high with sheets, comforter, towels and an assortment of clothing. He was pretty sure he recognized at least one pair of overalls in the stack, as well as some serviceable-looking high-topped leather work boots in what looked to be pretty close to his size. He was grateful for that; he wasn't sure his thigh muscles would have made it through another day of those knee-high rubber things.

With her usual abruptness Lucy picked up the basket by its handles and swung it his way, smacking him in the midsection with enough force to cause him to actually utter the word "Oof!" He grabbed at the handles, and just for a moment his hands tangled with hers, until they wiggled away out from under his and left him holding twisted wicker that was still warm from her touch. His heart gave a queer little lurch, which he put down to the general precariousness of his emotional condition. Right now, he thought, any physical contact at all would be dangerous.

He followed Lucy to the cottage and parted company with her at the bottom of the porch steps.

"Holler if you need anything," she said as she started off in the direction of the stockyards. Then she hesitated and turned back. "By the way, breakfast is at six."

"Six?" croaked Lanagan. "You got an alarm clock I can use?"

"Trust me, you won't need an alarm clock." She grinned. "Get a good night's sleep. Hard day's work tomorrow."

He watched her go, hands tucked in the back pockets of her too-big overalls. The wind, just a breeze at this time of evening, the early twilight hour, barely lifted the sides of her hair so they seemed to lift and float as she walked along, whistling a tune he didn't know. Off in the distance he could hear the squealing of the pigs in anticipation of her coming, and closer by, the contented chuckling of the last few straggling hens, dawdling into the chicken house to roost. The air felt soft and smelled of earth and grass and animals. He turned at last and went into the cottage, letting the screen door bang behind him.

Inside, he set the basket on the bare linoleum floor and surveyed his new home—his safe harbor. His hiding place. One room, a closet and a bathroom with a shower. A bed, a fat easy chair, a reading lamp, a low table and a small TV set. What more did a man need?

He was suddenly conscious of an overwhelming tiredness, tiredness that made his head swim and his legs shake, tiredness that felt like a weight too heavy to carry one step farther. He made up the bed after a fashion, with the sheets and comforter Lucy had given him, then undressed and lay down, sinking into the mattress as if it had no bottom to it. The feel of clean, smooth sheets felt strange against his skin. He lay with his eyes closed, floating, listening to the unfamiliar sounds of the country—lowing cattle and chirping frogs and singing insects—a disquieting din, it seemed, to ears accustomed to city noises.

The blank gray canvas of his mind began to fill with the day's images, jumbled images, so many, crowding in on one another…faces, Lucy's face, and Gwen's, and all the faces in the photographs in the parlor, the books, the knickknacks, the pictures on the walls….

And then, like a slow dissolve, it was *his* walls, the walls of his own home he was seeing, and the framed photographs that hung there. His father's photographs, each one sent from some faraway place between two sturdy pieces of cardboard, wrapped this way and that with layers and layers of tape and plastered with exotic postage stamps. He remembered the way his heart would leap with joy and anticipation whenever he saw one of those big flat packages propped on top of the mailbox. And later, how he would sit in the privacy of his room and hold the photograph in his hands, stare at it and ache with longing. Longing to have his dad home again, even if only for one of his brief, whirlwind visits. Longing to be out there, where he was, in the middle of whatever war or revolution or natural disaster he happened to be covering at the moment. For whatever the worst calamity or turmoil was in the world, that was where Sean Lanagan was sure to be, his cameras searching out and unerringly finding the searing, unforgettable images that in his tragically short career had won him a reputation as one of the greatest news photographers of all time. His second Pulitzer was awarded posthumously: Sean Lanagan had died in a helicopter crash during the Tet Offensive, leaving his young son with only a few hazy memories and a wall full of photographs. The photos were all he would ever have of his father. He'd picked out the matts and done the framing himself. And now they were gone.

So were his books, so many books—a lifetime's accumulation, from childhood favorites through college textbooks, a set of leather-bound classics he'd bought at a garage sale and always intended to read someday, literally hundreds of paperbacks and, worst of all, the well-thumbed dictionaries, thesauruses and reference books without which he couldn't function as a writer.

And the shoebox full of Matchbox cars he'd played with as a boy, and had saved to pass on to his own sons someday. His stereo. His computer, with all his notes for columns he'd meant to write someday.

His tax records.

That godawful sweater Monica had given him last Christmas.

His passport. Birth certificate. High school yearbooks. His maroon-and-gold USC sweatshirt, old and comfortable, faded to mauve, with the holes in the shoulder.

Gone. Everything was gone.

A shudder passed through him, pain and loss and loneliness too overwhelming for tears. He put a forearm across his eyes and concentrated on breathing, slowly and deeply, breathing past the pain the way he'd learned to do as a child, a boy-child raised in a time when it was considered unmanly for boys to cry. A boy forced too soon to take on the responsibilities of a man.

After a while, a long, long while, he slept.

On her way back to the house Lucy stopped to shut up the chickens for the night. Passing the cottage she hesitated, wondering if perhaps she ought to check in on Mike, just to make sure her new hired man had everything he needed. She stepped up onto the tiny porch beneath the rose trellis and raised her hand to knock, then slowly lowered it again. Inside all was quiet, so quiet she could hear the knocking of her own heartbeat. She stood very still for a few moments, listening, then went quietly down the steps, pausing to break off one rosebud that was more advanced than the rest, just cracking red, a harbinger of glories to come.

In the kitchen she took a glass from the cupboard, filled it with water and put the bud in it, even though she knew it wasn't mature enough to open and bloom. Then she turned off the lights and went upstairs to her bedroom. The door to her room was open, as always, and she went in as she always did, already slipping the straps of her overalls over one shoulder, one hand reaching to set the glass with the rosebud on top of the dresser before continuing on to the light switch. Light flooded the room, and the windows opposite became mirrors.

Remembering that the night beyond the windows was no longer populated only by livestock and stars, she hastily pulled her overalls straps back into place and, crossing to the windows, reached up to pull the shades. And stopped there, arrested by her own reflection in the glass. She lowered her hand and stood for a long time, gazing at what she saw there—a narrow face framed by dirt-brown hair, a neck too long and a body too scrawny for either grace or sex appeal. Her fingertips traced the arch of her nose, touched the sun creases at the corners of her eyes, then pressed against her lips and felt them tremble slightly before they hardened into an ironic little smile.

"Who am I kidding?" she muttered to herself. "I just hope..." But what it was she hoped for she had no idea.

Down below, the cottage was silent and dark. Leaving the shades up, she turned her back on the windows and slipped out of her overalls, then went down the hall to the bathroom in her underpants and T-shirt to wash her face and brush her teeth. When she came back she turned out the light as she came through the door, then got into bed and lay in the dark instead of reading for a while, as she often did.

Somewhere on the other side of the house the moon rose, thinning the darkness in the room to gray and revealing the shapes of familiar objects. Mom's cedar chest and rocker, the overalls discarded on the floor, the ghostly flutter of white window curtains. The dresser by the door. And one barely opened rosebud in a glass.

She curled her hand beneath her cheek and stared at the rosebud for a long time. And after a while, a long, long while, she slept.

Lanagan dreamed of fire and sirens and woke up sweat soaked, shaking with adrenaline. But for some reason the siren was still screaming. He jerked himself more completely awake, propped himself up on his elbows and swore into the murky light of dawn. Then it all came to him and he fell back again, groaning a protest, with his arm across his face.

It was a damned rooster, that's what it was. Crowing. Crowing right over his bed, or so it sounded. He took his arm cautiously away from his face and tipped his head back, expecting to see it perched right there on the headboard. Instead he saw a small window, brown-laced with cobwebs, and beyond it some green leaves and a whitewashed wall in need of paint. The chicken house, that was it. Right—his new neighbors. How could he have forgotten something like that? On the other hand, nobody had told him about roosters.

Trust me, you won't need an alarm clock.

Remembering that and thinking of Lucy, he suddenly found that he was smiling, and not only that but feeling rested, energized, eager, the way he used to feel when he was just getting started on a new story.

He swung his feet over the side of the bed and sat up, hissing in surprise as his muscles protested the abuses of the day before. And even that didn't dismay him. He hurt all over, but it was a good hurt, the result of good, hard, honest labor. He felt ennobled by it. He began to think that in the long run all this was going to be good for him. His current situation was sort of like a vacation, or like checking into a health spa. Sure—instead of going to California he'd stay right here and get lean and hard and healthy while his mind rested and his emotions healed, until the day when he felt ready to go back and tackle his life again.

He got briskly out of bed, did a few back and torso stretches, then showered and dressed in the clothes Lucy had given him—her brother's, she'd told him, although he thought probably the overalls had belonged to her father; he couldn't imagine anybody of his own generation wearing them by choice. Teenagers, maybe. He smiled to himself as he put them on, thinking about Lucy again, and the way she looked in them, like a little girl playing grown-up.

Just before he went out the door he picked up his old brown fedora and stood for a moment, turning it around and around in his hands, shaping the crown with his fingers. He put it on finally and struck a pose as he caught a glimpse of himself in the bathroom mirror. Geez, he thought, overalls and a fedora? He looked like something out of *Tobacco Road.* He took the hat off and resettled it at a more jaunty angle, giving the front of the brim a downward tilt. There, that was better. Now he looked more like himself again.

Mike Lanagan, newspaperman—that's who he was and all he'd ever wanted to be. He'd known that since high school, which was when he'd started wearing the hat, more or less as a joke in the beginning. Being pretty full of himself and his position of power as star reporter and editor in chief of the school newspaper, he'd seen *The Front Page* maybe twenty times, counting all the remakes, and had taken to imitating certain stars of the thirties and forties, like Gable and Bogart and his favorite, Spencer Tracy. Naturally, as a result he'd been considered something of a weirdo among his peers—he preferred not to think *nerd.* It hadn't bothered him particularly. He'd felt good about himself in spite of it, doing what he believed he was meant to do, and believing what he did was important.

By God, he still did. And although he might have dropped out of his life temporarily, or been forced out, it was still the only life he'd ever wanted to live and he meant to return to it one day. He *would* return to it.

You could count on it.

He snapped the brim of the hat with his finger and opened the door, almost bowling over Lucy, who was standing on the porch with her hand raised to knock.

"Oh..." she said. "You're up." And immediately thought, Gee, Lucy, that was brilliant.

She didn't know what she'd expected. Certainly not the twisting sensation she'd just experienced, right under her ribs, or her heart suddenly going ninety miles an hour. She'd housed hired men of all shapes and sizes in the bunkhouse cottage, but she couldn't recall any of them ever filling up its doorway quite the way this one did. Just for a moment she felt overwhelmed by the warm scent of freshly showered, clean-shaven man.

"Didn't have much choice." Her hired man smiled ruefully and stepped out through the door, closing it behind him, making it way too crowded on the little porch, curtained and canopied as it was by the rambling rosebush. She backed hastily down the steps into the open and gulped a breath of fresh air to clear her head.

"Told you you wouldn't need a wake-up call," she remarked as they made their way around to the back of the house.

He glanced at her as he fished in his shirt pocket for his cigarettes. "But you were going to give me one, anyway?"

She caught the gleam of his eyes in the shadows under the brim of his hat, and her breath gave an involuntary little hiccup. To cover it she said flippantly, "Hey, you're the greenhorn, remember? I didn't want you to get lost on your way to breakfast." He gave a wry snort of laughter and didn't bother to reply.

"Do you have to do that?" she asked after a moment, staring pointedly at the cigarette he was just inserting between his lips. Not that she was an antismoking fanatic, but she was cranky about the way her vital signs were behaving, and looking for something to be irritated about.

She saw his eyes sort of widen for a second over the flame of his lighter before he hastily snapped it off. "Sorry," he muttered, and turned his head away from her to puff out the smoke.

Okay, he was being nice about it, damn him. She didn't want him to be nice. "Why don't you just quit?" she asked snappishly.

"Trying to reform me?" But his tone was teasing rather than resentful. He seemed to be in unquenchably good humor this morning.

She flashed him a look, certain he was humoring her and in no mood to be humored, but for some reason her eyes lingered on his face, noticing, in spite of all her best intentions, the way his mouth curved and reshaped itself in a quirky little smile. She also noticed that his lips seemed very smooth. And firm. She liked a man with firm lips.

Her irritation ebbed away, leaving her feeling vaguely depressed instead. She shrugged and muttered distantly, "Wouldn't dream of it. It's your lungs."

"Hey, don't worry about me. I'm used to smoke-filled rooms." Mike's tone was still good-natured, but now there was something dry in it—a particularly bitter irony she didn't understand. "It's all this fresh air I'm not sure about."

She noticed that he took only a couple more puffs on the cigarette before he threw it down and ground it fastidiously into the dirt.

Smoked-filled rooms. But that could mean anything from barrooms to boardrooms, she thought, stealing uneasy glances at Mike as they went up the back porch steps and into the kitchen. She hated the fact that she still wondered about it after a long, restless night of troubled dreams, and even more that for all her wondering it was impossible to conclude which seemed the more likely.

Especially the way he looked right now. Pop's overalls and a brown fedora—what an ensemble! Something so familiar to her, evocative of comfort and security, combined with something so exotic, vaguely threatening, disquieting as a stranger's touch. Yesterday morning he'd been just an intriguing little ripple in the customary pattern of her days, a bit of storm flotsam, a moment of excitement, like finding a bird's nest that had blown out of a tree. Today he seemed very different. Bigger, for one thing, which might have something to do with the clothes he was wearing, overalls being bulkier than a pair of too-tight jeans. And a lot more sure of himself, which was good—she didn't have much use for men she could push around. Other than that it wasn't anything she could put her finger on, but all the same, she wondered why on earth she'd ever thought it was such a clever idea to take on a complete stranger as her new hired man.

Hoping he wouldn't notice, she sneaked another hard look at him, trying to figure out what it was about him that had made her do such a thing. A nice pair of shoulders? Trustworthy eyes? Not likely. Half the time she couldn't even see his eyes under the brim of that hat, and male bodies held no secrets for her, and consequently no great fascination, either. And furthermore, she didn't know whether she *did* trust him. Or if she'd hired him in spite of the fact that she didn't.

After Lanagan had enthusiastically put away his second cholesterol-laden breakfast in as many days, Lucy took him out to show him the routine of morning chores. He could tell she was still in a snit, but it didn't trouble him greatly. He was used to women's moods, and had learned that most of the time the best way to handle them was to ignore them.

Besides, his mind was busy with more interesting things. A reporter to the bottom of his soul, he considered himself first a gatherer of information, and second but of only slightly less importance, a writer. Circumstances had landed him in a world as alien to him as outer space. Now that he'd recovered from the initial shock, everything about it fascinated him. Consequently, his mind was constantly busy seeking out and soaking up new information and impressions and distilling them down into paragraph form.

He bombarded Lucy with questions and, as she had the day before, she answered most with patient amusement and an economy of words he thought was just natural to her personality rather than grudging. If she thought it strange that he should have so many questions she didn't say so.

Her cattle were mostly Charolais, she told him—burly, white, amiable-looking beasts with broad faces and dark, limpid eyes. The cows and calves were all out grazing on the lush hillsides—the green dotted swiss he'd noticed yesterday—but several huge bulls were confined to a large enclosure near the barn, which Lucy called "the bullpen" with a droll glint in her eyes, and had to be fed. At Lucy's direction Lanagan dumped several flakes of alfalfa and oat hay over the fence into their feed box, then leaned his arms on the topmost rail and watched them come to breakfast with unhurried gait and ponderous dignity, switching away flies with their long, busy tails.

One behemoth the approximate size and conformation of a buffalo, apparently more curious than hungry, wandered over to the fence, thrust his broad, moist nose between the rails and fixed Mike with a shiny, distrustful stare. For a few long moments Lanagan held his breath and returned the stare, eyeball to eyeball. Then, in awe, he reached out and touched the animal right between the eyes, where the white hair curled around a natural vortex. The bull instantly lowered his massive head, snorted gustily and took a step backward, pawing up a cloud of dirt with one great hoof.

"Hey, they really do that," said Lanagan in a fascinated tone, recalling all the Bugs Bunny cartoons he'd enjoyed in his childhood, wherein angry bulls were always depicted huffing smoke from their nostrils like runaway locomotives.

"Perhaps later we can find a little baby one for you to pet," said Lucy facetiously, climbing up on the fence beside him.

But Lanagan was finding everything much too interesting to take offense. He just grinned at her and nodded toward the bulls, all now placidly munching and tossing hay into the air. "How come you have just the one black one?"

"The black Angus? I keep him mainly to service the first-calf heifers."

"Ah..." said Lanagan. "Ha..." He searched wildly for a comeback question and finally settled for "How come?"

"Angus are a smaller-boned breed, especially the head." She glanced at him, then patiently explained, "That makes the calves smaller, easier to give birth to."

"Ah," said Lanagan. And after a moment, frowning, "Why do you keep the bulls separate from the cows? How do you know when to, uh..."

Lucy gave a small, raspy chuckle. "Oh, a cow'll let you know when she wants the bull. If I had a cow in season right now, trust me, she'd be down here at the fence, trying her best to get through it."

"Ah-huh," said Lanagan, and choked a little. The last thing in the world he'd ever have thought of himself as was a prude, but he wasn't used to discussing procreation with a woman in quite such unequivocal terms. He glanced over to see if she was teasing him, trying to shock him or make him uncomfortable, but her face was absolutely straight—bland, even. His masculine pride once again at stake, he coughed and inquired with equal sobriety, "Don't the, uh, bulls fight each other for the, uh, privilege?"

Lucy hunched her shoulders in a shrug. "Oh, sometimes they square off and paw up some dirt. Nothing serious." Now he caught a glimpse of her elusive dimple. "In general, they'd rather make love than war."

Lanagan chuckled obligingly. "So, how do they, uh, decide who gets to, uh..."

Lucy waited with raised eyebrows for him to finish it, then apparently took pity on him. "They don't. I do," she informed him with what was becoming a familiar look of tolerant amusement. Then, before he could think of another question to ask, she added with a hint of exasperation, "Well, for heaven's sakes, Cage, I do have to keep records. I have to know which calves are sired by which bull, after all."

She jumped down from the fence and waited for him to do the same. "You know," she said, looking up at him with one eye closed against the glare of the morning sun, "a lot of the big cattle operations don't bother with this stuff at all. They artificially inseminate from frozen sperm."

Lanagan landed beside her with a soft grunt. "Seems awfully clinical."

"Oh, I don't know. Makes good economic sense, anyway. Don't have to waste good hay and corral space on bulls—just keep the sperm and dispose of the rest." She tossed her hair back and blatantly showed him her dimple. "After all, it's absolutely the only thing they're good for, isn't it?" She headed for the barn without waiting for his reply. There was a sassy little swing to her walk.

God, she's ornery, thought Lanagan. He felt slightly out of breath, but couldn't for the life of him think why.

From Mike Lanagan's Personal Files
NOTES FOR FUTURE COLUMNS

Ever wonder about certain quaint old expressions? Where they came from, how they got to be such clear and colorful adornments to our language? A lot of 'em seem to have farm origins, maybe not too surprising when you consider that there was a time when everybody lived on farms, or not very far from them. So when you called somebody pigheaded, pretty much everybody knew the person in question wasn't only stubborn as a mule but ornery besides. That's something you're never going to fully appreciate until you've actually spent some time trying to get a pig to do what you want it to.

Other examples to explore:

Sweat like a pig. Note: Pigs don't sweat!

Bullheaded.

Pretty as a little spotted calf.

Chapter 6

Lucy slid back the two-by-four that held the barn's big double doors shut and hauled one side open a couple of feet, pausing a moment to hide a smile. She just wished she'd had a camera handy when she made that crack about the bulls, because the look on Mike's face would have been worth money. Or maybe it was priceless.

In any case, she had her confidence back now, which was worth more to her than any amount of money. And it sure was good to feel like herself again, with familiar ground firm under her feet. She didn't much care for the way she'd been feeling lately, particularly last night and this morning, sort of jumpy and tense, off balance and vulnerable. She didn't know why, but there was something about Mike that made her feel like that—as if she was riding on a roller coaster. Lucy didn't like roller coasters, or any kind of so-called thrill rides, for that matter. She'd always hated the idea of somebody else being in charge of which way she went and how fast. She preferred to have the controls firmly in her own two hands, thank you.

She slipped into the barn through the narrow opening and Mike followed close behind. It was dim inside after the brilliant sunshine, warm and airless, full of familiar animal smells mixed with the faint, alien odor of petroleum from the car that sat in the wide center aisle like a beached and bloating whale. A rectangle of sunlight from the window in the hayloft fell right across its raised hood, spotlighting its waterlogged innards.

Mike, like a typical man, made a beeline for his car and immediately started poking around under the hood, to no perceivable effect.

Lucy gave both him and the car a critical once-over. "I hope you put a tarp down. I don't want any oil spots on my floor."

He grunted in a preoccupied way and wiggled the battery connections a few more times before he looked up at her. "I did. One of the plastic ones that were folded up over by the haystack. Hope that was okay."

"Yeah, that's fine." She paused a moment, then asked grudgingly, "How bad is it?"

His snort was eloquent, and so full of self-castigation she felt sorry for giving him a hard time about the tarp. "We could still take it up and put it in the garage," she offered gruffly. "Be easier to work on there."

"Nah, I don't want to be in your way." He pulled a bandanna handkerchief out of the pocket of his overalls and wiped his hands with it, and her heart did a queer little flip-flop. She'd seen her dad do that very same thing, probably with that very same handkerchief, more times than she could count.

"Besides," Mike added, "it's apt to be a while before I can do much with it. Have to earn some money for parts first." His lips twisted in a skewed attempt at a smile; she couldn't help but notice once again how nice and firm they were.

And as soon as she did that, she heard the faint but unmistakable rumble of a roller coaster, and felt its vibration deep in the pit of her stomach.

"Well, it's not in anybody's way where it is," she said, doing a quick pivot turn so she wouldn't have to look at him any longer. "I'm not using the barn right now, anyway."

"What do you use it for?" Mike asked in that interested way he had. "Just storage?"

Lucy nodded. "Mostly." She could feel him behind her, moving closer, so she moved on, too, keeping some distance between them. "Used to use it for the horses...the milking, things like that."

"Gwen told me you don't keep horses anymore. How come?"

She shrugged and fingered back one side of her hair, smiling a little at the nostalgic pain that flashed through her, along with memories of hot, dusty rides on a razor-backed old strawberry roan named Micky. "Mom was the horse person. She always insisted on having a few around for kids to ride. I've never been fond of them, myself—more of a nuisance than anything. Not to mention expensive to feed."

"What about milking cows? With all these cows having calves all the time—"

Lucy wrinkled her nose. "I *hate* to milk. When I was a kid I had to help with the milking every morning before school and again every night whether I had homework or not. It was probably a necessity when Mom and Pop were alive and the boys were both home, but now it's just me, so..." She discovered that she'd run out of room, fetched up against a stall gate. Coincidentally, it was the same one she'd found Mike sleeping in just yesterday morning; she could still see the imprint of his body in the clean straw. Her stomach lurched and then dropped, like a roller coaster going over a steep hill.

"So?" He'd reached the gate, too, and leaned on it with one elbow so he was half facing her.

"So...what?" It was very quiet in the barn, and stuffy. There didn't seem to be enough air for two people to breathe.

"What do you use the barn for now? Looks like you keep these stalls ready for something."

The space between them seemed to shrink. With the rush and roar of the coaster loud in her ears she looked up, bracing herself for the impact of his blue, blue eyes....

A breath hissed softly between her teeth, half relief, half chagrin. Mike's eyes were bright with curiosity, nothing else, and focused somewhere above and beyond her head. She gave her head a quick shake, to clear it of the roller-coaster noise as much as anything, and said offhandedly, "Oh, yeah, you know, sick animals, babies, anything that needs doctoring or is too weak to go outdoors with the rest. Cows that have had a difficult time calving. Things like that."

Mike nodded. A pained look flickered briefly across his features, and Lucy's stomach righted itself once more. He'd gotten that same look, she remembered, when she was explaining what the squeeze-chute was for, and especially when she'd mentioned having to occasionally employ the block and tackle to pull a calf. That was men for you—it was always the biggest and strongest ones that turned green around the gills at anything having to do with birth. She couldn't understand it, herself. Birthing was probably what she enjoyed most about farming. She didn't think she'd ever get over the wonder and excitement of it, whether it was helping a new calf or litter of pigs into the world, or watching a chick peck his way out of an egg. It never ceased to fascinate her.

And right now it seemed to be just what she needed to restore her self-confidence and put her back in control. She felt...empowered somehow, imbued with that secret superiority women enjoy as the sole givers of life and bearers of future generations. It was an interesting discovery, and she made a mental note to remember it from now on. To keep the upper hand with Mike, she had a feeling she was going to need every weapon she could muster.

"Well, Cage," she said briskly, filled with new energy and inexplicable high spirits, "we've got work to do. I want to show you—"

"Wait a minute. Do you hear something?" Mike's hand snaked out and caught her by her bare upper arm. The contact was so unexpected she jerked away from it...and instantly felt a disturbing sense of regret.

"Hear what? I don't—"

"There, can't you hear it? It sounds like some kind of bird."

"That's not a bird," said Lucy. "It's a cat."

"I didn't know you had a cat."

"I don't." They stood side by side gazing up at the loft. The sound came again, unmistakable once identified, drifting down to them as if borne on the ladder of dust motes that slanted from the window high in the barn's eastern wall. A tiny, heart-shaped face appeared at the edge of the loft, a harlequin face, half black, half orange, with enormous black ears and a white triangle nose.

"I think you do now," said Mike. "How do you suppose it got up there?"

Lucy gave him a withering look and went over to the ladder. "Hello, kitty-cat," she called coaxingly as she climbed. "Come on, kitty-kitty." But whoever she belonged to, the cat obviously wasn't shy or in the least inclined to bolt. She paced the edge of the loft eagerly, encouraging Lucy's progress with chirps and trills, and as soon as she could reach it, gave Lucy's nose a welcoming bump with the top of her head. Bubbles of husky laughter rose in the back of her throat.

"Friendly little thing, aren't you?" she murmured as she scooped the lithe body up, cradled it in one arm and started back down the ladder. The cat's ecstatic purring seemed to reverberate all the way through Lucy's chest.

"Whose is it? Do you know?" The expression on Mike's upturned face was bemused.

Lucy shook her head. "Probably wandered in here the other night for the same reason you did—to get out of the storm." She stepped off the last rung of the ladder and handed the cat over to him. She wasn't sure why, it just seemed like a very natural thing to do. The way the cat cuddled right up in Mike's arms seemed natural, too, and watching his big hands and long, strong fingers stroke and burrow through the mottled calico fur made Lucy's throat feel as if she'd swallowed hay dust. Once again she could hear that damned roller coaster rumbling in the distance, coming closer.

"Another orphan of the storm," Mike murmured, fondling the cat's throat. Ecstatic purring seemed to fill the barn. "I wonder where she—*is* she a she?—came from. One of your neighbors?"

"Calicoes are always females," Lucy informed him, clenching her teeth as she took the cat from his arms and set her on the floor. She didn't think she could stand to watch those hands of his stroking and petting that silky, sinuous little body one minute longer. There was just something so *sensuous* about it. "I don't think she's one of the neighbors'. Somebody probably just dumped her off on the road."

Mike said, "You're kidding." He looked appalled.

"People do it all the time. City people—" she flashed him an accusing glare "—seem to have this idea their unwanted pets will have a better chance of making it on their own out here in the country. Lots of mice and rabbits and little creatures to eat, right? They don't seem to realize there are all sorts of *other* animals out here that not only eat mice and rabbits, but don't mind making a meal out of a cat now and then. Then, of course, there are the cars and various kinds of farm machinery—hay mowers, harvesters. They eat up stray cats, too."

"Good Lord."

Lucy watched the cat weave figure eights around Mike's legs. It had been a long time since she'd had a cat around the place—not since the last old gray mother cat had gotten hit by a car last summer. She'd been meaning to ask the Andersens to save her a kitten... She took a deep breath and headed for the door. "She's awfully thin. I'll stop in at the house and tell Gwen to bring her something to eat."

"Doesn't look thin to me," said Mike, bending over to give the cat's ears another rub. His voice was a low murmur, almost a croon. Lucy looked down at the top of his brown felt hat and swallowed, tasting hay dust. "In fact, she looks downright plump."

"She's not plump," she said flatly. "She's pregnant. Probably why she was dumped."

Mike's head shot up and his mouth dropped open. His blue eyes pierced the shadows under the brim of his hat. "*Pregnant?* You mean—"

"That's right," said Lucy with great satisfaction. "From the looks of her, any day now."

Mike straightened up, wiping his hands on the legs of his overalls as if he thought the cat's condition might be contagious. Lucy smiled at him, feeling both superior and slightly pitying. "Don't worry, Cage, Gwen will take good care of her. Let's go walk some fields before it gets any hotter." The sound of the roller coaster dwindled, then died away altogether.

"Walking the fields," Lanagan discovered, meant inspecting the young corn and soybean plants for weeds, insects and diseases that might affect the crops. Their number and variety astonished him. By the time they paused to rest by an old split rail fence that made a barrier between one cornfield and the next, he'd begun to feel awed and humbled by the whole farming thing. It seemed to him there was something almost biblical about the plagues—drought, floods, locusts, winds, hail—a farmer had to do battle with in order to produce the food he took for granted.

"Before the white settlers came," Lucy told him, leaning on the top rail of the fence, "this was all open prairie as far as the eye could see. The topsoil was two feet thick, and the prairie grass held it in place. Then the white men came and plowed up the grass, and now every year the wind blows more and more of the topsoil away." She didn't sound regretful, just resigned.

Lanagan watched a hawk, balancing on the ever-present wind, looking for gophers, and thought for a fleeting moment of the cat—hunter of one and prey of the other. "The white men—meaning your ancestors?"

"Yep. Right over there—see where those trees are? That's where the original sod house was. That's where Lucinda Rosewood lived when she set fire to the place and climbed down the well with her baby in her apron. Of course, there weren't any trees then. Nothing but prairie grass, as far as the eye could see." She slapped the silvered wood that supported her forearms and said with an air of quiet pride, "My great-great—I don't know how many greats—granddaddy built this fence—brought the wood all the way from the river in a wagon."

So many generations, all in one place.... Lanagan's eyes followed the zigzag line of the fence to where it disappeared into a distant copse of trees. For reasons he couldn't begin to figure out he suddenly felt restless and argumentative. "Wouldn't these fields be easier to plow if you took it out?"

"Sure they would." She turned around and leaned her elbows on the rail, squinting at him in the midday sun. "Some things you just like to keep around, for some other reason besides convenience, or even good sense. My mom and her horses, for instance."

The wind, coming from behind her now, spread strands of her hair like ribbons across her face. Nerves in his right hand and arm jumped in unexpected response, but before he could transfer the impulse into action she'd lifted her own hand without conscious thought to tuck the strands away behind her ear. He was left feeling startled by what he'd almost done, and obscurely shaken.

Oblivious to his confusion, she tilted her face to the sun and drew in a deep, contented breath, seeming to savor the scent of warm, burgeoning earth as if it were the sweetest perfume. "This fence reminds me where I came from. Just in case I forget who I am and where I belong."

"Which is..." But he knew what she was going to say.

"Right here." Her voice seemed huskier than usual. She glanced over at him and smiled. "I'm a farmer. It's in my blood."

It's more than in her blood, he thought. She's part of it, this land. When he looked at her he saw its colors, the rich, earth shades of brown, the golden glow of sunshine, and felt an inexplicable sadness.

"So you've never thought about leaving here?" asked Lanagan, watching the hawk dip and soar, zigzagging away into the blue sky until he could no longer see it. "Going someplace else?"

She shook her head, and the wind snatched jealously at her hair.

"What about your brothers?" he persisted, speaking as softly as she had been, as if, he thought, they were speaking of intimate things. "It's in their blood, too, and they both went their own ways."

She shook her head again, her smile maddeningly serene and knowing, uncannily like Gwen's. "Well, they think they have. For now. Sooner or later I have a feeling that way's going to lead them right back here."

Lanagan shook his head, still with that strange feeling of combativeness, as if he needed to convince her of something. "One's off fighting wars overseas and the other's heading for the state house. Seems to me like they're both a long way from the farm."

She gave a complacent shrug. "It may take a while, but they'll make it eventually. Just watch and see."

"You sound awfully sure."

"I am." She pushed away from the fence in that abrupt way she had, brushing dust and splinters from her hands. "Look at me. Took me a while, too, but I came back."

It took him a moment to catch her meaning. "You mean, you—"

She laughed, an edgy, ironic little chuckle. "Sure, I left. What did you think, I've never been off the turnip truck? Hey, believe it or not, I've been to college. Degree and everything."

He felt chided, but before he could apologize she dismissed it with a shake of her head, saying softly and with a half smile that wasn't really a smile at all, "I was young. And like any kid I thought there had to be something better someplace else. I went off to college meaning to find it. For a while there I even thought I had."

It was Lanagan's job to know how to insert questions unobtrusively into sensitive places. He kept his voice gentle and very soft and said, "What changed your mind?"

"What changed my mind?" Her lips twisted. She looked down quickly and kept her face averted from him until she had it under control again. Then she fingered her hair back and said in a thoughtful voice, "Well, I guess I was forced to choose. And when it came down to a choice between...someone...and my farm, I suddenly realized what was really important to me. I knew I didn't want to leave this place, after all."

"Maybe it just wasn't the right...person," Lanagan ventured stubbornly. "I bet if you loved somebody enough, you'd leave."

"Maybe," said Lucy flatly. She pushed away from the fence with an air of finality, then hesitated and added a parting shot over her shoulder as she left him. "And maybe what I want is somebody who'd love *me* enough, he wouldn't ask me to."

She was good at having the last word, thought Lanagan as she took off for the house and the dinner that was waiting for them there, Dodger trotting placidly at her heels. But although he was hungrier than he could remember being in a long time, it was a while before he bestirred himself to follow. As he watched Lucy walk away from him, slim and supple in jeans—no overalls today—and a blue work shirt with the sleeves cut off, hair blowing in the wind, he could feel his attention being tugged along after her as if it had been captured by a powerful magnetic force. The longer he watched, the narrower and sharper its focus became. He could *feel* it happening. All his interest and curiosity about the alien world he'd stumbled into was being refined and distilled down to one single aspect of it.

Lucy.

She was so full of contradictions. She was beginning to fascinate him.

"I've been thinking," said Lanagan.

"You have, have you?" Gwen responded alertly, looking as if she couldn't wait to hear what wonders that activity might have produced.

Such gentle and good-natured sarcasm was wasted on Lanagan this morning. He dipped his brush in the can of white paint and turned back to the side of the chicken house, frowning at the progress he was making. "It's about Lucy."

There was a dry puff of laughter. "Well, I'm not surprised. You've been here two weeks," said Gwen without looking up from the nesting boxes she was filling with fresh straw; she had two setting hens with eggs due to hatch in another week or so and wanted to be ready. "I told you, she can be hard to work for."

"Not that hard." He thought about it, studying his hands, where healing blisters were already turning into calluses. "Of course, she works rings around me," he said in real admiration, adding with a snort of irony, "Makes me feel like an idiot most of the time."

"She has a way of doing that," said Gwen sympathetically.

"Yeah, but she makes me laugh, too."

"Yes," said Gwen, smiling, "she has a way of doing that, too."

"What I was wondering is..." Lanagan gave the rough wood planks a couple of swipes with the paintbrush before he stepped back with a deepening frown. "Why is it she's doing this all alone? It's a lot of work for one person, man or woman."

"Didn't have much choice," Gwen said simply. "When her folks were killed, and with her brothers both gone..."

"That isn't what I mean. It seems to me... it just seems strange that she isn't married."

"Married!"

He propped the paintbrush in the can and turned to find the old lady's brows up and her shrewd, amused eyes regarding him quizzically. "I mean, with everything she's got to offer..."

"Like this place, for instance?"

Lanagan grimaced and shook his head. "Lucy'd never fall for somebody who was after her for her land. No, I was thinking about just her. You know, she's got intelligence and strength, she's self-sufficient...."

"Men usually find those things kind of off-putting in a woman," Gwen observed, twinkling gently.

"Oh, no," Lanagan protested, slightly offended at the implied insult to his own gender. "Not at all. Hey, don't kid yourself. Men *like* a woman with brains. All that stuff about men going for the gorgeous bimbos—that's just a stereotype. Listen, Lucy's got a great personality, and she's..." He paused, recognizing the stinginess of what he was about to say, and already feeling guilty about it. "She's attractive, too."

Gwen's eyebrows flew up again; her voice rippled with laughter. "Attractive?"

The subtle mockery made him squirm, but the truth was, he couldn't allow himself to say out loud what he really thought. He didn't even dare to think it too long or too hard, because the last thing in the world he could afford right now was to find himself attracted to a woman. Especially one like Lucy.

"In her own way," he qualified stiffly. "Of course, she tries her level best to hide it. Now, if she'd just—"

"But," said Gwen, "you just said beauty didn't matter."

He winced at the word *beauty,* remembering all too vividly the moment he'd realized it could be applied to Lucy, and in more ways than one. It had been about three days after they'd found the cat in the hayloft. He'd slipped into the barn one morning after chores as he often did, just to check on his car, see how things were drying out. He'd left the windows rolled down so moisture wouldn't build up inside during the hot afternoons and mildew the seat covers. When he'd walked in he had seen the cat's funny little clown face peering out at him from the side back window. As soon as she'd seen who it was, she'd jumped down and come to wind around his ankles, begging to be fed, but when he'd tried to pick her up to pet her she'd jumped out of his arms and right back through the window, into the back seat of his car. That was when he'd heard it—the silvery, almost birdlike chorus of tiny mews.

He'd muttered something appropriately awed and probably profane and had gone to investigate, and there she was, her mottled orange-and-black body just curling protectively around a nestful of roused and squirming kittens. He'd done the natural thing, under the circumstances. He'd hollered for Lucy.

He could still see her face, the way she'd looked as she'd approached him as he'd stood there helplessly beside his car—the gleam of excitement in her eyes, the little smile that had made him feel inept, strangely humbled, almost...extraneous. He'd seen her hands as she'd reassured the worried mother and deftly examined and counted her babies. "Newborn," she'd announced in the softest of murmurs. "Still damp. She's got four. Looks like three males, one female." There had been no cooing, no foolish baby talk, but her small, capable hands had cradled each kitten with infinite tenderness.

And her face... That was it, the moment he'd known what he should have seen that very first morning, if he hadn't been so shell-shocked and preoccupied. Bending over the newborn kittens as she'd bent over the box of baby piglets, stroking back her hair to expose her profile to the slanting shaft of morning sunlight...she had the kind of beauty that makes the throat catch and the eyes burn. It was a moment that had made Lanagan wish for a camera, or the ability to paint timeless masterpieces.

But that was only part of it, a rare kind of beauty that was art, rather than perfection. There was an earthiness about the vision that touched something far more primitive and compelling in a man than his soul. *She should have babies.* That was the thought that had come to him then, as naturally as his next breath. If ever a woman was born to be a mother, Lanagan thought, it was Lucy. He could see her with that same look, gazing at an infant nursing at her breast, hear her rusty laughter as she gently pushed a breathless child in the old rope swing, see her hands as they deftly braided a little girl's hair. The images were so vivid to him, so real, he almost felt as if he'd seen the child somewhere before. As if he *knew* her.

More and more in the days after that he'd thought about what a shame it would be if Lucy never had children. What a terrible waste. She should be married, he told himself. She should have somebody.

"Beauty doesn't matter—not physical beauty, anyway," he said to Gwen, laying his paintbrush down on the chicken-house steps so he could use both hands to illustrate his point. "But a person's appearance is still the first thing you notice about them, right? I just think, you know, if she'd make more of an effort to look nice, maybe get out more, she might meet somebody. Somebody nice. Somebody..." He stopped there, because beyond that his vision had simply refused to go.

"It's an idea," said Gwen, somberly twinkling. "Have you suggested it to Lucy?"

"No," said Lanagan, taking a deep breath. "But I think I will."

At lunchtime Lanagan was in the driveway rinsing out paintbrushes when Lucy drove in from the fields on her big red International tractor, pulling the planter and a cloud of dust behind her. She parked at the machine shed and came over to him, heat-rosy and dusty, but grinning.

"Finished it?" asked Lanagan.

"Almost. Another couple hours." She stuck out her hands and he obligingly held the hose for her while she washed, hands first, then her arms clean up to her shoulders, then her face and neck. "Hot out there," she explained, smiling at him through the water stream. She straightened up, shook off her hands, wiped her face with them, then took the hose from him and leaned over once more, this time putting her lips to the cold, clear stream. Her hair fell forward, sticking to her wet cheeks and getting in her way, and she used her free hand to hold one side of it back while she drank.

Lanagan watched for a moment with a peculiar rumbling in his midsection he hoped was only hunger. Then he reached up and fingered the other side of her hair behind her ear, as he'd seen her do so many times. Her eyes flew open wide above the silvery water, reminding him of a startled deer.

"You ever think about getting it cut?" he asked in a casual, friendly kind of way.

She put the hose down and straightened warily, wiping her mouth with the back of her hand. "Cut? Why?"

He got up, brushed his hands on his shirtfront and put one on either side of her head, surprising her so much that although she gasped softly, she didn't pull away, even when he pushed his fingers deep into her hair. Her scalp was sweat-damp and sun-heated. Her face seemed very small between his hands, all wide, wary eyes, with pupils so large they looked almost black.

He cleared his throat and said, "Yeah, see, like this—kind of feathered short around your face...one of those pixie cuts, I guess you'd call it. Then it wouldn't keep getting in your way all the time."

"So what are you, a hairdresser?" she demanded suddenly in a hoarse, raspy voice, and pulled back from his hands like a horse who wasn't about to let herself be bridled. She gave him one brief, puzzled look, holding her hair back from her face with her own two hands, then stalked off toward the house.

She didn't speak to him all during lunch, and afterward, when she went back out on the tractor to finish the last of the planting, he noticed she was wearing a baseball cap.

USA Today, May 17

Front Page

CHICAGO—Authorities announced today that they are expanding the search for missing *Chicagoan* columnist Mike Lanagan in the wake of the firebombing that destroyed his southside residence more than two weeks ago. According to police, Lanagan spoke with them immediately following the incident, and thereafter apparently vanished into thin air.

While widespread speculation continues linking the bizarre case to organized crime, police maintain that they have no evidence to support the theory, and no suspects at the present time.

Chapter 7

The next day was Friday, and that evening after supper Lucy gave Lanagan his pay.

"Don't spend it all in one place," she said gruffly as she handed it over, in cash, as he'd asked.

He smiled wryly and tucked the folded bills away in the pocket of his jeans. "I'm afraid that's just what I'm going to have to do. Know a good auto parts store?"

"There's one on Main Street—Sam's. You'd be better off going to K mart for the oil."

"Thanks," said Lanagan. He went out onto the porch. Lucy followed diffidently, hands in her pockets. He pushed open the screen door. "You coming out?"

She hesitated, then shrugged and slipped past him. "Might as well. I have to check on the sows... shut up the chickens."

That was the way things had been between them ever since the episode in the driveway yesterday noon. Polite and careful.

He paused on the top step to take his flattened cigarette pack out of his shirt pocket and his lighter out of his pants. He felt the pack, counting how many were left. Just two. "Aw, the hell with it," he muttered, and put it back in his pocket.

He went on down the steps and across the strip of grass to the driveway. After a moment he heard the crunch of Lucy's footsteps in the gravel behind him and turned and waited for her to catch up with him.

"What's the matter?" she asked in that brusque, belligerent way she had. "Out of cigarettes?"

"Naw," he said, "I quit." Then impulsively he held out his lighter. "Here—present for you."

She hesitated, then took it from him with a wary, suspicious glance. "What would I want with this?"

He shrugged. "Keep it. You never know." And he wouldn't be tempted. He drew a long, deep breath of the evening air and observed, "Nice evening. No wind."

"It always dies down this time of day," Lucy mumbled absently. She was still rolling his lighter around in her hand and suddenly he felt a sick lurch in his belly, remembering. His girlfriend—the one before Monica—had given it to him for his birthday. It was silver and onyx, and had his initials engraved on it. He could see Lucy's thumb rubbing thoughtfully back and forth over the spidery silver "L." Too late he thought dismally, wishing she'd ask him about it so he could at least offer her a convincing lie, tell her he'd borrowed it from a friend, maybe. The fact that she didn't ask confirmed what he'd already suspected: He wasn't fooling her a bit.

He strolled on down the driveway, intensely conscious of Lucy just a step or two behind him. A vague restlessness seized him, along with a sense of isolation and an itchy kind of loneliness. Memories from his past life, once begun, kept flickering through his mind. He thought about smoking, suddenly wanting to, badly, now that he'd made up his mind to quit. He didn't feel like watching TV until he got sleepy, or reading one of the books he'd borrowed from Lucy's parlor, which was what he usually did after supper. For some reason, what he found himself thinking about with an intensity that bordered on yearning was that very first evening in the parlor with Lucy, playing the piano and laughing together like old, easy friends. He remembered the way his arm had brushed hers, the way he'd felt her warmth even though there'd been space between them.

At the corner of the house he turned right, into the front yard, instead of left to his cottage. Behind him Lucy's footsteps crunched once, twice more on the gravel driveway. Then they, too, were muffled in the thick lawn grass.

It was Lucy's favorite time of day. Her favorite time of year, too, between the hectic rush of spring and the summer doldrums, but tonight she felt tense and restless, as if a storm were brewing. She looked up into the dusky sky, almost wishing it was only that, but the first stars were already winking on, the air was light and soft, with only innocent promises of summer, and she knew she was kidding herself.

It was Mike who was causing her to feel this way, of course. She was certain of that. In her pocket the lighter burned against her thigh as if it were his hand that touched her there instead. She felt his nearness the same way she did thunderstorms, with a thrill of fear along her spine, a keening in her ears and a high-voltage tension vibrating along every nerve. And as certain as she was of her own feelings, she knew equally well that *he* felt nothing at all. Just as he'd felt nothing yesterday when he'd combed his fingers through her hair.

She sat in the swing, hearing the old rope creak and stretch with her weight. Mike heard it, too, and turned back.

"So," she said, toes braced in the grass, idly rotating, "you're not going to go off and paint the town?" Her voice sounded harsh and artificial to her own ears.

"Paint the town?" He came closer, thumbs hooked negligently in the front pockets of his jeans. His chuckle sounded relaxed and faintly ironic. "You mean there's a town to paint?"

"Oh, sure." She leaned back, watching the leaves overhead stir and shiver with the returning wind. "Friday night? There's all kinds of action. Let's see. The new shopping center has a four-screen movie theater. You'd have to go a little farther to find a bowling alley, but the pool hall should be jumping. If you like honky-tonks, the Cross Bar has live country music on weekends. At least, they used to. Just be careful somebody doesn't try to pick a fight with you—these local farm boys can get pretty wild on Friday nights." She didn't know why she was doing this. She felt bitchy and mean; if she were a man feeling like this *she'd* probably go to the nearest honky-tonk and pick a fight.

Mike wasn't biting—she could hear a chuckle in his voice. "Honky-tonks aren't exactly my style."

"Oh, yeah?" she drawled sarcastically, "what is your style, Mike? Bright lights, big city, right?"

He didn't answer. It had gotten too dark to see his face; she wished she could tell what he was thinking. The silence was an emptiness rapidly filling up with the sounds of the evening... frogs in the creek bottom, crickets, a cow bawling down in the stockyards.

She straightened her legs abruptly, pushing herself back, then picked up her feet and let herself swing forward. "Sometimes there's a dance at the VFW Hall. I could check the paper for you if you're interested."

"No, thanks," he said dryly, "I'll pass." He caught the rope, stopping her. "What about you, though? Maybe you should go."

"Me?" Again she wished for more light so she could see his face. He'd surprised her. She wondered what he was leading up to.

"Yeah. You ever go and...what did you call it—paint the town?"

She laughed irritably, annoyed that her heart had begun to beat faster. "Why would I want to do a thing like that?"

She saw him shrug. His body was a silhouette, very big and very near. "Why would anybody? A little change of scenery, some fun, socializing...."

"You mean dates, don't you?" Her throat felt dry, and her voice came out even more raspy than usual. "Look, Mike, if you want to know if I date, why don't you just ask me?"

"Okay," he said. "Do you?"

"No, not much."

"Why not?"

It was her turn to shrug. "Look, it's hard to think of somebody you've wrestled, had fistfights with, in terms of dates, if you know what I mean. Most of the guys around here have known me since I was in pigtails. I've even punched a few of 'em in the nose a time or two. That's not something a man forgets."

"Why?" His voice was very soft all of a sudden.

"Why...you mean, why did I punch them? Oh, heavens, I don't know, it was a long time ago." She shrugged again. "Probably just wanted to prove how tough I was. I was little and a girl besides. It took a lot of proving."

"Is that what this is all about? Proving something?" That soft, gentle tone—he had a way of doing that, she'd noticed, when he was asking questions. Especially questions he had no business asking.

She tugged on the swing, trying to free it from his grasp. "What 'this'? What are you talking about?"

"This...all this. Running this place all alone. Doing everything yourself. Setting things up so you can handle them without any help from anybody, if you have to. You still trying to prove something?"

She muttered resentfully, "I hired you, didn't I?"

He gave a soft, self-derisive snort and she thought for a few moments she'd managed to shut him up. Then he said in that same quiet way, "A hired hand's just a hired hand. It's not the same as sharing the burden and responsibility with someone. Must be hard sometimes."

"My choice. It's the way I want it." She got up from the swing, only to find that he was still holding the ropes and that consequently she was trapped between his arms, with the wooden seat bobbing gently against the backs of her knees. Panic assailed her, thinly disguised as anger.

"Look, Cage, you've stepped way over the line here. I've been real patient with you up to now, but let's get something straight. Okay? My life doesn't need fixing. My hair's the way it is because I like it that way. I'm alone here because I like that, too. I don't have to prove myself, because I've already done that. You think I act tough? Mister, I've got news for you. I *am* tough. I've had to be—" The last part was a whisper, ending in a hiss of surprise and of hemp as his hands slid down the ropes and captured hers. And seemingly choked off her breath, as well.

His hands were so much bigger they completely covered hers. His thumbs loosened her grip on the ropes gently, with almost no effort at all.

"Yeah, I know you are," he said in a thoughtful, musing way, turning her hands palms up in his and stroking across the calluses there with his thumbs. "For what it's worth, though, I don't think it goes much deeper than these."

She'd been sorry about it being too dark to see his expressions. Now she was desperately glad it kept him from seeing hers. She didn't know what was wrong with her, why she ached so dreadfully inside, but she knew nothing in the world could have kept it out of her face.

"Don't push your luck, Cage," she croaked with gratifying calm, and pulled her hands from his grasp. She had to, before he could feel them tremble.

She could still feel him watching her all the way down to the farrowing sheds, even though she knew it was impossible, that he couldn't have seen beyond the crown of the hill even if it had been broad daylight. The pain in her chest felt as if something had lodged there, something too big to swallow.

The next day was Saturday. Lanagan had the day off, so he hitched a ride into town with Gwen when she went to do the grocery shopping, to see what he could find at the auto parts store.

The town was pretty much what he'd expected. Grain elevators, farm machinery stores and livestock auction lots on the outskirts, along with some new-looking fast-food places and video stores; lots of churches on tree-lined streets; genteel houses turned into doctors' offices and beauty parlors; a dusty downtown crowded with pickup trucks and even an occasional tractor, but with a good many empty storefronts.

He spotted the auto parts store on Main Street, across from a defunct five-and-dime with vacant, clouded windows and next door to a café advertising a daily lunch special for $2.99. Gwen dropped him off at the corner, saying she'd pick him up at the café when she was finished with her shopping. A few people recognized Gwen's Bronco and waved, giving Lanagan sideways glances and trying hard not to appear nosy. He tipped his hat to a couple of people he met on the sidewalk and muttered, "Morning" as he went into the store.

He bought a case of oil and a filter, a battery and a set of spark plugs, which left him just about enough cash for the lunch special next door. On the way into the café he stopped to browse the newspaper racks, which offered the Des Moines *Register, USA Today* and a local weekly. Balancing his oil on top of the rack, he dug change out of his pockets

and bought a copy of *USA Today*. Then, since the local was only a dime, he bought that, too.

The day's special was Salisbury steak and mashed potatoes. He ordered and, while he was waiting for his coffee, leafed through the local paper. He couldn't get interested in the crop news, or the notices of weddings and funerals, church services and club activities, but he did take note of the fact that the farm wives' association was planning to put on a fund-raising dance on Memorial Day weekend. He looked at that particular item for a long time, thinking about last night with Lucy on the front lawn...remembering her hands, how small and vulnerable they'd felt when he'd held them, the way they'd trembled slightly, like captured birds....

He folded the weekly and tucked it into the sack with his filter and spark plugs, then picked up *USA Today*. It was weird, realizing how out of touch with the world he'd been lately. He found that he was really looking forward to catching up, but before he could unfold the paper his lunch arrived, and since Salisbury steak took two hands to eat, he had to postpone the pleasure. When his plate had been cleared away and he'd refused pie for financial reasons, he picked up his refilled coffee cup, spread the newspaper out on the counter and got comfortable.

The headline was small and on the lower half of the front page, but it jumped out at him and startled him so badly he spilled hot coffee on his leg.

Search For Missing Chicago Journalist Widens.

Lanagan went cold first, then hot, burning with the same intense awareness of his own vulnerability he'd felt as a child of ten when called upon, utterly unprepared, to recite a poem before his snickering classmates. Kiplings "If"—he remembered it well, *now*. "If you can keep your head..." It popped into the blankness of his mind as clearly as if the printed pages of his English textbook had been there before him instead of the newspaper that bore, in incredible and terrifying black and white, his own name. He'd never felt so exposed. It was like one of those nightmares where you find yourself inexplicably stark naked in a public place.

Somehow this development had never occurred to him. He was a reporter. He was used to writing the news, not making it. It had caught him completely off guard. The *national* news, for God's sakes! And what else? He hadn't watched the news in two weeks. For all he knew, in all likelihood, in fact, his picture had already been broadcast from coast to coast on network television. God, he might even have made "Unsolved Mysteries" or "America's Most Wanted." This was Iowa, not the back side of the moon. *Anybody* might recognize him. He began to see a new and sinister significance in the glances that had been cast his way out on the street. What if somebody had recognized him already and was even now passing that information along, for good or ill? What about Gwen? Lucy? Did they know?

He wasn't ready. *Not yet.* He still couldn't see his way out of the danger he'd gotten himself into; there were things he hadn't figured out yet, pieces of the puzzle he couldn't fit together. The stench of his burning home was still in his nostrils, the roar of the flames deafening in his ears. *I'm not ready.*

For what seemed like forever he sat there feeling like a hunted animal flushed from its hiding place, stunned and half-paralyzed. Utterly helpless. The $2.99 lunch special churned in his belly; cold sweat formed on his brow.

In reality, according to the big clock above the counter with the words Coca-Cola across its face, it was only a matter of seconds before reason and a measure of calm returned. Lanagan drew in a breath—not quite steady—and folded the paper neatly and tucked it into his sack along with the oil filter and spark plugs and news of local interest. He paid his check, left a modest tip, gathered up his purchases and left the café, tilting his hat even farther over his eyes than he usually did. Just to be on the safe side.

Gwen was pulling up to the curb, head in, the old-fashioned, small-town way. She gave him a look as he got in beside her, and said, "You all right? You look a little peaked."

Lanagan gave her a close look, but couldn't see anything more knowing than usual in her eyes. He made a face, then grinned lopsidedly. "I don't know, maybe something I ate. I guess maybe your cooking's got me spoiled."

Her response was her usual musical ripple. She nodded at the bag he was settling between his feet. "I see you picked up a paper."

"I figured I ought to see what's happening in the world," he said casually, making a production out of getting comfortable and settled.

Gwen put the Bronco in reverse and half turned in preparation for backing up. She paused a moment to look at him. "Anything interesting?"

Lanagan met her gaze and for a long moment didn't say anything, but it seemed to him that some sort of understanding did pass between them in that small span of time. He also knew it could have been his imagination. He wondered if he would ever begin to fathom the wisdom and insights that lurked behind those serene and youthful eyes.

He gave his shoulder belt a snap and said, "Nah, same old stuff. You know how it goes."

She just smiled and pulled out into the street. When they were straightened out and heading home she nodded once more toward the bag between Lanagan's knees. "Is that a local paper I see?"

"It is." He pulled it out and unfolded it. "This is some exciting place you've got here."

She gave a light laugh, and him the briefest of glances. "Don't kid yourself, Mike. There's all kinds of excitement.

We have our share." He was beginning to recognize the subtle nuances her voice carried along with the laughter.

"Huh, look at this. Did you know Farm Wives are putting on a dance Memorial Day weekend?" He said that as if he'd just discovered it.

"That's right," said Gwen as if she believed he had. "It's a potluck supper dance."

"No kidding?" After a moment he asked, elaborately casual, "Lucy belong to this, uh, Farm Wives organization?"

She threw him a look that said plainly, "You've got to be kidding!" and chuckled. "No, but I do."

"Uh-huh." Seconds ticked by. Gwen braked for a tractor that was pulling out onto the road, then waved at its driver and went on around. Lanagan resettled his shoulder belt and cleared his throat. "Do, uh, people ever go stag to these things?"

"Stag?" The question seemed to truly surprise her. "Certainly they do. All sorts of people go, old, young, married, single. Families."

"They have a band?"

"Sometimes. Or a disc jockey. They're a pretty big deal around here, Mike. Why, you thinking of going?"

"Me? Nah." And after a moment, "Lucy ever go?"

"Lucy?" She had a way of answering his questions like that, repeating the principal word with a lilt of incredulous laughter, and he was beginning to find it unnerving. "Not in a good many years. Why?"

"I was just thinking maybe she ought to."

"Ought to..."

"You know, like I was saying. Get out more. Meet people."

"Maybe she would," said Gwen pointedly, "if you asked her."

"Me?" He shifted his shoulders, feeling obscurely defensive, as if he were having an argument with himself, and said bluntly, "I can't do that."

"No?"

"No. Uh-uh. I don't think so. It wouldn't be a good idea."

"Why not?"

"Well, because..." *Why not?* He shifted restlessly under his seat belt. Of course, there were a dozen good reasons, none of which he could tell Gwen about. Like the fact that he didn't dare show his face in public, for example. But the main thing was, Lucy—or any other woman, for that matter—was simply off-limits to him right now. She was a friend to him, that was all she could be. No matter how attracted to her he might be. He was just interested in her well-being, like any friend would be. He wanted to see her happy. He wanted...

Rounding up his straying wits, he coughed and launched doggedly into his excuses. "For one thing, I'm her hired man. It wouldn't look right. No telling what people would think was going on."

"That's true," said Gwen, nodding agreement.

Encouraged, Lanagan pressed on. "And then, I'm just here temporarily. The whole idea's for her to meet somebody, right? Somebody who's going to be around for a while. How's she going to do that if she's with me? No," he said firmly, warming to it now that he had the idea sorted out and spoken up, "what she needs is to go to that dance stag. Dressed fit to kill. Show these guys what they've been missing. A dress, high heels, something slinky." He could see it in his mind—those arms of hers, neck and shoulders bare... taut, supple little body defined in shimmery... red. Yes, definitely red. But short, baring those slender legs to midthigh, and high heels to give the calves an elegant curve.... He cleared his throat and finished somewhat thickly, "Those guys wouldn't know what hit 'em."

"Probably not," said Gwen softly. After a moment she looked over at Lanagan with her eyebrows pushing wrinkles into her forehead. "She'd never do it, you know."

"You could talk her into it."

She shook her head. "She'd hate it."

"No, not if we do it right. I've been thinking—"

"You're dangerous when you do that," said Gwen dryly.

"No, listen." It was an idea that had come to him in the night while he was lying awake after that strange encounter with Lucy under the trees, keyed up and restless and looking for ways to mute the disquieting images in his mind. Images of Lucy, sun rosy and grinning, with water droplets clinging to her face and bare arms, dripping from her chin and dampening the front of her T-shirt...Lucy's face, unexpectedly small between his two hands, her eyes unexpectedly vulnerable, mouth unexpectedly soft-looking... He gulped a breath and came out with it in a rush, before he could begin to have second thoughts about it. "These guys around here have all known her since she was a kid, right? So they all think of her as some sort of pesky little sister, still in skinned knees and pigtails. They've seen her that way so long they can't really see her any other way. What if she played it as a joke—you know, like in *My Fair Lady?* Maybe they wouldn't even recognize her all dressed up. It would be fun to find out, wouldn't it?"

"Yes," said Gwen, "I guess it would."

"So?"

She sighed. "She'll never go for it."

"I can't believe I let you talk me into this," Lucy grumbled.

"To tell you the truth," said Gwen mildly, "I'm a little surprised myself."

Lucy turned from the dressing table to give her a hostile look. "No, you're not. You've been pestering me for two weeks, both you and Mike. What was I supposed to do? *Damn.*" She began to pace, fanning at her underarms. She was wearing only panties and a bra and was fresh from a long, thorough shower, but she felt as if she'd just come in from a hard day in the fields. "I just wish I could quit *sweating.* Why did it have to turn so humid? Oh, God, I hope it's not going to storm. Do you have any baby powder?"

Gwen got up from the bed and went to look. Lucy leaned over to examine her face in the mirror one more time, hoping for miracles. Unfortunately, the features that looked back at her were the same ones she'd come to expect when she looked in a mirror: the nose, of course—the Rosewood family nose, which a staunchly loyal friend had once told her could be called "regal"; sharply pointed chin and just a little too much jaw; a mouth that wasn't bad except when she smiled, when it had a tendency to cut her face in two and show off the teeth that hadn't been *quite* crooked enough for braces. And, of course, there were those wrinkles at the corners of her eyes. She leaned closer, trying to erase them with her fingers, like pencil marks. She hadn't put on any makeup yet—she supposed she'd have to, for all the good it would do. She wished she'd taken better care of her skin, used moisturizers, worn sunglasses, anything. She was too young for wrinkles! Not even thirty, just twenty-nine. *Twenty-nine.* Today.

Today was her birthday, and she was going to celebrate it by making a fool of herself. Mike Cage, or whatever your name is, she thought with an audible whimper, I hate you. I truly do.

Oh, how I wish I hated you.

Gwen came back with a pink cardboard cylinder filled with talcum powder. "What is this?" Lucy asked as she sprinkled it liberally in all the appropriate places, coughing a little in the dust cloud. "Smells nice."

"Old-fashioned roses," said Gwen. "It was your mother's."

Memory and loss rose stinging to her nose and eyelids as quickly and acutely as the need to sneeze. Glowering fiercely, she thrust the talcum at Gwen and turned to the open closet. "I don't know what I'm going to wear to this thing. I don't have anything. A dress? Give me a break. I've got a couple of sundresses or my Sunday suit. Take your pick."

Gwen shook her head firmly. "What's that back there?"

"What? There's nothing but old stuff from high school."

"No, right there, that red thing. I don't think I've ever seen you wear it."

"This?" Lucy hauled the dress out of the closet, laughing as she turned with it held at arm's length. "You've got to be kidding. Do you know what this is? This is the dress I bought for the Sweetheart Ball, my senior year. It was girl's choice. I got up enough nerve to ask Brent Weatherby—remember him? Oh, man..." Remembering, it was half groan, half sigh...rueful, pain filled, but forgiving of the silly girl she'd been. "He was point guard on the basketball team, and I had the biggest crush on him. Nobody was more surprised than I was when he said he'd go with me...." Her voice trailed wistfully off. She turned to the mirror almost without intent, the dress held in front of her on its satin hanger, shimmering under plastic.

"What happened?" Gwen asked softly.

"I think the teasing got to him," Lucy said, frowning at her reflection, carefully keeping the remembered hurt and humiliation under wraps, like the dress. "He came down with the stomach flu the day of the dance." She tossed the dress away from her, onto the bed.

Gwen picked it up and remarked thoughtfully, "Brent Weatherby might very well be there at the dance tonight. I've seen him show up before, more than once."

Lucy snorted and managed about half a smile. "With or without his wife?"

"He can still look, can't he?" said Gwen placidly. "All the better to say, 'Eat your heart out.'"

Lucy's surprised laugh erupted with a little twinge of pain, like a bubble bursting.

"Here," Gwen insisted, "put it on. See if it fits."

"Oh, Lord..." Her hand crept forth of its own volition to take the dress from her aunt's outstretched hands. Laughing silently, she doubled it over and held it pressed tightly against the fluttering knot just below her ribs.

"Now," said Gwen in a businesslike way, "what about shoes?"

Lucy closed her eyes, took a deep breath and sighed on its shuddering exhalation. "On the top shelf. Sling-back pumps... open toes... dyed to match."

The Chicagoan, May 30

Front Page
by Ralph Buncomb, staff writer

CHICAGO—Federal authorities announced today that they are launching a full-scale investigation into the affairs of the Westside Development Corporation, following recent charges and allegations of corruption and ties to organized crime. While FBI sources maintain the agency has suspected for some time that the Chicago corporation may have been a front for a midwestern crime syndicate, they admit that the current investigation was prompted in part by the unexplained disappearance of *Chicagoan* columnist Mike Lanagan shortly after he announced plans to investigate WDC in his column, "My Kind Of Town." Lanagan has not been seen or heard from since the May first firebombing of his home on Chicago's south side, and police have admitted they now believe it "highly unlikely" that the columnist will be found alive.

Chapter 8

Lately Lanagan had taken to sitting on the front porch steps in the evening, where it was nice and peaceful and conducive to unstressed thinking. With Gwen busy in the kitchen and Lucy avoiding him whenever she could, there was nobody to interfere with that activity except Dodger. The Border collie would come up and nudge his knee to demand his evening's ration of affection, and then they'd settle down together in easy comradeship to watch the sun set behind the barn.

But the past couple of days, with the weather turned sultry and unsettled and thunderheads piling up every afternoon in the west, there hadn't been any sunsets. And this evening there was only a heavy, brooding twilight with occasional slashes of crimson bleeding through holes in the clouds, and restless little dust devils stirring in the lane as if at the whim of a sulky child.

His own inner restlessness had been increasing lately, as well, which he supposed was only to be expected. What he didn't understand was a heaviness inside him that seemed to match the weather, a reluctance that had nothing to do with foreboding, or dread of what might lie ahead, but rather an aching certainty that he was about to lose something he already had, if only he knew what it was. It served to put a rein on his restlessness, but he knew the wind was changing in spite of it, and that there wasn't anything he could do about it. Before, when he'd thought about going back to Chicago to pick up the banner he'd dropped in his ignominious flight from the field of battle, his heart had cried out in protest, *Not yet...not yet!* Now it whispered a promise, *Soon...soon.*

His broodings were disturbed by the crunch of footsteps on the gravel driveway. When Lucy's voice called through the twilight, "Mike, are you out here?" he realized he'd been waiting for her.

Dodger got up immediately and went to meet her, but for a few moments Lanagan stayed where he was, watching his newly hardened and callused fingers snap thorns from the stem of a rose he'd picked from the bush that grew over his door. Then he drew a careful breath and laid the rose on the wooden step beside him and called back, "Yeah—around front."

She came around the corner of the house, teetering a little as the heels of her shoes punched unpredictably into the lawn he'd mowed just that afternoon. He stared first at those shoes, at the flecks of fresh-cut grass clinging to the shiny red satin, the sheen of nylons clinging to high, elegant arches, slender ankles and well-defined calves. They were something, those legs, not the long, graceful lines he usually admired, not the sleek, indolent curves that brought to his mind images of long, languid afternoons in satin sheets, but pert, sassy, taut-muscled legs, playful as a romp in the hay, sexy as a wink.

"Well, don't just stand there. Tell me what you think."

Lucy's voice, snappish and raspy as always, jerked him out of an impossible reverie. He said, "Ghar..." or a close approximation of it, and groped blindly for cigarettes, simultaneously remembering and cursing the impulse that had made him decide to give them up.

"The dress," said Lucy patiently, in the manner of one speaking to a dim-witted child. "What do you think of the dress? Is it all right, or do you think it's too much?"

She was standing hip-shot with a hand on her waist, a pose he realized was defensive rather than deliberately provocative. There was nothing whatever of the vamp about Lucy. She had no idea the way the clingy red fabric—what there was of it!—molded itself to her high, firm breasts, pulled diagonally across her flat stomach and tucked in under her round little bottom so it defined each and every curve and hollow as if she'd been all-over dipped in red sugar glaze, like a candy apple.

"Too much?" he croaked, cleared his throat and tried again. "Too much? No, I don't think it's too much. It's..."

"It's too damn dressy," Lucy groaned. "It doesn't even fit me. I feel like a fool." She lifted her hands and let them drop, a gesture so forlorn it shook Lanagan out of the daze he was in.

"No! Hey, come on, it's perfect." He got up and went toward her, managing to tear his eyes away from the dress and focus for the first time on her face. And that was when something happened to his heart that had nothing to do with pulse rate and blood pressure, both of which had already gone off the scale.

Her chin was cocked at a valiant angle, and it was a long, vulnerable sweep from there to where the flame red fabric of the dress began. In the violet dusk her mouth was a scarlet blur, pouting self-consciously in the unaccustomed lipstick in a way that reminded Lanagan suddenly and poignantly of a little girl who'd been playing with her mother's makeup. Her hair was almost but not quite as usual, parted low on the side and tucked behind one ear as always, but kept there with something invisible—a comb or a clip of some kind. The other side was still free to fall forward across her eye, but she made no familiar gesture to push it back. Instead she seemed almost to hide behind it, her eyes peering out at him, dark smudges of reproach.

"It's perfect," he repeated in a reassuring tone, and put his hands on her shoulders, a gesture that was meant to be brotherly. But his heart gave an alarming surge, disposing of that absurdity once and for all. Snatching his hands hastily from that searing contact, he turned, swooped down upon the rose he'd left lying on the steps, plucked it up and turned back again, camouflaging his shortness of breath in dramatic gestures. "Except for one... last thing. The final touch..."

He heard the sharp intake of her breath just before she caught and held it. He was holding his own breath, as well; it nearly burst his chest before his clumsy fingers finally found and opened the clasp that held her hair in place above her ear, closed and fastened it again over the thornless stem of the rose. He stood back, oxygen starved and dizzy, to mumble, "There, now it's perfect."

Her fingers fluttered upward, pale as moths, touched the rose and fluttered down again. He heard the rush of her exhalation. "Mike, I don't want to do this."

"Sure you do," he said robustly. He touched the point of her chin delicately with his closed-up fist, falling back as he'd done at certain times of stress in his adolescence upon his heroes from another era. Bogart this time. "You're gonna have a ball, kiddo. All those guys that still think you're a scrawny little kid in pigtails—you're gonna knock 'em out."

She turned her face away from his touch. Her voice cracked, leaking uncertainty. "What they're going to do is fall down laughing."

"Trust me," said Lanagan fervently. "Nobody who sees you in that dress is going to be doing any laughing."

Something of the visceral quality in his voice must have gotten through to her. Her face swiveled slowly back to him. Her eyes intently searched his, all her attention suddenly focused on him instead of her own misery and self-doubt. For a long time she just looked at him, saying nothing, and there didn't seem to be anything for him to do but look back at her, while his heart thumped a quick, suspenseful rhythm, like the tapping of an impatient foot.

When she finally did speak, it was so faintly he barely heard it. "Mike... come with me."

He flinched, then shook his head, unable to comprehend why those words should make him hurt so much.

"Please, I need you." It was barely even a whisper, but the pain inside him grew.

"That would kind of defeat the purpose, wouldn't it?" he said finally, trying on a lopsided Cary Grant-type smile. "The whole idea is for you to walk in there and dazzle those guys. Knock their eyes out. Be the belle of the ball. Right?"

She kept looking at him as if she didn't believe a word of it, and all the while searching his eyes for something else, something he desperately hoped she wouldn't find. Apparently she didn't, because after a moment she made a small sound of resignation and turned away.

"I'll take a dance now, though," he heard his own voice—an unrecognizable croak—say. "If you'll do me the honor..."

She paused, looking at him as if he'd lost his mind. He held out his hand, nodding encouragement, the very picture of confidence, a man who knew exactly what he was doing. But every nerve in his body was thrumming like the plucked strings of an out-of-tune guitar.

"Dance? *Here?*"

"Sure, why not?"

She shook her head, but her hand slowly lifted and found its way into his, almost as if it were being operated by someone else. He pulled gently. She started toward him, then stopped, looked down at her feet and quizzically back at him. Then she simply stepped out of the red satin shoes and left them there in the grass, with the heels spiked deep into the turf.

Afterward he wondered where the music came from. It seemed to surround him, part of an enveloping blanket woven of soft, purple twilight, the sweet scent of roses, and heat that had more to do with hormones than weather. A well-remembered heat, reminiscent of adolescence and desperate fumblings in the back seats of cars, it bloomed in his cheeks and burned along the back of his neck and soaked through the fabric of his shirt where she touched him. Lord, that fire! He'd forgotten what a torment it was.

It seemed to him as though they weren't moving at all, that instead the oak trees revolved slowly around them while they remained still, two beings merged into one, a single focal point, the center of the universe. He wasn't holding her close at all, there was space between their bodies, and yet he felt as if she were melting in the heat of his fire, dissolving... merging with him until he was afraid that in another minute he wouldn't be able to tell where he left off and she began, or ever to separate himself from her without suffering grievous damage to himself. Panic seized him. He tried desperately to right himself, to stop the world from spinning once more out of his control, even though deep in his heart a voice was already crying, *Too late, too late.*

To further torture him, an impish breeze picked up a wisp of her hair and tickled his lips with it, wickedly teasing, *Kiss me... kiss me.* Kiss Lucy? He'd never wanted anything so much, or seen so clearly that it was something he couldn't do. Laughter, the excruciating kind that sometimes takes the place of sobs, bubbled through his chest, and instead of kissing her he pressed his lips lightly against the top of her head and muffled its residue in her hair.

She pulled back instantly to demand in a breathy, suspicious voice, "What's funny?"

"Nothing," he mumbled, his tongue thickened and sticking to the roof of his mouth. He moved his hands to her shoulders and kept them there, holding the two of them apart and himself together. "It's late. Better be on your way."

She was looking down at her hands, which had come like homing birds to rest on his chest. She plucked them away and stood back from him, giving her head a slight, unconscious toss. "Yeah, I guess I'd better do that."

It was almost dark; the dance would be in full swing by the time she got there. Perfect for a grand entrance. Lanagan swallowed a knot in his throat and said, "Don't forget your shoes."

She threw him a look he thought was probably meant to be scornful and plucked them out of the grass with a single sweep of her arm, hooking her fingers in the heel straps.

"Better put 'em on," he said gently. "You'll run your nylons."

She did so without a word or any help from him, hopping a little for balance, then straightened and looked back at him, her face a pale blur in the almost-darkness. She looked like a banished waif.

"Break a leg," he murmured. She uttered a soft sound that might have been a laugh or a whimper and turned away.

As he watched Lucy totter across the lawn in her treacherous spike-heeled shoes, Lanagan was suddenly swept by a fire storm of emotions, raw and powerful emotions, primitive emotions, all having something to do with mating, possession, sexual imperative and jealousy. Here he was sending her off like a proud papa to find a mate, when the very idea of her in the arms of another man made his blood seethe and boil. He suddenly realized that what he wanted to do was run after her, grab and claim her as *his,* carry her off somewhere and seal his claim with a coupling more binding than any vow. Brand her with his body, imprint himself on her heart and soul....

He'd never felt anything like that before. Sex had always been to him something lighthearted and fun, or loving and cozy, occasionally even just an itch that needed scratching. In any case, his partner had always been someone he liked, perhaps even loved, whose company he genuinely enjoyed. Certainly he'd always respected the women in his life as individuals, understood their separateness from himself. Freedom was a declared part of his relationships. Nobody owed anybody, or owned anybody, and if it did hurt like hell when his partners inevitably exercised that freedom, he told himself that was the way things were supposed to be. The whole idea of possessiveness and jealousy shocked him. It went against everything he believed in as an enlightened, sensitive man of his time. But he'd felt it tonight—still felt it now. Oh, boy, did he. And it terrified him.

He stood stunned and silent, watching Lucy's car roll crunching down the driveway, its taillights flash at the bottom of the lane, then wink out where the highway dipped and curved near the creek. He heard the rumble of far-off thunder. A fitful wind lifted his hair, smelling of ozone and distant rain. He groaned and whispered aloud in stark dismay, "Oh, Lord, what have I done?"

"Oh, Lord," said Lucy as she pulled into the VFW Hall parking lot, "what have I done?"

She didn't want to be here, had no business being here. It was her birthday, and she felt bad and mean, and she hadn't even really stopped shaking yet, after that business with Mike on the front lawn. Plus, no matter what he said, she did look ridiculous, dressed up like somebody she wasn't, not that it mattered. There wasn't anybody here she was interested in impressing anyway, and the man she did want to impress was too stupid to notice a good thing when it was sitting right in front of him, just because most of the time it happened to be wearing overalls.

She was all set to turn around and go right back home, but just then Jeff from the feed store and his wife June walked by and recognized her, and of course they had to stop and say hello.

"I didn't expect to see you here," said June when Lucy had rolled down her window. She liked June, even if she was from back East and had a fondness for Ralph Lauren and reportedly bought all her clothes through the mail from Bloomingdale's and Saks. "Are you going in? We'll wait and walk with you."

Oh, boy, thought Lucy, here goes. She opened the door and sat there for a moment, debating the best way to get herself out of the car without displaying her underwear. Finally she swung both legs around, squeezed her hips past the steering wheel and stood up while simultaneously tugging her skirt back down more or less where it belonged.

"That's sure a pretty dress you're wearing," said Jeff, sounding as if he were coming down with a cold.

Lucy muttered, "Thanks," and leaned across the driver's seat to get her dish for the potluck supper.

June said brightly, "Is that some of Gwen's cheesecake? I sure do love her cheesecake—don't you, Jeff? It's that lemon juice and almond flavoring that make it so good." Lucy couldn't help but notice that she maneuvered herself so she was standing between her husband and Lucy.

She also noticed that while they were walking from the parking lot to the hall, Jeff kept sneaking glances at her across his wife's shoulders.

In the foyer she stopped at a table to pay her four dollars. The cash box was being manned by Martha and George Swensen, who were both in their sixties and had known her since she was a baby. When she leaned down to write on her name tag, she noticed that George's face sort of went bright red. He'd always had a ruddy complexion, and had probably just been out in the sun a lot lately. And if it wasn't that, thought Lucy, then he ought to be ashamed of himself.

"Surprised to see you here," Martha commented coolly as she stamped the back of Lucy's hand. "Did Gwen come with you?"

"No," said Lucy grimly. "Just her cheesecake."

The music coming from the hall was a popular song that Lucy recognized—a DJ, then, not a band. The lights were dim and people were dancing, but as she skirted the floor to the table where the potluck dishes were spread out, she felt as if she were on a great big stage with a spotlight trained on her. Every eye in the place had to be on her dress, which sort of gave off a glow all its own, and which she could feel creeping farther up her thighs with every step she took. Her leg muscles were starting to cramp from trying to walk on the slick hardwood floor in the damned spike-heeled shoes without teetering like an adolescent in her first pair of pumps. Or worse, slipping and falling flat on her fanny.

"Lucy—Lucy Brown, is that you?" rumbled a masculine voice. A pair of masculine hands came from nowhere to remove the glass baking dish from her hands.

Lucy blinked and looked up into the face of Terry James, the ag teacher at the local high school. He'd been out to her place a dozen times at least, buying calves and feeder pigs for his FFA kids to raise for the fair. The expression he had on his face was one she'd seen plenty of times before, but only when he was looking at her livestock.

"Here, let me take that for you. Mmm, is that some of Gwen's cheesecake I see?"

Before she could answer that, another pair of hands fitted themselves to her elbow and the small of her back. They belonged to Harvey Kittler, who had been her partner for three interminable weeks of square dance class, and they still felt unpleasantly warm and moist, just like they had back in fifth grade. "Hullo, Harvey," she said without enthusiasm.

Harvey's forehead had risen a bit since the last time she'd seen him, and it looked every bit as warm and moist as his hands. He smiled, showing too many teeth and reducing his pale blue eyes to slits. "It's been a long time since we've seen you at one of these affairs. You come all by yourself?"

Lucy sighed, regretting that fact more and more all the time. "Yes, I'm afraid so."

Terry the ag teacher came strolling back her way, having deposited the cheesecake on the refreshment table, and was looking her up and down and rubbing his hands together. "My, my, Lucy," he said, "you sure are looking nice tonight."

"Thanks," she said warily. Any minute now she expected him to start feeling her arms and legs for muscle tone. If he did, she was prepared to deck him on the spot.

"Lucy, where've you been keeping yourself?" Another masculine voice claimed her attention. Yet another large hand fell hot and heavy upon her almost bare shoulder.

Why, she wondered, did everyone suddenly seem to think he had the right to *touch* her? She looked around in annoyance, then smiled with relief as she recognized a friend of her brother Earl's. What was his name...Kyle, or something—no, Ken. Kenny, that was it. At least, she thought, she wouldn't have to worry about *his* motives. The kid was at least five years younger than she was, and the last time she'd seen him, he and Earl had been up to their elbows in grease and motorcycle parts, and neither one of them would have noticed if she'd walked by stark naked.

"What do you hear from Earl these days?" said Kenny, smiling down at her in a very friendly way. "He still down there in Africa?"

"Yes, he's..."

Kenny's gaze slipped downward and didn't bother to come back up. He was unmistakably blushing.

Lucy made a small sound of utter exasperation and cast a quick look around her, hoping to find some unobtrusive avenue of escape. She was stunned to discover that she had become the center of a crowd. More accurately, of a crowd of men. Not all of them were looking at her, at least not directly. Quite a few—the married ones, mainly—were standing sort of sideways to her, sipping punch from plastic cups and trying hard to look as if they weren't interested.

Terry the ag teacher offered to get her some punch. The music started up and somebody—it *had* to be Harvey, of course—grabbed her arm and asked her to dance.

"Now, wait a minute," someone else said. "What's your wife gonna say, Harvey? Come on, Lucy, you better dance with me so you don't get him into trouble."

Another voice hooted and said, "Yeah, listen to him. He's a fine one to talk!"

The voices tumbled together and merged into babble. The circle of bodies around Lucy seemed to whirl slowly, while her gaze skipped from one hovering, sweat-shiny face to another in utter bemusement. The situation was completely beyond her range of experience. She didn't know whether to burst out laughing or scream and run.

Just when it seemed the second option was most likely going to win, a strong, self-confident voice boomed, "Sorry, you're all out of luck. She's dancing with me."

The babble subsided to background murmurs. The crowd stopped spinning. "Who said that?" she demanded, thinking maybe she'd go along with whoever it was, even if he was an arrogant so-and-so, just to restore order.

"I did."

Lucy's mascara'd lashes flew wide, then fluttered partway down. "Brent Weatherby," she breathed, feeling a little like Scarlett O'Hara, and wishing she had something to fan herself with. Then she recovered and inquired coolly, "Why would I want to dance with you?"

"Hey, don't tell me you've forgotten," he said, taking her arm. "You owe me one. You were supposed to go to a dance with me, remember? Only you canceled out on me at the last minute."

She opened her mouth to tell him in no uncertain terms that *he* was the one who seemed to have forgotten a thing or two, but his smile was still *so* cool, his eyes still boyishly long lashed and charming, and she found herself smiling back instead. "That was a long time ago, Brent."

"I know, and I've been waiting a long time for my dance."

He guided her out among the dancers, an arm encircling her waist. He turned toward her and pulled her close—too close. She stiffened and murmured, "Where's your wife tonight?"

"Oh, she's home. One of the kids has the flu."

Must run in the family, thought Lucy. She felt a bit unwell herself, sort of shaky and fragile. Brent's body was very warm against the front of hers, and she wondered if that was why.

"You sure have changed since high school," he whispered in her ear. His voice was husky and his breath smelled faintly and not altogether unpleasantly of beer.

"Not all that much," said Lucy dryly, wondering what he'd say if she told him about the dress.

From Mike Lanagan's personal files
NOTES FOR FUTURE COLUMNS

To be added to list of quaint old expressions with farm origins: Madder than a wet hen.

Chapter 9

Lanagan spent most of the evening in the barn tinkering with his car, even though he'd already gotten it pretty well dried out and cleaned up. It really only needed a little bit of fine tuning. It wasn't lack of transportation that was keeping him here walking cornfields instead of going back to Chicago and the *Chicagoan,* where he belonged. Where he should have gone weeks ago, before he'd gotten himself into another mess he couldn't handle.

He'd been doing a lot of that lately. And this time he had a feeling the consequences could turn out to be a lot more painful than just the loss of his home and all his worldly possessions.

How could he have been so stupid?

What could have possessed him to try to change Lucy, when he already liked her so much the way she was? Remembering her now the way she'd looked tonight, walking away from him across the lawn, wobbly as a newborn calf in those damned high-heeled shoes, the way she'd looked back at him in silent reproach, missing all the sparkle and sass that made her so interesting to him in the first place, he felt sick at heart, sick in his belly, as if he'd broken something he didn't know if he could fix.

Ordinarily the intricacies of an internal combustion engine had the power to soothe his soul and crowd troublesome thoughts from his mind; some people he knew used alcohol or TV sitcoms for the same purpose. Tonight, though, no matter how hard he tried to concentrate on his engine's rhythm and cadence, no matter how hard he listened for the slightest flaw in the timing, he kept hearing dance music instead. His mind insisted on wandering off to a crowded dance floor, one that in his imagination looked a lot like a honky-tonk. A dark, smoky honky-tonk. Full of wolves. Wearing farmer's overalls. And right in the middle of it all was Lucy in that flame red dress, looking a lot like Little Red Riding Hood.

Please come with me. I need you.

It was all his fault. He'd done this to her, stripped her of her weapons and armor and then sent her out to face the wolves all alone. He'd never forgive himself if she got hurt. If any of those bastards so much as laid a hand on her... When he thought about that possibility he felt as if he wanted to take pieces out of his engine and chew on them.

A small trill of sound broke in on his black thoughts, like bird song after a long night. "Hullo, kitty-cat, where've you been?" he murmured as he bent to pet the little calico mother cat, who was twining energetically around his ankles. She gave his hand an affectionate bump with the top of her head, then touched it with her cool, moist nose in the tiniest of kisses. For reasons Lanagan had never been able to figure out, the cat seemed to adore him above all others, even Gwen, the one who usually fed her. She was an affectionate animal and loved to be petted and cuddled by anybody who'd take the time to do so, but he and only he was the recipient of these small caresses.

It seemed to him there was something almost possessive about the cat's attitude toward him. Remembering what Lucy had said about the likelihood she'd wandered into the barn during the storm, as he had, he wondered if perhaps the little animal considered him somehow her savior. And who knows, maybe he had been—maybe he'd even opened the door for her. God knows, the shape he'd been in, he'd never have noticed one rail-thin waif slipping like a shadow past his ankles. And then he'd barely made it to the empty stall before he'd collapsed. Now he wondered if the cat had adopted him and kept watch over him while he slept.

"You've been out prowling, haven't you? Left the kids home alone again?" he accused as he scooped the little animal into his arms. She gave his chin a playful bat with one paw and tipped her head back to expose the velvety white underside of hers for him to scratch. There was something therapeutic, he discovered, in petting the creature, stroking the warm, vibrating body, the soft, silky fur. Gentling his hands helped to gentle his mind. As the cat's purring reached buzz-saw intensity he felt his own body relax, his jaws unclench. He even laughed a little as he set the cat back down on the floor, laughing at himself for his own foolishness.

It's just a good friend's concern—a big-brotherly protectiveness, he told himself as he watched the cat jump up to the open window of his car, balance there for a moment, then drop down onto the back seat where her four kittens slept in a multicolored and indistinguishable pile. He and Lucy had twice tried to move the family into a straw-filled box in one of the empty stalls, and both times the mother had moved her kittens right back again into the car. She'd chosen her place, and there she would stay.

Of course, he thought, almost dizzy with relief. That's all it is. Just like the cat's adopted me, I've adopted Lucy. Of course he felt protective toward her. After all, it was a role that felt familiar and comfortable to him. It was just like when he was a kid. *Pick on somebody your own size.*

He went back to his car's engine whistling, conveniently forgetting all about the wild, primal urges that had swept through him just a little while before, urges to mate and possess that were about as far from being brotherly or a kid as it was possible to get.

Sometime around eleven Gwen came down to the barn, blowing in through the small, west-facing door on a gust of wind that set the electric lamp he'd slung over the beam above his head to swaying as if it were on a ship in a rough sea, and elastic shadows dancing across the floor. Lanagan looked up in surprise and said, "Where'd that come from? Is it going to storm?"

"Looks like it," said Gwen. The wind caught the door and slammed it shut at her back. Beyond it Lanagan could hear thunder growling and snapping like thwarted wolves. She leaned against the door to catch her breath and gestured with the napkin-wrapped plate she held in her hands. "Brought you and the cat some cheesecake."

He pulled his arms out of the car's innards and shut off the motor. "Thanks," he said, grinning at her as he took the plate from her, "but if you think I'm sharing this with that cat, you're crazy. Besides, she's busy at the moment."

It was the best cheesecake he'd ever tasted. Gwen watched him appreciate it for a while in silence, then said in her usual light, lilting way, "I'm surprised Lucy's not back. She'll want to be home before this hits."

Lanagan gave her a quick glance, then a longer one. Her face, which so often seemed to smile even in repose, now had a fragile, artificial look, like a smile reproduced in porcelain. He shrugged. "She's probably just having a good time."

Gwen shook her head and didn't say anything. But with the brief glance she gave him he had the strange feeling she was as vexed with him as he was with himself. The next moment, however, he thought it must have been his own guilty conscience that made him think so, because both her eyes and voice were gentle with sympathy when she nodded toward his car and said, "Looks like you've about got it fixed."

"Yeah." He shrugged. "Good as it's ever been, anyway."

"Does that mean you'll be leaving us soon?"

He couldn't answer her, and instead turned to poke casually and needlessly at the tangle of wires and cables under the hood. Presently his hands stilled and he muttered to the silent engine, "It's not the car that needs fixing."

"You know you're welcome to stay as long as you need to," said Gwen in a careful, searching kind of way. "Lucy can always use the help."

"Lucy." Lanagan snorted and shook his head, still gazing into his car's engine as if it were the cause of his ironic laughter. "She's got this place set up to be a one-man—excuse me, woman—operation. She doesn't need anybody's help." He paused and felt his mouth twist with an unexpected spasm of pain. "Just ask her."

The old lady's smile was gentle, forgiving him the note of bitterness he hadn't been able to keep out of his voice. "That's just Lucy. That's the way she is." There was a pause before she added, "Would you want her any different?"

He jerked his head around to look at her, unnerved to hear so close an echo of his own guilty thoughts. Her eyes regarded him steadfastly, fathomless and wise. "No," he said grudgingly. "I wouldn't."

"You always hear people say they want to be needed," she remarked in a thoughtful tone, "but I don't think that's necessarily such a good thing. It's being *wanted* that counts. And most of the time when people say the one, it's the other they really mean."

Lanagan didn't say anything. He was hearing Lucy's voice pleading with him once again. *Please come with me... I need you.*

Gwen turned to go, and he caught a fleeting glimpse of former grace and ageless beauty and realized with a sense of shock and discovery, *This is how Lucy will look when she's old.* And he realized that he desperately wanted to be there to see it. So stunned was he by that revelation that he didn't think to help Gwen with the door, even when the waiting wind rushed in howling through the crack to wrest it from her grasp.

"Mercy!" she exclaimed above the noise, grabbing for the door with one hand while the other flew automatically to hold down her hair. "I hope Lucy gets home before this storm hits. I don't like the looks of it."

She went out, still struggling with the door. Lanagan jumped belatedly to help, but the wind had already slammed it shut.

He went slowly back to his car, the moving shadows from the swaying lamp making him feel slightly off balance, as if the earth were heaving beneath his feet. He remembered the same sensation from his childhood, long ago in California, and his mother telling him it was an earthquake. There'd been other quakes after that, of course, but never one that had rocked him quite like that first one, when that most fundamental faith, his innocent belief in the solidity and permanence of the ground beneath his feet, had been forever shaken.

Once again he tried to concentrate on his car, even tried to think about what he was going to do when he got back to Chicago, what he was going to do with those documents in his briefcase, and when. But something—or rather, someone—kept getting in his way.

Lucy.

Dammit, she was all he could think about, all he could see. Lucy in overalls, hay dusty and grinning, sassy as a jay;

Lucy as Madonna, bending over a nestful of newborn kittens, luminous and lovely as a medieval painting; Lucy like a little girl drinking from the water hose, with her hair sticking to her cheeks, eyes wide and vulnerable; Lucy in that damned red dress, smelling of roses....

He broke out in a sweat; he felt hot, half-suffocated. He wanted to yell at somebody. He wanted to argue—loudly—that what was happening to him *couldn't* be happening. That was when it suddenly struck him that it had never happened to him before, not once in his whole life. Incredible, but true—he'd never been in love before. And for it to choose this time and these circumstances to happen to him seemed a cruel, impossible joke. He couldn't deal with this now. He couldn't. His life was a mess. He had nothing ahead of him but fear and uncertainty. And to make matters worse, it had to be Lucy. *Lucy.* A woman who neither needed nor wanted a man in her life, and even if she did... Oh, yes, he knew only too well that for Lucy, this land would always come first.

When he heard the rush and howl of the wind again, he thought it must be Gwen, returning for the cheesecake plate they'd both forgotten and which was still sitting precariously balanced on the front fender of his car. He whirled, mouth opened, already armed with futile denials, primed for the battle that had been raging silently inside him.

And there instead, as if he'd conjured her from his feverish thoughts, was Lucy. Lucy, roused and windblown, cheeks flushed, eyes catching the glow of the swaying lamp and shooting it back at him like sparking coals.

The door crashed behind her, cutting off the wind in midhowl, and for a moment she leaned against it just as Gwen had, slightly knock-kneed and breathing hard.

Outside the barn the thunder had become an almost continuous rumbling, like an artillery barrage; inside it seemed deathly still. Lanagan felt transfixed, dumbstruck, as if he'd been caught in the act of some unspeakable transgression.

There were so many things going on in his mind that he simply didn't know what to say.

Which definitely didn't appear to be Lucy's problem. It seemed she'd only been taking a moment to marshal her forces before she gathered herself and let fly with a veritable volley of words.

"Men are so... *stupid!*" she yelled, underlining the last word by ripping the rose from her hair and hurling it at Lanagan. It hit him squarely in the middle of his chest, catching him by surprise. He watched dumbfounded as it tumbled onto the back of his hand, which was lying palm down on the fender of his car.

"Such... *idiots!*" This time the punctuation was provided by one of the red spike-heeled shoes, which, since he was a little better prepared for it, he managed to duck. It sailed an inch or so wide of his ear and he heard it crash against a stall gate.

"Hey, now wait a minute," he began, holding out a restraining hand.

"Jerks!" The second shoe sailed high and landed somewhere in the straw, almost without a sound.

And then he realized that she was crying—tears of rage, to be sure, but tears nonetheless. Fear and remorse assailed him. His plan had backfired. Something must have happened at the dance. Something terrible. "Lucy, I'm sorry," he choked out, and started toward her.

"You," she breathed with eyes narrowed and blazing, stopping him in his tracks. "What is it with you men? You're all alike. Shallow... insensitive... stupid... *jerks.*"

"Good God, what happened?" he ventured, horrified. "Did something—"

"What happened? What happened? I'll tell you what happened. Just exactly what you thought would happen, that's what. I hope you're satisfied." She gave a sharp, outraged laugh. "They were all over me. You'd have thought I was a bitch in heat! Guys I've known all my life—married ones, even. Some I haven't seen in ages. *Years,* Cage. Not one of them ever looked at me twice before, and all of a sudden they're just dying to dance with me. *Me.* Geez, they all seemed to want to put their hands on me. Brent Weatherby—my God, I had such a crush on him in high school. He got the flu so he wouldn't have to go out with me. *Brent Weatherby.* He actually suggested we ought to 'get together' sometime. Geez, he's got a wife and two kids!"

She had her hands pressed to her forehead as if in total disbelief, and the words were spilling out of her so rapidly he couldn't tell anymore whether she was laughing or crying. A little of both, he suspected.

Then she suddenly threw her arms wide and demanded, "Why do you suppose that is? Why, Cage? You tell me. Because of this stupid *dress?*" She lifted her arms, reached awkwardly behind her and began squirming and tugging furiously at something, a fact Lanagan registered without immediately comprehending its purpose. "This dress. Dammit, I'm the same person I was yesterday, last week, all my life. Except I'm wearing this stupid dress. Well, this isn't me, dammit. If anybody wants me, he'll just have to take me the way I *am!*"

The final word was accompanied by the faint but triumphant screech of a metal zipper. By the time Lanagan realized that she meant the red dress to follow the way of the rose and satin shoes, it was almost too late. He leapt forward and managed to get his arms around her and pin her arms to her sides just as the dress, laid suddenly open all the way down the back, fell forward over the rounds of her shoulders. Only his chest pressed tightly against hers kept it from slithering all the way down to her ankles.

"Get...your...hands off me," she seethed between clenched teeth. Her body was stiff as a post in his arms.

Gazing down, he said in a wondering tone, "You're not wearing a bra."

"That's none of your business," she hissed, still seething. But it was impossible to seethe and remain stiff, something they both seemed to be discovering at about the same time. In the closeness of his embrace her body was inevitably heating, softening, developing curves. And just as inevitably, his body was responding to that development.

"Well, it seemed to me," Lanagan said huskily, "you were just about to make it my business."

Her chin jerked up a notch, but her eyes stayed glued to the middle of his chest, as if she couldn't quite bring herself to meet his eyes. He could barely hear her mutter, "Didn't think you'd notice."

"I'd have noticed." The barn seemed close and airless. Outside, the thunder grumbled a counterpoint to his pounding heart. He could feel her heart beating, too, against the sensitive place just below his ribs. He could feel her body heat soaking into his shirt, see a fine sheen of sweat across the bridge of her nose and the tops of her cheeks. Her lashes were longer than he'd realized; she'd darkened the sun-bleached tips with mascara. They fluttered slightly, like the first stirrings of a newly born moth's wings.

"Then why," she asked in the same, barely audible voice, "did you stop me?"

He didn't answer right away, partly because he wasn't quite sure himself why he'd stopped her—it might have been just his old Sir Galahad instincts, alive and well. But then again, he had a strange sense of something fragile and wonderful happening, as yet out of sight, just below the level of conscious thought, like the small miracles of seeds germinating beneath the soil's surface. He didn't want to trample them in his clumsiness before they'd even had a chance to sprout.

He cleared his throat and said carefully, "I wasn't sure you knew what you were doing. Wouldn't want you to hate me when you came to your senses."

She gave that a moment's consideration, then murmured just as carefully, "I guess that would depend . . ."

"On what?"

"On what your reaction was." Her lashes fluttered once more, then lifted bravely. Her eyes looked straight up into his.

There was another long, suspenseful silence inside the barn, while just beyond the doors the wind howled and the thunder rolled and grumbled. Lanagan felt as if that same turbulence was inside him, rumbling in his belly and chest, and skating along all his nerves. He felt a fine trembling begin and didn't know whether it was hers or his, or just the buffeting of the storm. *My reaction?* Oh, Lord, what could he possibly say to her?

"I mean, if you would've burst out laughing . . ."

"Laughing was the farthest thing from my mind," he growled.

"Yeah?" she whispered, as if her mind wasn't on it. He noticed that her eyes had gone wide and startled, and realized that, with her body pressed so tightly to the front of his, she couldn't help but notice what *was* on his mind.

"Yeah." He sighed and kissed her.

He'd have sworn he hadn't known he was going to. He'd been treading so cautiously, trying so hard not to do or say the wrong thing, which wasn't easy when the signals she was giving him were so confusing. What decided him, if something that volatile could be said to have anything to do with decision at all, was the realization that in spite of her pinioned arms, her hands had somehow come to be resting on his sides, right at his waist. Lightly, perhaps unconsciously, but there beyond any doubt, a small and intimate warmth soaking slowly through his shirt just above the waistband of his jeans. From those places shards of sensation lanced downward into his groin and legs. He closed his eyes, uttered a sound like a moan of pain, and the next thing he knew her whimpered breath was in his own mouth, and the storm's thunder was in his ears and its heat and electricity in every part of him.

Their arms simultaneously shifted, seeking more sensual alignments. Lucy's, released from captivity, slipped instantly around him as if that was their natural form and place. Her hands flattened against the back of his shirt, then grasped it in greedy handfuls.

His hands, seeking something to hold him to reason and sanity, instead met the softness of skin, and the delicate undulations of back muscles and shoulder blades. He slid his hands downward slowly, reveling in her softness, conscious of their roughness, the rasp of his calluses on her unflawed nakedness. Conscious, too, of the way her body arched into his, not flinching, following the path of his touch the way the cat's back had arched beneath his petting hand... realizing instinctively that her skin was shivering with responses, every nerve awake and hungry, and that she reveled in the roughness.

His hands moved down, down, following the gentle curve of her spine to where the zipper ended and the red fabric of the dress still clung precariously to her hips. They didn't stop even there, but dipped under the giving fabric to palm and mold the taut, nylon-slippery swell of her bottom...and finding the nylon raspy and unforgiving to his touch, and past thinking of the consequences of such intimate trespass, he pushed beneath it and found at last the anchor he'd been seeking.

Secure in that possession, now with regret he relinquished his claim on her mouth, lifted his head, opened his eyes and looked down into hers, still half-dazed and unbelieving, half expecting to see disaster there in spite of all his other senses' evidence to the contrary. What he saw were pools of bewilderment, pupils dilated almost to black, shimmering with a fragile glaze of shock. Just about then he realized that she was trembling, trembling so hard he was sure that if he released her she would fall. And trembling, moreover, almost in concert with the thunder outside, fresh shudders seizing her with each new crack and rumble.

He made a guttural sound, low and concerned. His body responded instinctively, gathering her in and tightening protectively around her. But before he could ask her what was wrong, she clutched at his arms and lifted her mouth again to his with a desperate, whimpering cry. He took what she offered without hesitation, and tasted passion, heady and strong as warm whiskey. And the unmistakable salt-tang of tears. His response to the one was visceral and wrenching as a hot knife to the groin; the other involved parts of him that were considerably more complicated, and capable of causing him infinitely more pain.

It seemed as though he'd become caught up in everything that was happening, in the storms that were raging both inside and outside the barn. He felt buffeted and dizzy, pulled by forces it would take all his strength and will to resist. And certainly there was a part of him that didn't want to resist—the visceral part, passion-ruled, that would have reveled in the storm and ridden it joyfully wherever it might have taken him. It was the other part, the complicated part, that made him finally pull his mouth from hers and lay his cheek against her hair and cry out with a sound like tearing cloth, "Lucy, Lucy, for God's sake, tell me what's wrong."

He never knew what she might have answered, or if she would have done so at all. Because in that moment there was a flash, and a tremendous crack of thunder that shook the barn to its foundations. Lucy made a tiny sound like a hurt animal, and tried to burrow her face into the front of his shirt. The light flickered, dimmed and then went out, and it was in the total darkness that Lanagan suddenly saw everything clearly.

She was afraid. Terrified.

"Lucy—" His arms tightened convulsively, protectively around her.

"The animals! I have to... get the animals." She pushed him away so forcefully he staggered backward against the fender and upset the cheesecake plate that was precariously balanced there. It slid to the cement floor with a small, splintering crash, like wind-driven rain on glass.

He cried out to her again, but his voice was swallowed up in another deafening *crraack,* and once more the barn shook and rattled around them. The lightning was almost continuous now; he could see Lucy moving away from him, struggling with the zipper of her dress, her movements jerky in its strobelike flickering. He was lurching toward her, reaching for her, when a new and dreadful sound froze them both where they stood. It was like nothing Lanagan had ever heard, a sound like the death scream of some gigantic beast, and it seemed to come from the very ground beneath their feet, as if the earth herself were dying in terrible agony.

His hands gripped Lucy's shoulders, his head bent close to hers so she would hear what he was about to say. Whatever that might have been he never knew, but he was able to hear her say, somewhere between a gasp and a whimper. "Oh... God." And then, in sharp urgency, "Help me—hurry!"

He understood. His fingers sought and found the metal tab and he tore the zipper upward and closed with considerably more dispatch and efficiency than he'd ever opened one. He groped for the barn door and found Lucy's hands there ahead of his. Together they pushed it open and surged out into the maelstrom of wind and rain, light and sound.

Sound. Oh, the sound! For a moment he felt as if it was happening to him all over again. He could hear it—the roar of fire, the awful snapping and cracking of collapsing timbers. Then Lucy was running and he was, too, running blindly up the lane through sheets of rain and howling wind and flashing light and darkness toward the crashing sounds that were not thunder.

He caught up with her at the top of the lane and grabbed her arm to hold her back. She fought him for a moment—out of reflex rather than reason—then staggered back a step and stood braced, almost like a boxer taking a defensive stance. Ahead of them the night seemed to be alive, filled with wild thrashings and flailings, with the creaks and snaps and crashes of countless things breaking. Then all at once it was over, and the storm seemed almost gentle, the chaotic night peaceful by comparison.

"It's a tree," Lucy shouted, trying to wipe rain from her face so she could see. "I think the swing tree. It's down.... I can't—"

"It's okay," Lanagan yelled back. "It's down across the drive. I think it missed the house."

"Well, it hit *something*. Damn this rain. Damn it all to hell!" She pulled from his grasp, and with the next lightning flash he saw her with her fist upraised, shaking it at the sky as if at an unseen enemy.

"Lucy—"

He reached for her, but she evaded him, sobbing wildly, "I can't *see*. I have to get a flashlight." And she disappeared into the darkness.

He groped his way forward, muttering under his breath. Where was lightning when you needed it? As if in reply to that question, a great silvery shaft rent the blackness overhead, split into a fork and danced with lurid glee toward the horizon, like a taunting prankster. Lanagan, surveying the bleached and glistening scene laid out before him, felt a crazy desire to laugh. Not again, he thought as the darkness descended once more, thicker than ever. I don't believe it. *Not again.*

The little white cottage with the rambling rose growing over the door—his cottage—lay crushed beneath a tree limb as big around as a man's body. Beyond it, the chicken house was all but invisible, buried under a maze of branches and leaves. I don't believe this, he thought, with the beginnings of outrage. My house—twice, in less than a month! *My house!* It wasn't as if he had anything left to lose. The only things he had left to call his own, besides his car, of course, were his hat and his briefcase, and they were—

My briefcase.

He felt his way along the fallen limb and began to claw at the wreckage of the porch, tearing his fingers on rose thorns. He heard shouts, heard a screen door slam. Twin flashlight beams swam toward him through a curtain of water, and Gwen materialized before him, a tall wraith in a long pale nightgown, with silvery hair streaming down her back.

"Here, take this," she shouted, thrusting one of the flashlights into his hands. "What're you doing in there?"

"My briefcase," he gasped. "Got to...find my brief-case."

She shouted something he couldn't hear, except for the word *chickens*. He felt her fingers squeeze his arm as she moved past him, and then he heard her crashing through the branches that covered the chicken house.

He hesitated, started after her, then swore and dove back into the rubble, aiming the flashlight beam toward the place where he knew the briefcase should be. *There.* Right where he'd left it, under the bed. He could reach it, if he crawled in under the limb....

A few splinters and torn sleeves later he had it. His hat had gotten pretty badly caved in during the scramble, but otherwise seemed to have survived. He jammed the brief-case under his arm and went to look for Gwen. He found her in what was left of the chicken yard, with her nightgown gathered up in one hand like an apron. It was full of baby chicks. Below it, he could see that she had on a pair of men's work boots, laced to her bony ankles.

"Where's Lucy?" he shouted.

"Seeing to the pigs. Here, take these chicks to the house. I've got to get to the others before they drown!" And she held out her gathered-up nightgown.

For a moment Lanagan just stared at her, utterly at a loss.

"Your hat!" she yelled. "Give me your hat!"

So he whipped off his precious fedora and held his briefcase over it like an umbrella while Gwen filled it to the brim with sodden baby chicks. He raced to the house with his awkward little burden, and found that Gwen already had Coleman lanterns lit in the kitchen. By their chilly light he located a laundry basket, lined it with towels, dumped in the miserably cheeping chicks and draped another towel over the top. Then he ran back outside for another load.

For the next few hours Lanagan was busy rescuing chickens and baby pigs and getting them bedded down in the barn, lashing down sheds and mending fences and helping corral terrified livestock—too busy to think at all about the other storm that had broken that night... the storm inside him. It was a night he knew he'd never forget, full of almost surreal images, some of which would stay with him as long as he lived. Gwen, with her men's boots and streaming white hair, scooping half-drowned chickens into her kilted-up nightgown. And the little dog Dodger, darting here, there and everywhere amongst the hooves of frightened cattle and somehow keeping them from bolting through their flattened fences.

But the most unforgettable of all was Lucy. Lucy, with her flame red dress plastered to her body, barefooted, hair torn by the wind, rain coursing down her face like tears... shaking her fist at the heavens in rage and defiance.

The Chicagoan, June 1

Front Page
by Ralph Buncomb, staff writer

CHICAGO—A new mystery has surfaced in the FBI's ongoing investigation of Westside Development Corporation. The *Chicagoan* has learned that certain records and documents pertaining to the Chicago-based corporation's business and financial dealings, as well as all records of communications between the corporation and the city's planning commission, have apparently turned up missing. FBI sources admit they now believe the documents, which are considered critical to the investigation, may have been in the possession of *Chicagoan* columnist Mike Lanagan at the time of his disappearance following the firebombing of his home last May first.

Chapter 10

"Are you still out here?" Gwen called softly, coming out onto the porch with a Coleman lantern. "Why don't you come in now? There's nothing more you can do until daylight."

"Yeah, I will. In a minute." Lucy's voice sounded hard and loud in a night filled with gentle sounds: the drip and trickle of water, the softest sigh of wind, like whispers of apology. She turned away from the screen door and wrapped her arms across her body, holding herself tightly together. "Where's Mike?"

"I put him in Earl's room. Right now I believe he's taking a shower."

"A shower? With the power out?"

"Forty gallons of warm water in the tank—no point in letting it go to waste, especially with the both of you soaked and chilled to the bone. Don't worry, I warned him to save you some."

"What about you?" Lucy said almost angrily. "You're as wet and cold as anybody else."

Gwen dismissed that with a single, bell-like note of mirth. "These old bones can take a lot of chilling. But look at you, in nothing but that scrap of a dress." She shook her head ruefully. "I think it's seen its first and last dance. What'd you do with your shoes and stockings?"

"They're in the barn," Lucy mumbled.

"The barn! Why on earth did you leave them down there?"

"I threw 'em," she muttered, glowering at the memory. "At Mike's head." The nylons she'd taken off later, after they'd already been torn to shreds.

"I wondered where you were," said Gwen mildly, apparently not finding anything too surprising in such behavior. "I saw the car lights pull in. How was the dance?"

The dance. It seemed like a long time ago to her now. And not very important. She even smiled a bit ruefully as she reported, "The dance was great. A ball. The dress was a big hit, almost as big a hit as your cheesecake." She began to make her slow and gingerly way to the kitchen, still keeping herself tightly wrapped in her own embrace and shaking like a leaf in spite of it.

In the kitchen she paused, surrounded by shadows and the soft rustlings and peepings of baby chickens, and waited for Gwen and the lantern to catch up with her. "You know, once the shock wore off, I actually kind of enjoyed it. Anyway, at first. Then I got mad. I'm not sure why, I just got... it made me so..." She let go of herself long enough to make a gesture, but her teeth started chattering and she had to grab hold of herself again so she could finish talking. "*Mad.* You know what I mean? I mean, here were all these guys going nuts over a stupid dress. I just wanted..." She paused, unable to keep the smile from coming back. And growing. "Well, actually, I guess I kind of did."

"Did what?" asked Gwen in a fascinated tone.

"You know Brent Weatherby? You were right, he was there—his poor wife was home with a sick kid. Well, he got me while we were slow dancing, and he propositioned me."

"No!" said Gwen.

"Oh, yes. We happened to be pretty close to the refreshment table at the time, and I—"

In a hushed, fascinated tone, Gwen said, "Lucy, what did you do?"

"I shoved him into the punch. I'm not sure what part of him landed in it, because I left right after. I thought you ought to know," she said soberly. "You might want to let things die down a little bit before you show up at another Farm Wives meeting."

"Oh, dear," said Gwen, trying without much success to stifle laughter.

Then she said in real concern, "Lucy, for heaven's sake, go get in the shower. I don't hear the water running, so I'm sure Mike's out of it by now. You'd better get out of that dress and get yourself warmed up before you catch your death."

Lucy nodded and wobbled toward the door, all of a sudden shaking too hard for speech. But she wasn't cold, and she knew there wasn't enough hot water in the world to make those shivers go away.

She didn't bother with a lantern, since she knew her way around the house blindfolded. When she opened her bedroom door she was surprised to see that it wasn't really dark in there at all, but a silvery twilight that defined shapes and shone palely through curtains and gave mirrors and glass-covered photographs a dull, metallic sheen. She went straight to the window, wondering if it could possibly be dawn already, but instead, low in the west, there was the moon, a fat three quarters, just breaking out of the scudding clouds. *The moon.* The storm was really over.

Except that Lucy knew it wasn't. Not for her.

She hated storms. She'd always hated storms. They left her feeling exhausted and drained. But nothing like this, never like this...except—oh, yes, once before. The night of the accident. The night her parents were killed. It had been storming that night, too, she remembered. And she'd stood like this, alone at the window after everyone had gone away and Earl was sleeping sedated in his room down the hall. The room where Mike was now. She'd stood for such a long time that night, looking out the window, wrapped in her own arms, so numb and stiff, afraid to move, afraid to let go of herself for fear she'd fly apart in a million pieces.

It wasn't the storm. At least, not only the storm. She knew that.

Eventually, just as she had that other terrible night six years before, from somewhere she summoned the will to make her arms move, to peel them away from her body, to force stiff fingers to grasp the zipper tab, and nerveless hands to draw it down. The flame red fabric fell of its own damp weight onto her bare feet. *Stupid dress.* She stepped out of it and kicked it angrily away. Stupid dress, stupid dance, stupid idea. Stupid men, of course.

Stupid me.

That was the worst of it—wondering how in the world she could have done something so dumb. How could she have let it happen? She, Lucinda Rosewood Brown! *Always keep your wits about you, Lucinda, and you'll never have to be afraid of anything.* Well, she had tried to keep her wits about her, and she really wasn't afraid of anything.

Except falling in love.

She couldn't understand it. She'd had everything all planned out, her finances squared away except for that one small loan at the bank, the farm set up so she could manage it by herself with just a hired man for the busiest times. She'd had everything under control. But for some reason that hadn't kept her from behaving like a complete fool. It hadn't kept her from falling for a man she didn't even know, a man who, for all she knew, could be wanted by the law, a common criminal, a fugitive from justice. For all she knew...

All she knew was the way she'd felt tonight when he'd touched her. Danced with her. Kissed her. All she knew was the way she felt right now, remembering. It was much, much worse than any roller coaster ride. She felt shocked...hollow and quivery in the middle. Terrified. Hungry and restless as a tiger in a cage.

Cage. Mike Cage—yeah sure. It wasn't even his real name. The monogram on that lighter proved it. Why, oh, why, hadn't she gone and checked his wallet when she'd had the chance?

She stalked to the closet, her movements clumsy and misaligned, like an old-fashioned windup toy. She needed a robe. Didn't even know if she owned a robe. She'd had no need of one in years, not with just her and Gwen rattling around in the house, two women alone. But she couldn't very well go trotting down the hall to the bathroom in her underpants with a man in the house, now, could she? Even if it was pitch-dark and he was probably sound asleep by now, anyway. What if the lights came on all of a sudden? What if he came out of his room?

Groping around in the back of the closet she found an old terry-cloth robe that was probably left over from college. She couldn't find the tie, but slipped it on anyway and wrapped it across her front and held it in place with her arms. It had a faintly dusty smell.

She crossed the moonlit room to the door, slipped through it and tiptoed down the dark hall like a cat burglar. She wondered why she was tiptoeing, when Gwen was still downstairs nursing her baby chickens and Mike was probably...well, of course he'd be asleep by now—why shouldn't he be? There in his room, the boys' old room, right across the stairwell from her old room, which was Gwen's now, since she'd moved into her parents' room in the front, with its view of the lane and barn and the livestock yards.

She knew he was asleep, but she stopped at his door anyway, felt briefly for the panels and lifted her hand to knock, stiffly and mechanically, as if she were a wooden puppet and someone else were pulling the strings. She waited, head down, shivering.

The door opened with a faint sound and a slight draft. "Lucy? What in the world—"

"I hope I didn't wake you."

"No, I was just—"

"I j-just wanted to see if you n-need anything."

"I'm fine." His voice seemed to crack. She felt his hand on her elbow. "Lucy, what's wrong? My God, you're shaking. You need a warm shower. I left—"

"I d-don't w-want a sh-shower. I j-just want—I need—"

"Get in here." His voice was low and guttural. She felt his nearness—the warm puff of his breath on her forehead, the heat from his body. She held out her hand, reaching toward the heat as if it were a furnace on a cold winter's day.

"I need..." The words seemed to choke her. She struggled and finally got out the barest whisper. "...you to hold me. Please."

"Here, come on."

At last. She felt his arms come around her, and herself being lifted up and carried, and then she was sitting cuddled on his lap with her knees drawn up and her face nestled against his bare chest. She put her arms around him and burrowed her face into his hair. It was soft and tickly. His skin smelled good, so good. Like soap. She couldn't get enough of it.

"Shh," he said. "Shh... it's okay."

"Hold me," she pleaded.

"I will, I will. Is it okay if I take this off?" He tugged on her bathrobe. She nodded, and after a moment's hesitation, only because she couldn't bear to let go of him for even that long, took her arms from around his body and let him pull the bathrobe over her shoulders and shuck it down and push it out of the way.

He felt so good, so good. She flattened her hands against his back and slid them over his smooth skin, every nerve quivering and hungry. She pressed her fingers into his muscles and almost laughed out loud with the joy of such a small, exquisite pleasure. Her breasts shivered and grew taut at their first contact with his naked chest; she uttered a soft gasp of pure shock, then pressed closer and felt them flatten and warm, and the warmth pool deep inside her. She felt his hands on her back...*yes—like that.* Oh, how good it felt, just as she remembered. The rasp of calluses on her skin... how rough his hands were. And how gentle.

She couldn't get enough of touching him; she felt as if she wanted to climb inside him somehow. She couldn't believe how hungry she was, simply for touching. Before tonight, how long had it been since she'd been...touched? And yet, the touch of strangers had sickened her. It was *his* touch she was starving for, no one else's.

She lifted her face to his by degrees, searching blindly, fumblingly, as if it were something she'd never done before and had to learn as she went along. When she found his mouth she tasted cool, salty moisture, and whimpered a little.

"Shh," he whispered. "Don't cry."

"I'm not," she growled. "I *never* cry."

His chuckle was gentle, not mocking. His lips took the moisture from hers in tiny sips, obliterating it in his own warmth and essence. She held herself very still, lips parted, trembling inside, aching with the wonder of it.

"Lucy..." His hand, stroking slowly down her back, rasped over the thin covering of nylon on her bottom and suddenly stopped. "I want to make love to you."

She listened to the sound of his swallow, her own wildly thumping heart, and whispered, "I thought that was what we were doing."

"You said you wanted to be held. I just wanted to be sure we were both on the same track."

"I do. We are. But thanks for asking."

Her hand rode upward along the sloping ridge of his shoulder to find the curling tips of his hair, still damp from the shower, and under them the strong, warm column of his neck. With no more urging than that he took what she offered him, sinking into her mouth with a deep-throated groan, searching with his tongue for that joining from which there would be no retreat. No pulling back. No pretending this hadn't happened, or that things between them weren't forever changed.

At the same time his fingers hooked the elastic of her panties and tore them roughly down over her hips and, with her enthusiastic cooperation, all the way down over her thighs, knees and ankles. Then those same fingers, those wonderfully rough-gentle fingers, trailed slowly, slowly up again along the inside of her legs, and she shifted naturally to allow him access, her body molding to his touch, melting in the warmth of his hands. But when he touched her most sensitive place she found that it was too much, bright and sharp, like pain, while the parts of her that weren't being touched felt cold and bereft. She arched and hissed softly, and pulled her mouth away from his kiss.

"Sorry," he muttered, and pulled her close, as if he understood.

"Hold me," she whispered into the hollow of his neck, wishing *she* did. "Make love to me."

"I will." His voice was tender. His fingers stroked her hair back behind her ear. "There's just something I have to do first, okay?"

He kissed her forehead and shifted her onto the bed. She lay alone and shivering, listening to the sounds he made in the darkness, straining to see him. It was so dark in the room she knew he must have pulled the shades. She heard the pad of footsteps, the rustle of clothing, the snap of the fastenings on his briefcase. After what seemed like forever the edge of the bed sagged with his weight.

"What are you doing?" she asked. And then, as the embarrassment of realization came, whispered hoarsely, "Oh. I didn't think of that."

He chuckled. "I'd have been surprised if you had. I doubt that you have anything, either. Do you?"

"No." She propped herself on her elbows. "You mean you had that in your *briefcase?*"

"Yeah." He sounded preoccupied.

"Cage, answer me one question."

"Yeah, what's that?"

"You don't even have a toothbrush to your name, and you carry condoms in your briefcase? Does that make sense to you?"

He was silent for a long time, and in the dark she couldn't tell whether he was evading, or just thinking about it. Then he said, "Sure it makes sense. Cavities won't kill you."

"Oh..." She let her breath out. She felt young and inept, and wondered what he must think of her. "Yeah...."

He shifted around so he was facing her. She could feel his thigh alongside hers, but other than that he didn't touch her. "So, now that you've cooled off a little," he said gently, "do you still want to do this?"

"What makes you think I've cooled off?" she asked, her voice thick and husky. But she had, a little, in a way that in no way diminished her hunger for him. There was something—an element of fear, a daredevil feeling that she was crazy, going to hell in a hand basket and didn't care—that had been there before but was suddenly gone. She wasn't thinking clearly enough right then to put together the why of it. It was only later that she'd draw reasoned conclusions about the sort of man who not only carried condoms around in his briefcase but cared enough about her to remember to use them, even in the heat of unexpected passion. Right then she just knew that inside her where the cold, hollow shivering had been, now there was a quivery *lightness,* like warm champagne.

She found Mike's leg in the darkness, warm, hard muscled, furred with hair, and slid her hand upward, daringly, toward his groin. His breath hissed softly through his teeth, but he didn't stop her. Instead he followed her lead, mimicking her caresses, his hand a sweet abrasion on all the nerve-rich places . . . the back of her knee, the inside of her thigh . . . the hot, tender places. But again she found his touch there too much, too soon, and instead of opening to him she sat up suddenly and went into his arms in a rush that was almost panic.

"Please, Mike. Make love to me now."

For his answer he kissed her deeply and for a long time, until she felt drugged and groggy, then laid her gently back, stroking her hair away from her face with both hands. But when he would have pulled away from her to realign his body with hers, she found herself once again clinging to him almost with desperation. "No, hold me. Close."

"Lucy . . ." His whisper was hoarse, his laugh a little pained. "I can't . . . I'm too heavy." But even as he was speaking she was moving around him, coming quickly to straddle his lap, so that her nipples nested in the hair on his chest and her belly caressed his with every breath she took. His words ended with a small, surprised gasp.

"See?" she murmured, her confidence growing. "How's that?"

His reply was inarticulate. His arms were wrapped around her tightly and his face was buried in her hair and she could feel his body shaking with laughter. She wanted to ask him what was so funny, but before she could she felt herself being lifted and centered, and the unmistakable hardness of his body, and then it was her turn to gasp. She was moist and ready, there wasn't any pain, but the penetration was a shock nonetheless. It had been a long, long time. He entered her with a steady, inexorable pressure that drove the air from her lungs and brought tears springing to her eyes. She hadn't the slightest idea why. Shudders cascaded through her. She clung to him and drew a long, trembling breath against his damp, silky hair.

"Easy," he whispered. "Easy..."

"It's all right—I'm all right," she said in a high, rapid voice. "It's just... I don't know—"

"I know," he said. "I know."

The tenderness in his voice made her ache inside. She didn't understand what was happening to her. She pressed her lips together and shut her eyes as tightly as she could, but the tears squeezed through anyway, and ran into his hair. She held on to him like someone falling over the edge of a cliff.

"Just stay like that for a while," he told her softly. "Don't move."

And he wrapped her close in his arms and stroked her hair and after a while began slowly, slowly rocking her, back and forth, until gradually she relaxed and the rocking became, in a very natural way and without ever breaking the closeness between them, something else. Their hips moved now in opposing rhythms, and she could feel the hard, hot length of him deep inside her. His arms slipped down around her hips, holding her hard and tight against him. The heat and pressure inside her grew and grew, and she wanted to increase the tempo but he wouldn't let her. He made her keep it slow and gentle, and the tension became intolerable. She wanted to scream with it.

And then she did scream, a small, high sound she didn't recognize as her own, while Mike caught her hair in his hand and stifled her cries with his mouth. She hung on to him desperately, but it didn't help; she truly felt as if she were on a roller coaster, plunging off a cliff, falling headlong, out of control, terrified.

He held her, absorbing her shudders and spasms, and then, while she was still covering his face with relieved, whimpering kisses, suddenly groaned and caught her around the hips and pinned her hard against the force of his thrusts. She felt the surging strength and power of his body and was filled with a strange kind of awe, and wholly unexpected tenderness.

He held them both still for a moment longer, drawing deep, quieting breaths, and then they collapsed together onto the bed, arms and legs still tangled, laughing as if they'd just managed somehow to escape disaster unscathed.

"Wow," Mike said presently, a single, deep-throated syllable, like a tiger's purr.

"Shh. Gwen might hear you," Lucy murmured, but her heart wasn't in it. She had a feeling the damage was already pretty much done.

"Regrets?" His voice was very soft; his hand rasped lightly up and down her arm.

Her hand rode the diminishing swell of his chest like a gull on a wave. "No," she whispered, "no regrets." But a strangeness, certainly. Oh, heavens, what must he think of her? Her fingers curled in his chest hair. Her hand felt achy and prickly, as if the circulation in it had been cut off, and it took every ounce of willpower she had to lift it away from his body.

"Where are you going?"

She paused, already half-sitting, her body tensed and curled. "I thought...you'd probably like to get some sleep."

"Hey, come 'ere." He gathered her back in, tugging and tucking blankets around and over them both. "I can sleep fine just like this."

She was stiff and resisting at first. "I'm not too heavy? I don't want your arm to go numb."

"Don't worry about my arm." He pulled her leg across his and tucked it between them, then cradled her head in the hollow of his shoulder, stroking her hair back with his fingers, weaving it behind her ear. "There, now," he crooned, the words slurred and exhausted. "Go to sleep…."

She sighed, then shook with a strange, involuntary little chuckle. Once again those inexplicable tears came from nowhere to puddle beneath her eyelashes as she slipped, drained and achy, into sleep.

Lanagan woke up alone in bed with the first light of morning in his eyes. For one wild moment he wondered if he'd dreamed Lucy there, dreamed making love to her in the craziness of last night. But then a shadow came between him and the light and a voice low and husky with self-consciousness said, "Morning."

He pushed himself up on his elbows. She was standing with her back to the windows, holding an ancient terry-cloth bathrobe closed with her folded arms. He cleared the morning rasp from his own voice and murmured, "What time is it?"

"Early. Sorry, I put the shades up. Didn't mean to wake you. It's just that my body clock's set to the light."

"'S all right." He couldn't remember pulling them down, but he supposed he must have. An automatic city thing.

He didn't realize he was frowning until she gave an uncomfortable little shrug and said sardonically, "Regrets?"

"Regrets?" He scooted a pillow up against the headboard and leaned back on it, laughing softly. He was feeling about as far from regret as he figured it was possible to get, warm and wired at the same time…whiskey and sunshine. "I was thinking more along the lines of miracles."

"Miracles?" Her arms shifted, pulling the robe closer. Her chin had an uncertain look.

"I thought I'd dreamed you." He could actually hear her swallow from clear across the room. He looked at her in silence, wanting her with such intensity he thought surely she must feel it and come to him of her own accord, like a bolt to a magnet. Then he remembered how it had been, how *she'd* been, her terrible vulnerability. He said gently, "Are you always like that during thunderstorms?"

"Like what?" Her voice sounded breathless and defensive. Even in the pale lavender light he could see a dark blush spring into her cheeks and spread downward like a stain.

He smiled. "Scared."

"Oh." She shrugged and moved tentatively closer to him. "Well, I've never liked thunderstorms much." There was a pause. "My parents were killed in one."

"I know," said Lanagan. "Gwen told me."

She took a deep breath and sat on the edge of the bed, but with barely enough weight to put a dent in it, like a bird poised for flight. "It was six years ago—just. The year my brother Earl graduated from high school. This is his room." She paused briefly to look around as if she'd never seen it before. "It was awards night at the high school. Earl was a terrific athlete, and a good student besides, so he was up for all sorts of awards and scholarships. The whole family was supposed to go, but..."

Lanagan brushed her forearm with the backs of his fingers. "But you didn't?"

She shook her head. "I'd just gotten home that day, just finished a rough week, with finals and everything." She looked down at him and smiled crookedly. "Plus, I was never very big on going back to my old high school, seeing all those people...well, you know. And then, we'd missed my birthday, and we were going to celebrate it when they got back."

"Your birthday!" He sat up abruptly. "When is it?"

Her voice was dry. "Yesterday." She glanced at him, then quickly away, dismissing it. "Anyway, the storm broke while they were gone. When they didn't come home I thought it was just because they'd decided to wait for it to pass. But I waited and waited, and finally one of the neighbors came and brought Earl home." Her voice seemed far away, almost dreamy. "He'd been in the back seat. He wasn't hurt at all, not a scratch. Just a few bruises."

Lanagan tightened his hand on her arm, but she didn't seem to notice, pulling away from him anyway as she drew up her knees and wrapped her arms around them, curling her bare toes into the sheets on the edge of the bed. "It was kind of ironic. I was going to tell them that I was thinking about getting engaged. That night when they got back. I never got the chance." She took another deep breath, the way someone does when they have an ache they can't reach. He waited without saying anything, and after a while she went on in that faraway voice. "Paul came out for the funeral. He wanted me to go back with him then, but Earl couldn't have handled the place by himself, even with Gwen here. It was summertime. There was so much to do. I told him I'd see him in the fall—I had one more year to go for my masters—and we'd make our plans then. But by the fall Earl had decided to give up his scholarships and join the marines instead of going to college or staying on here. Rhett didn't have any interest in the place, so that left me with three choices. I could lease it, sell it, or..."

"Stay," Lanagan finished for her.

She nodded without looking at him, and he watched her throat jerk with her swallow. "Paul called with an ultimatum. I told you about that. So..." She let her legs down and her breath out at the same time. "I didn't know it at the time, but that was the last time I would ever see him—at the funeral." She coughed and looked down, blushing again. "It was also the last time I, uh... well."

The last time you had sex? How about the last time anyone touched you with love? thought Lanagan. Anyone at all. It seemed incredible to him, but at the same time entirely probable. Who had there been, in all that time, to give her a warm embrace, a neck rub, a friendly hug? Her brothers didn't sound like very likely sources of comfort, and even Gwen, for all her innate warmth, was of a generation not much known for physical demonstrations of affection.

"Lucy," he said hoarsely, reaching for her hand. But she stood abruptly, and instead he caught the bottom edge of her robe.

"So," she said in a bright, false voice, "now you know. All about me." She looked down at him. Her lips trembled slightly, then tightened, and he could see the rest of it in her dark, troubled eyes. *And I don't know one damn thing about you.*

His throat tightened with sympathy for her. How hard this must be for her... how fragile she must be feeling. He wanted to tell her the truth, tell her *something,* at least, but he didn't dare. If he told her anything at all he'd have to tell her everything, and how could he do that, how could he involve her in something that might put her in danger, even get her killed? Even *he* didn't know what he was dealing with! He couldn't even tell her how he was beginning to feel about her. He didn't have the right. So all he said, in a voice guttural with pain, was, "Do you have to go?"

She looked away from him and made a tiny, wordless sound. He tugged gently on her robe, and she finally sighed and whispered, "I should. It's morning."

"I don't think Gwen's downstairs yet. If she's in her room and you go now, she'll hear you for sure." He pulled harder on her robe, and suddenly, as if in surrender, she lifted her head and let her arms drop to her sides, and the robe came off over her shoulders and fell to the floor. He caught his breath, stunned at the vision of her small-boned, beautifully proportioned body, backlit and gilded by the first soft rays of the morning sun.

"What?" she demanded in that breathlessly suspicious way she had.

He laughed out loud in sheer delight as he caught her hand and tumbled her down on top of him. There wasn't much he could tell her, but one thing he certainly could, and maybe atone a little for his past stupidity. "You're so beautiful," he said, husky with emotion. "So incredibly beautiful."

She paused in her halfhearted struggles to stare at him, eyes fierce and slightly crossed. "You're incredibly crazy."

"Uh-uh. I was, but I've come to my senses. Come in here. I'll show you."

"How crazy you are?"

"No, how sensual." He pulled the blankets away from between them and settled her again, sighing at the exquisite pleasure of her body, draped full length on his.

Her eyes widened. "Are you always like this in the morning?" she asked, mimicking him.

"Like what?" She wriggled excruciatingly, making it hard for him to breathe, much less talk. "Oh," he gasped. "That. Yeah, as a matter of fact, I am. Most of the time. It's a common male phenomenon, I believe."

"I wouldn't know about that," said Lucy, looking thoughtful. And after a moment, "It seems a shame to waste it."

"That's what I thought," said Lanagan.

People magazine, June 3

New Mob Mystery In Chicago:
Where is Mike Lanagan?

The crusading columnist was known as a champion of the underdog, until he tried to take on the mob. Now his disappearance has all of Chicago in an uproar and authorities wondering if they might have another Jimmy Hoffa on their hands.

Chapter 11

"It'll have to come down," Lucy said as she gazed up into the canopy of oak leaves, dappled now with sunlight and shimmering a little in the warm morning breeze.

Lanagan was silent, listening to the trilling of a bird rejoicing in the storm's passage. The swing dangled between them, and each of them was holding on to one side of the rope, each looking everywhere but at the other. After a moment he said, "Looks like the biggest half's still standing. Can't you save it?"

She shook her head, with regret but firmly. "Beetles and borers will get into it, hollow it out, weaken it. Sooner or later another storm'll take it, and who knows where it'll land next time? Might land on the house, one of the cars. Next time it might kill somebody."

"Seems a shame," Lanagan murmured in sympathy. "This tree must be a hundred years old, at least."

He glanced at her finally, then let his gaze linger in newfound fascination on the top of her head, with its endearingly ragged and off-center part, and red-gold highlights coming and going with the shifting patterns of sunlight. God, he could still smell her hair, still feel the silky tickle of it on his face as she lowered her mouth over his, feel her body lightly astride him, hot and tight around him. He felt the heat and pressure of wanting her all over again, even though it couldn't have been more than an hour since they'd lain tumbled together in sun-warmed sheets.

Feeling his gaze, she looked at him, the bleached tips of her eyelashes catching the sun like flecks of golden chaff. He heard the softest intake of her breath and saw the rosy wash of awareness flood her skin, and knew she was thinking of the same things he was. But he saw no smile for him on her lips, no secret joy in her eyes. Just the poignant uncertainty and insecurity of a woman who knows she's given away the secrets of her body to a man, while the secrets of his heart remain locked away from her, far out of reach.

She shrugged and said distantly, "Nothing lasts forever. Things change, things die. That's life." She let go of the swing and moved away from him, leaving him with an inexplicable sadness and an aching sense of regret.

Nothing lasts... things change. It was something she'd grown up with, he supposed, that awareness of the fragility, the temporariness of life, living year in and year out so close to the earth, witnessing over and over again the cycles of birth and death, the ebb and flow of seasons. But for him the awareness of his own mortality had come only recently, only a month or so ago. And along with it the growing realization that between the beginning and the end of his life there was a vast emptiness he had yet to fill. He knew he wanted to fill it with something of value and significance, something that would justify and validate his having lived at all, but what that something was he had no idea. Except that, during the past twenty-four hours, and especially this morning, the feeling had begun to grow in him that it had something, possibly everything, to do with Lucy.

He thought again of that moment of epiphany in the barn, when he'd watched Lucy with the newborn kittens. He wondered now how he could have seen some things so clearly that morning, and completely missed the most important things of all. Sure, he'd known then that she was truly beautiful, but hadn't had a clue that he was falling in love with her. In his visions he'd seen her as a mother, but what he hadn't understood was that he was seeing in her the mother of his own children.

"God, I hate storms." She stood in the steamy sunshine, hugging herself as she surveyed the devastation, reminding him of the way she'd come to him, shivering in the night.

Lanagan went to stand behind her, wishing things were right enough between them that he could wrap his arms around her and tell her she didn't have to face it all alone. "It's not so bad," he said. "Except for the tree."

She laughed bitterly. "And the cottage, and the chicken house, and the fences and the sheds. And who knows what else."

But the damage was less than Lanagan would have expected. The yard was a wreck, of course, the lawn strewn with small branches and twigs, leaf clusters and broken blossoms. Some of the stockyard fences were down, but they'd moved the cattle into the pasture last night, and he could see them there now, placidly grazing. The roof was off the hay shed, and a few of the farrowing houses had blown over. The sows had been contained in the hog yard, but the little pigs were making the most of their first taste of freedom and were rooting happily in the cornfields' soft, rich earth. He could see a hen that had somehow managed to escape last night's roundup scratching away in the grass along the lane. It really was amazing, he thought, how resilient the animals were. More so, apparently, than people.

"Lots of work to be done," he said softly. He was thinking that it made an excuse for him to stick around awhile longer. Lucy turned her head to look at him, holding his eyes for a long, uncomfortable time, as if he'd spoken the thought out loud. He swallowed a knot of unexpected guilt and quickly asked, "What about the crops?"

She looked away again. "I haven't checked. At least there wasn't any hail. This time."

"The animals seem fine," Lanagan ventured. "No lasting traumas." Her only response was a short, unhappy little laugh. Unable to go on not touching her any longer, he put his hands on her shoulders and began to massage them gently. "I'm not at all sure about you, though." She gave him a quick, wary glance, but he persisted in his soft, careful way, using his interviewer's skills without remorse. "Why do you hate storms so much? Is it just because of your parents—the way they died?"

She laughed suddenly and lifted her hands to comb back her hair with her fingers, subtly evading his touch. Then she turned on him, her smile tense and strained. "Why do you do that?"

"Do what?"

"Ask questions most people would consider were none of their business? And the darn thing is, you do it so quietly it seems like I'm answering before I even stop to think that it probably *isn't* any of your business."

"Sorry," Lanagan said with a shrug and a smile, more of acknowledgment than of apology. "I'm a—" I'm a reporter, he'd almost said. It comes naturally to me. Hastily he substituted, "A curious person. People interest me, I guess. You interest me. I want to know what makes you tick."

"I wish..." She caught her breath and looked away, and he heard the rest like a distant echo. *I wish I knew what makes you tick, too.* After a moment she let her breath out and said in a remote, thoughtful voice, "I think I've always hated storms. I don't know." She shook her head, giving up her hair to the breeze. "It's just—I hate feeling so..."

"Helpless?" offered Lanagan softly. "Not in control?"

She looked at him, her expression quizzical and wondering. "Yeah, sort of. How did you know?"

Because, he thought in bleak understanding, that's the way you are, Lucy Brown. Even when you make love you need to feel you're in control. That's why you like to be on top, astride me, why you won't let me touch you with my mouth, my fingers, in all the ways I know of that might make you lose it completely. That's what you're so afraid of, isn't it? Losing control. Or perhaps more accurately, afraid to trust anyone—afraid to trust *me*—enough to relinquish it.

And why should she trust him? What could he say to her that might make her think she could? Just now, the way she looked at him, head slightly tilted, little half smile on her lips, the ghost of a frown deepening the fine lines at the corners of her eyes, he could see the questions gathering in her eyes like storm clouds. God, he almost wished she'd ask a few. That way at least he could express a modicum of sympathy. Of regret. *I'm sorry, I wish I could tell you, but I can't.* That in itself would be an explanation, of sorts.

But she didn't ask. And he felt more and more dishonest and fraudulent.

He wondered if she would come to him again that night. He lay awake in the quiet house, listening for her step in the hall, instinctively knowing she'd be awake, too, and wondering the same thing.

It would have been so much simpler if he could have gone to her instead, but he knew that was one thing he could not do. He had no right to ask for or presume anything more than she was willing to give him. He shouldn't even be touching her; he was acutely aware that he hurt her every time he did, even though she might have wanted it as much as he did. He'd never been in a situation like this before, never known an affair to be so complicated!

He found himself thinking about Lucy in ways he'd never thought about a woman before, thinking about her needs and wanting more than he'd ever wanted anything in his life to be able to fulfill them. She needed control? He could give her precious little else, but at least he could give her that. So he lay in his bed in the darkness with his door slightly ajar and his senses straining and every nerve in his body singing like high-tension wires, and waited.

She came so quietly he felt the slight stirring of air from the movement of his bedroom door before he heard anything at all. Then the door closed with the smallest of sounds, and she whispered, "Mike? Are you asleep?"

"No," he said. "I was wondering if you'd come."

"I wasn't sure I should." Her voice was jerky with nervousness. He wondered if she was shivering again.

"Why not?"

"Well, after last night...and this morning..."

He laughed softly, feeling warm and wired again, with relief, anticipation and a terrible tenderness all mixed up together. "If you doubt my stamina," he murmured, "come over here and let me put your doubts to rest."

He'd left the shades up this time, and although the moon hadn't risen there was enough reflected starlight for him to see her as she left the shadows near the door and came toward him, a pale wraith in a white T-shirt, slender legs bare. He threw back the covers and made room for her, then held his breath while she paused beside the bed and drew the T-shirt off over her head. He could see that she was wearing white panties. He thought about telling her she might as well take them off, too, while she was at it, but didn't. He thought he understood why she hadn't, and anyway, it was her call.

She slipped in beside him, trembling only slightly this time, probably no more than he was. "I feel like a sneak thief," she muttered with a low, guilty giggle. "Or a teenager."

"Who do you think you're kidding?" Lanagan gathered her close and buried his face in her hair, muffling laughter. "Don't you think Gwen knows about this already?"

"I think she knew about it before we did," Lucy said, suddenly somber. Her body went still for a moment, as if she was listening to the echo of her own words.

But of course, being Lucy, she would never be still for very long. She took the initiative as she had the night before, moving quickly to lie full length on top of him, giving a small, contented sigh as if she'd found the place where she rightfully belonged.

Which was fine with him. Her body was light and limber, and in that position he could caress her back, the whole supple length of it, and feel her muscles grow taut and her slender waist writhe beneath his hands. He could slip his hands inside her panties and mold and knead her buttocks, stroke the backs of her thighs, coax her legs apart and explore the warm, tender places between.

But before he could do any of those things she slipped from his grasp again, wriggling her body so that he shifted his legs to make a place for her between them, then sliding lightly downward. He felt it as an excruciating, all-over caress, and groaned aloud as her tight-budded nipples teased the sensitive skin on his belly, then the ticklish places at the top of his thighs. And then her mouth...

He whispered her name hoarsely and plunged his hands into her hair, clutched at her shoulders and tried desperately to remember to be gentle.

For a long while after that he didn't say anything at all, because it took every ounce of his concentration and willpower just to keep from losing control himself. Just when he thought he would lose it anyway she wriggled out of her panties and moved up over him again, trailing kisses across his heaving belly and chest, her legs taut and silky along his sides. It would have taken very little guidance on his part to fit her to him then, to the part of him she'd already made wet and slippery with her mouth, but as much as he wanted to do just that, he knew he couldn't. Not yet. Not yet.

With his stomach muscles rigid as wood, jaws clenched, silently cursing the necessity for it, he reached out with one arm and opened the drawer in the table beside the bed. When she realized what he was doing she gave a small cry, an inarticulate protest that was part whimper, part groan. He raised his head and shoulders from the pillows and kissed her fiercely and hard. "I have to," he rasped. "You know—"

"I know...I do. I wish—"

"So do I," he said fervently. "Believe me."

She didn't make it easy for him, either, kissing, stroking, fondling, distracting him so that he felt drunk and inept as a teenaged virgin fumbling around in the back seat of his father's car. By the time he was ready for her he was close to exploding, hot and rigid almost to the point of pain, wanting nothing but to plunge himself deep inside her and feel her sweet softness enfold him, to surge into her again and again, fast and hard, until the spasms of climax took his breath and reason away and left him utterly and completely drained.

Oh, he was ready for her, more than ready. But as eager as she was to have him inside her, impatient, even, he was almost certain she wasn't ready for him, not physically. With the natural glazing she'd given him covered now by an unforgiving sheath, penetration wouldn't be easy for her. And he had an idea that after this morning's lovemaking she might be a little tender and sore. It had been a long time for her; she wasn't used to it. He wanted her hot and wet and wild, so wild she wouldn't feel any discomfort at all, only pleasure. Pure, primitive, uncomplicated.

But of course, with Lucy nothing could ever be uncomplicated. He kissed her first, deeply, intimately, in all the most sensual, arousing ways he knew. And that was fine; she took all he gave her, greedily, as if she could never get enough of kissing him, until her eyelids seemed too heavy to lift and her mouth was hot and swollen and tasted almost like wine. He laid her gently over, then, in the cradle of his arm, and lowered his mouth to her breasts. He swirled his tongue around her small, tight nipples, rolled them roughly between his lips, sucked them hard and deep. And that was all right, too; she moaned softly, and her breath grew short and panting. She arched her back and pushed deeper still into the sultry heat of his mouth.

But when he lowered his head still farther and pressed his lips to her belly he found her muscles were tight and fluttery with tension. And when he stroked the insides of her thighs and pressed his fingers, oh, so gently against her soft, swollen folds, she suddenly quivered like a plucked guitar string and squirmed simultaneously away from his touch into his embrace, gasping, "Please, please—*now.*"

He gave up then, giving in to her pleas and his own desires, and drove himself into her the way he'd wanted to, gripping her hard around the hips and holding her fast against the force of his first powerful thrust. He had to steel himself against the inevitable breaking of vulnerable, unprepared tissues, her small, shocked gasp, which she instantly stifled. Firmly housed within her, he pulled her legs up and held them as wide as he dared, and pressed into her quickly, deeply and hard, again and again, forcing her breath from her body in short, quick puffs.

At first she clutched desperately at his shoulders, almost panic-stricken, seemingly caught off guard by his roughness. But then, gaining confidence, she raised herself and arched above him with her head thrown back, throat taut and breasts thrusting upward. She rode him with wild abandon, the way he imagined she'd ride a wild stallion, reckless and exhilarated, challenging him for dominance and control. It was a wild, exhilarating ride for him, too, unlike anything he'd ever experienced before. And his climax, when it came, was both sudden and devastating, as violent as riding full tilt into a wall. The spasms gripped him and would not let go. Dimly he felt Lucy's body rippling and pulsing around him, encouraging the convulsions that finally emptied him and left him limp as an old rag doll.

"Lucy, did you...?" he croaked helplessly. But now he could feel her trembling, feel the residual clenchings deep inside her, and knew he wouldn't have to ask, after all. She leaned down and kissed him languidly, sighing a little, then collapsed with relieved laughter onto his chest.

He cuddled her close, as he had before, and even laughed some himself when he'd regained enough of his strength. Then she dozed while he lay with her head tucked under his chin and watched leaf shadows dance on the moonlit ceiling. He didn't want to feel disappointed. But he did.

He was fully aware of the irony of it. After some of the most mind-blowing sex he'd ever experienced, he should have been feeling smug and comfortable as a cream-fed cat. Instead he felt hollow and achy inside, vaguely frustrated and inexpressibly sad. He felt that way because he knew, in spite of the intensity of their lovemaking, that things weren't right between Lucy and him, and because for the life of him he couldn't figure out how to make them right.

She was holding back. He knew it, and it hurt him immensely even though he knew and understood why she did. He knew she was protecting herself from him because she fully expected that eventually he would hurt her. That knowledge made him writhe inwardly with pure anguish, but he couldn't blame her for thinking it. She knew nothing at all about him—nothing. Not even where he came from or where he was going or how long he planned to stay. He hadn't dared tell her any of those things, of course, for fear of involving her in the danger he was in. But perhaps more important, he hadn't told her how he felt about her. He hadn't said a word about love—first, because he knew he didn't have any business falling in love with anybody right now, and second, because it just wouldn't be fair to her, under the circumstances. So how was she to know? She had no way in the world of knowing what kind of man he was, whether he was free to love, or even capable of it. Why should she open up to him? Why should she give herself to him without restraint? Why should she trust him, when in all probability he *would* only wind up hurting her?

And still he wanted those things from her, all of them. More than he'd ever wanted anything in his life before.

"Mike?" It was a sleepy mumble. She stirred, nuzzling the hair on his chest like a kitten. "Are you awake?"

"Mm, sort of."

"I should go."

"Stay," he said huskily. He wrapped his arms around her, pressed his lips to her hair and shuddered with the intensity of the emotions he couldn't voice.

He felt her head tilt back and knew she was looking up at him, wondering, trying to fathom the ripples in his body, the rasp in his voice.

"Stay," he whispered again with a sigh, and, closing his eyes, began to stroke and caress her, trying the best way he could to tell her without words that he could be trusted. With the gentleness of his touch he tried to tell her of his basic goodness and decency, and that he'd never willingly hurt her. He cherished her with kisses, with so much tenderness he ached with it, hoping that somehow she'd hear what he was trying to say to her, and understand.

Lucy was gone when he woke up. From the racket the pigs were making, he knew she was already up and out about the morning chores.

He dressed in guilty haste and wolfed his breakfast under Gwen's wise and watchful eye, then snatched up his hat and went to find her. He felt a sudden, urgent, almost adolescent need to see her, to remind himself in some tangible way of the night just past. It was a need so acute he wondered if he'd ever be free of it. Then he realized it was only a measure of all the things that were wrong between them, and that he probably wouldn't ever be free of that insecurity until he'd managed somehow to make them right.

Lucy was in the equipment shed, starting up the tractor. From a distance he watched her mount the big red International tractor and remembered that on his very first day here he'd had a vision of that small, feisty woman handling one of those powerful machines and thought it pleasantly erotic. He wondered why he hadn't known right then what would have to happen between them. He wondered again how he could have missed the signs so completely.

She backed the tractor out of the shed, then saw him and stopped and waited for him. "I'm going to go check on the soybeans," she said, her voice gruff and remote above the engine noise.

He got a grip on one of the cab struts and pulled himself up onto the step beside her. "I'll go with you."

She gave him a brief nod as she put the tractor in gear, and they rumbled off down the hill together, past the hog yards and onto the dirt road that followed the curve of the fields toward the creek.

He watched her as she drove, head held high, hair floating in the wind, and thought about the way she'd ridden him in the night, with wild abandon and even, he was sure, with a kind of primitive joy. But here in the bright morning sunlight he could see that what she was feeling deep inside wasn't anything at all like joy.

He hated the stretched, polished look of the skin across the bridge of her nose and under her eyes, as if she'd been crying in secret, although he didn't see how that was possible when she'd spent the entire night curled up beside him. The sharp, angular bones of her face seemed fragile and thin as eggshells. It occurred to him that it had been a long time since he'd seen her dimple.

He remembered the way she'd been that first day, when he'd followed her around the hog yards and the old white sow had chased them both over the fence, remembered her sassy arrogance, her downright *orneriness,* and how much he'd liked her that way. He tried to tell himself she was probably still depressed and upset about the storm damage, but he knew very well that *he* was the main reason for the change in her. When he thought about the way he'd tried to change her on purpose, he felt almost sick with shame.

I wish I knew what he's thinking, Lucy thought miserably. I wish I knew *him,* what he thinks of me. She could sense the sadness in him, the disappointment. And even in the hot June sunshine she felt chilled and wretched as a storm-tossed waif.

She was pretty sure the disappointment had been there last night, too, but she hadn't thought about it much then. It was easy not to think when she was lying in Mike's arms, and the whole world was his bed, curtained around with darkness. The way he made her feel then—she'd never felt like that before, couldn't even begin to put a name to it. How could she? How was it possible to feel both protected and scared at the same time? Oh, but the way he *touched* her. No one had ever touched her the way he touched her, kissed her the way he kissed her. Her insides fluttered and churned at the memory of it.

Oh, God, she thought, it was terrible to feel so helpless, so vulnerable! What was she going to do? She couldn't let him know how she felt about him. She *couldn't.* At night, lying in his arms, she felt as if it really would be all right, as if she could stay with him like this, safe and well loved, forever and ever. But that was a fantasy. A dream.

This—*this* was the real world. *Her* world. And he was an alien in it. Just look at him, she thought in unbearable anguish. He's a stranger! Even riding beside her on the tractor, even wearing her father's old overalls, it was obvious that he didn't belong here, and that he never would. She'd thought maybe it was just the hat. His big-city, tough-guy hat, a gangster's hat. But she knew it was more than that.

It was something in his eyes, something hard and haunted, as if they gazed at least part of the time into another world entirely, a troubled world, one she would never understand or care to be a part of. And she knew beyond any shadow of a doubt that he would return to that world someday.

When he did—oh, what would she do then? She gasped out loud, feeling the pain of loss already, like a knife thrust to her belly, and turned her head quickly lest he see the rush of tears to her eyes. She had to hold them back. She *had* to. The only defense she had against him was to keep her emotions private, locked away inside herself.

But of course, against her emotions she had no defense at all.

She jerked the tractor to a halt, wiping away the residue of moisture from her eyes with her forearm, as if it was only perspiration. "There," she rasped, and cleared her throat. "Washout. I was afraid of that. The whole bottom section is probably buried."

Mike jumped down from the idling tractor and walked over to where the storm's torrential rains had washed through the contoured rows on the hillside and carried the precious topsoil down to deposit it on top of the newly sprouted soybeans in the valley below. He paused and looked back at her, squinting in the morning sun. "Can't you replant it?"

"Sure," she said wryly. "When it dries out a little more." *You,* he'd said. Can't *you* replant it, not *we.* She had to accept that, when it came to Mike and her, there could never be a *we.*

Oh, but suddenly he was smiling at her, with heart-stopping sweetness, pulling off his hat to wipe sweat from his forehead. The familiar comma of hair hung damply across one eyebrow. He badly needed a haircut, she noticed. His eyes were brilliant with secret knowledge and shared intimacies.

Oh, God, she thought wildly as her heart quickened and her body's tender places throbbed in instant response, why do I have to make things so complicated? Why can't I just take him as he is, enjoy the heck out of his body and let it go at that?

A red-tailed hawk glided by, flying low over the furrowed hills, then soared high, calling twice as he climbed, his cries pure and silvery in the clear, warm air. Lucy shaded her eyes and watched him until she couldn't see him anymore, then said, "That washout needs to be fixed before it decides to rain again. I'll go back and get the shovels."

She backed the tractor around and drove away. Lanagan watched her go with an unrelieved fullness in his loins and a deep sense of regret in his heart. It amazed him how much he'd have liked to make love to Lucy just then, right out here in broad daylight under that ceramic blue sky, with nothing but warm soft earth under them and the sun burning hot on their naked bodies. He thought he'd have given just about anything to have the freedom to do that, plus a whole bunch of other things he was just beginning to think about doing. He could imagine making love with Lucy in ways and in places that had never occurred to him before. In the barn, definitely—on the sweet-smelling straw in the stall she'd first found him in. On that damned tractor. He'd have liked to try the swing, before they'd had to cut it down. The possibilities were endless and almost painfully arousing. Most of all he could imagine himself breaking through that reserve of hers, imagine her wild and uninhibited and passionate, as he knew she would be when she finally gave herself to him completely. *When...*

God, he thought, why did it have to be so complicated? Why couldn't he just enjoy the sex and let it go at that? He'd always been able to before. But he knew that Lucy wasn't the kind of woman who could ever be happy in a purely physical relationship. And maybe this time, for the first time in his life, neither was he.

He sat down right there in the soybean field, stunned to discover that it was true. For the first time in his life he wanted to share everything about himself—his past history, present thoughts and future dreams. And what a wicked little irony it was that the first time he really wanted to open up to a woman was the one time he couldn't. He also thought it ironic—the kind of delicious little conundrum he'd have relished as a writer—that Lucy should be the one to give of herself so freely in every way but the physical, while he did just the opposite, trying to give her with the intimacy of his touch what he couldn't give in words. With the result being, inevitably, that he was miserable and so was she.

Of course, Lucy wasn't the first woman Lanagan had made unhappy. He thought it had probably been the rule rather than the exception in his relationships up to now. But while it had grieved him each and every time a love affair had gone sour, now he knew it had been a selfish kind of grief, and the pain he'd felt solely on his own behalf. Seeing Lucy's unhappiness pained him in a whole new way. He found that he ached *for* her, not because of her. More than anything in the world he wanted her to be happy again, and he knew that he would do anything, give anything in the world to make her so.

The Chicagoan, June 8

Front Page
by Ralph Buncomb, staff writer

CHICAGO—Repercussions from the Westside Development scandal reached city hall yesterday, as Planning Commissioner J. T. Lowell responded to allegations that members of his department may have been guilty of accepting bribes in approving WDC's multibillion-dollar high-rise project. During a stormy session of the city council, Commissioner Lowell stated that if any member of his department was found guilty of wrongdoing, "immediate and appropriate action" would be taken.

Meanwhile, the FBI has widened its search for critical evidence believed to have been in possession of *Chicagoan* columnist Mike Lanagan at the time of his disappearance last May first.

"If the stuff didn't go up along with his house, he took it with him," said Detective Chuck Wilson, who has been heading the Chicago Police Department's investigation into the firebombing of Lanagan's southside residence. "Wherever he is right now, that's where those papers are. I just hope we get to him before the bad guys do. God help him."

Chapter 12

Lanagan threw himself wholeheartedly into the cleanup and repair work around the farm, trying in some obscure way by making the place right again to make things right for Lucy, as well. As he worked bare backed in the hot June sun he knew he'd never worked harder or felt stronger or been in better shape physically in his life. But all the while in his heart he felt meager and inadequate and, alongside Lucy, completely outclassed.

He'd finally been forced to face the truth. He, Mike Lanagan, so-called crusading columnist and defender of the underdog, who'd taken on heads of state, CEOs and celebrities of all kinds and both sexes with equal fervor and never a twinge of fear or regret, was nothing but a coward and a fraud.

Yes, he was a coward. He knew it, and it shocked him to the very depths of his soul. All those years, all those times he'd so heroically challenged the bullies and gotten punched in the nose for his pains—he knew now he hadn't been brave at all. He hadn't been brave because he'd never been scared.

That was the truth of it. He'd never really believed he'd get hurt. No matter how many times it happened, it had always come as a surprise to him when that fist connected with his nose. Then out of the blue a firebomb had destroyed his house and everything he owned, and it had hit him that someone had intended to destroy him, as well. For the first time in his life he'd understood that he could be hurt. That he could die! It had scared him badly. And what had he done? Run like a frightened rabbit to the nearest hole and pulled it in after him.

Then one night in the midst of a storm he'd watched one small woman stand her ground against the one thing she was most afraid of, and he'd finally understood what courage was. And how far short of it he'd fallen.

And unlike Lucy's, *his* enemies were only human, like himself—no more and no less. They could be beaten. What's more, he, and possibly *only* he, had the means to beat them. He'd had it all along. It was right up there in his bedroom now, locked in his briefcase. All he had to do was find the courage to use it.

He took off his hat, swept his forearm across his sweaty brow and looked up at the sun like a penitent begging for mercy. But there was no absolution for him there. He knew what he had to do to make things right with himself and for Lucy, and for the possibility of anything that might have started between them that stormy night, or long before. He bowed his head and stood for a long time gazing down at his hat, turning its crumpled, misshapen brim around and around in his hands. Finally he set his lips tightly together, put the hat on and settled it to a firm and businesslike angle.

"Lanagan," he said to himself as he began to gather up his tools, "it's time to go home."

Lucy had taken the side racks off the flatbed truck and had gone into town to get a load of plywood for the new chicken house. She'd asked Mike if he wanted to come along, but he'd declined, saying he thought it would be better if he stayed and finished clearing away the tree mess. So Gwen had decided to come along instead, and do a little grocery shopping while she had the chance. Might as well, she'd said. It would save her a trip.

"I know why he doesn't want to come," Lucy said flatly as they jounced down the gravel lane. "He's afraid somebody in town might recognize him." She glanced over at Gwen, but Gwen didn't seem to have much to say. She persisted anyway, feeling unaccountably cross. "He hasn't been away from here the whole time he's been here, has he? Did you notice that? Except for that one time he went with you to get his car parts."

"Just the once," Gwen confirmed with a slight nod. The arches above her eyebrows and the brackets around her mouth were carved into their usual perpetual smile, but her eyes looked filmy and sad. For the first time in her life it struck Lucy that her aunt was *old*. She felt a dreadful squeezing around her heart, and a bleakness she thought must be loneliness. She'd had it a lot lately. *Things change... things die.*

She tore her eyes away from her aunt's beloved face and looked in the rearview mirror instead. Mike was just crossing the driveway, carrying the chainsaw, not wearing a shirt. She saw that he had on Earl's old jeans this morning, which weren't quite as tight on him now as they'd been at first. They rode low now, on lean hips. He looked bronzed and fit, firmed up every bit as nicely as she'd thought he would. Hunger for him hit her like a wind gust, rocking her to the soles of her feet, overwhelming her senses with taunting reprises of the way his skin felt, so silky smooth, except for his hands, of course... the way he smelled, cool and shower sweet, or warm and musky with sleep and sex.... Her heart gave a flip-flop she felt in the floor of her belly.

"Well," she said, breathless and grumpy, "he can't go on like this forever."

"No," Gwen agreed softly, "he certainly can't."

Lucy swallowed and said nothing more. *Nothing lasts forever.* Something had to happen, was going to happen, and probably soon. She didn't know what that something would be, but she could feel a tension in the air, as if a storm was on its way. And as she did before a storm, she felt a sense of dread, a certain heaviness around her heart. She felt afraid.

The first thing she did when she pulled in to the lane with the load of plywood was look for Mike, but she didn't see him anywhere.

"Huh," she said with a sinking premonition in her chest, "I wonder where he is."

"Looks like he's finished with the tree," said Gwen.

Where the swing oak had stood there was only the stump, raw and pale as a fresh amputation, and piles and trails of sawdust blowing in the wind, sifting into the grass. The two main logs lay on either side of the driveway waiting for the truck to come and haul them to the sawmill to be cut into boards. The burnable wood had been stacked in the woodshed and the small, brushy debris had been carried around back to be burned. The wrecked cottage had been dismantled down to the floorboards. The surviving canes of the rambling rosebush stood alone and free, dipping and waving in the breeze.

When Lucy saw them she was suddenly overcome by a wave of memory and nostalgia that stung her nose and eyelids like pollen. Suddenly she was wrapped in the sweet scent of the roses and the soft embrace of twilight, with the cool kiss of rose petals on her temple, and Mike's fingers combing through the hair behind her ear.

There, now it's perfect.

The farm seemed very quiet. She thought she heard a faint rumble of thunder in the distance, but when she looked the sky was clear and blue, all the way to the horizon.

She helped Gwen carry in the groceries, then went upstairs to change into her chore clothes. Mike's bedroom door was standing open. As she went by, Lucy noticed his beat-up old hat lying on the made-up bed, looking as out of place as a bum sleeping on a manicured lawn.

She stuck her head through the doorway and called softly, "Mike? Are you in here?"

There wasn't any answer, but by then she'd noticed that his briefcase wasn't where it usually was, on the cedar chest by the window. She went on in, hardly even aware that her heart had begun to pound. She opened the closet. His city clothes were gone, too.

She went back downstairs and into the kitchen. "I think Mike's flown the coop," she told Gwen in a hard, hollow voice.

"Really!" Gwen turned from the cupboard with a can of soup in each hand. "Did you look to see if his car's still here?"

"No, but I will," said Lucy grimly. But she knew there wasn't any point in it. She knew what she'd find before she opened the barn door.

Mike's car was gone. The kittens were mewing in a box in one of the empty stalls. Even the tarp had been neatly folded up and left near the door. In the empty space where it had been, the little calico cat sat alone, looking bereft and forsaken. When she saw Lucy she uttered a small, brokenhearted "Meow?" and looked intently beyond her, as if she hoped to see someone else follow her through the door.

"Oh, kitty," said Lucy brokenly as she picked up the cat and buried her face in its mottled fur. But there was no comfort for her there; the cat's body was taut as a coiled spring. She kept staring into far corners with eyes big as saucers, ears cocked for the sound Lucy knew wasn't going to come. "He's gone," she whispered, wishing to God she could cry. "He left us both—the bastard."

She'd known he would, of course. She'd wondered what she'd do when he did, and now she knew. It was worse than dying. She was going to have to go on living, knowing what she was missing, how much she'd lost. *Damn you, Cage!* Rage burst through her like a supernova. Whatever else he might or might not be, the man was a thief. He'd come into her life like a burglar in the night and stolen her happiness away. She'd been *happy* before he came. She *had* been. Now she wondered if she would ever be so again.

She put the cat down and left her sitting there, still watching and waiting.

In a fine protective rage she stormed back into the house, banging the screen door. The rage carried her up the stairs and into Mike's room. There she snatched his hat up from the bed and sat down in its place, breathing hard.

A small piece of paper fluttered out of the hat and zigzagged down onto the floor. She bent to pick it up, and had to blink her eyes into focus through a red fog of fury before she could read it.

"Lucy," it said. "I have some unfinished business to take care of. Hope someday I'll be able to explain. Thanks for everything. Mike."

That was all. *Thanks for everything. Mike.*

She crumpled the note and sat for a long time with it burning in her fist like a lump of red-hot coal, rocking herself slowly back and forth, trying to cry. Wishing to God she could cry. After a while she made herself get up, and went downstairs to the kitchen where Gwen was still putting away groceries. She put the hat on the table and dropped the crumpled-up note beside it.

"Well, that's it," she said with a quick, steadying breath. "He's gone. The . . . bastard is really gone."

"Hmm," said Gwen, eyeing the note thoughtfully. "And he didn't say where he was going?"

"Ha! Nothing. Not a word of explanation. Just something lame about unfinished business. Serves me right, you know that? That's what I get for taking in a—a *drifter!*" She flung her arms out and began to pace, in short bursts with jerky turns. She hurt so badly inside every little movement hurt. But it was better than curling up in a ball, which was all she felt like doing. If she did that she was afraid she might not ever come out of it again.

"Oh, yeah, what do I do? I give him a job, a place to stay, feed and clothe him. Geez," she said, pausing disgustedly, "I even gave him a *toothbrush.* And then, just when he's finally starting to amount to something, what does he do? He goes off and leaves me high and dry." She brought her fist down hard on the tabletop. "How could he do that to me?" Her voice thinned dangerously. "How *could* he?"

"What did he do?" asked Gwen, looking surprised. "You've had hired men quit before. You can always get someone else." Lucy snapped her head around and stared at her aunt as if she'd just dropped through the ceiling. Gwen stared back at her, eyebrows arched. "Can't you?"

Lucy held the stare in silence for as long as she could hold her breath, then let them both go, quivering and tearful at last. "Oh, dammit... dammit."

Gwen watched her for a moment, then said matter-of-factly, "Well, what are you going to do about it?"

"Do?" She grabbed for a paper towel, got three by mistake and used them all to mop up her face and blow her nose. "What can I do?" she muttered angrily into the cascade of crumpled paper. "Nothing, that's what." She hiccuped and added in a wretched, despairing whisper, "You know something? I don't even know his real name."

Gwen suddenly became very busy at the counter, straightening up, wiping off, putting away. "What if you did?" she asked, sounding mildly curious. Lucy just stared at her, a wadded-up towel pressed to her nose. In the same tone of voice, without turning around or stopping what she was doing so energetically, her aunt said, "Would you go after him?"

"Hell, no," declared Lucy stoutly. "Absolutely not. Look, he left—that was his choice. A man's gotta do what a man's gotta do. If he wants me, he knows where to find me. I've got too much self-respect to go chasing off after a man if he doesn't want to stay."

Gwen's voice was light but searching. "So that's it, then? You think he doesn't want to stay."

Lucy stopped pacing and waving her hanky around and stared at her, suddenly feeling confused and lost, like a small child. "Yes. No...I—I don't know. How could he? Dammit, he left, didn't he?"

"So," said Gwen gently, "I guess you must be pretty sure he doesn't have any reason to stay."

"R-reason? Like what?"

"Like *feelings,*" said Gwen with infinite patience. "For you."

"F-feelings for me?"

Gwen sighed. "Love, Lucinda. Does he love you?"

"Well..." She groped for the back of a chair and held on to it. "He never said he did." Oh, but how could she tell Gwen about the way he touched her? All the ways he held her and caressed her and made her feel safe, secure, cherished...and, oh, yes, definitely *loved.* It couldn't all have been a lie, could it? Could she have misunderstood? Or maybe, she thought in sudden, heartsick awareness, it was *he* who'd misunderstood.

"The thing is," she whispered, "I'm not sure...I gave him any reason to think he should."

Gwen turned from the counter at last, her eyes compassionate and wise. "So, I guess you never told him you love him, either."

Lucy whirled away from that steady gaze before her tears could start again, gulping air like a netted fish. "Oh, God, no. How could I? Gwen, he never told me anything. *Any-*

thing. Not who he is, where he came from, what he does..." Again she added the clincher in a hopeless whisper. "Not even his real name."

Her aunt shrugged and said pragmatically, "Well, he probably had his reasons." She paused. "Then, of course, there's the matter of pride."

"Well, I have pride too, dammit!" shouted Lucy.

"How much?" Gwen's voice was soft. "Enough to ruin your whole life?"

Lucy managed to hold it in for a moment or two longer before she sank into the chair, suddenly hurting too much inside to keep up the pretense. "No," she whispered, warm tears pouring down her face faster than she could stanch them with the already soggy towels. "You want to know the truth? I'd go after him in a minute, if I knew... if I knew—but I don't even know where to start. And I don't know if he'll ever come back. Maybe he loves me and maybe he doesn't, but even if he does, he might not think—I don't know if I gave him any reason to think... I know I held back, because... because I didn't want to get hurt. I didn't think I could trust him. I mean, how could I? We know he's got to be some kind of fugitive, who knows what kind of a scoundrel, and, and probably a criminal to boot—"

"Oh, for heaven's sake," said Gwen briskly, drying her hands on a dish towel with an air of finality, as if she'd reached an important decision. "A bit of a scoundrel he may very well be—which isn't such a bad thing, if you ask me—but he's certainly no criminal."

With that she stalked off to the washroom, leaving Lucy staring after her, baffled and sniffling, but with her heart beginning to trip over itself in a mad rush toward hope.

In a moment Gwen was back, and slapped something down on the table at Lucy's elbow. It was a small laminated card, about the size of a driver's license. Lucy thought it even looked a little like a driver's license. It had a picture on it.

She sniffed and said, "What—?"

"Go on, pick it up," said Gwen in a lilting tone, like music. "Take a good look at it."

But Lucy's eyes were blurry. She wiped them and made an effort to focus. "That's Mike," she said, not brilliantly. And then, "But this is—"

"It's a press card, is what it is. I found it in his coat pocket that first morning. You don't think I'd have let you take a possible crook and lowlife under your roof, did you? His name's Mike Lanagan. According to that, he works for *The Chicagoan.* I suspect if you wanted to, that's where you'd find him."

"Oh, my God, a *reporter?*" Lucy felt as if she'd just had the wind knocked out of her—sort of like being hit in the chest with a bowling ball. "You mean he—he was—that son of a—"

"I very much doubt he was here looking for a story," Gwen said mildly, with a trill of her old laughter. "As for what he was doing here, I guess you'd have to ask him that." She paused, then added, "If you wanted to, that is."

"Well, I..." Lucy straightened herself up slowly, still numb and wondering. "You mean you think I should..."

"It's up to you," said Gwen serenely.

"Go to Chicago?" She lifted both hands to comb back her hair with her fingers, then clamped them tightly to her head, feeling as if she'd lose it completely if she didn't hold on to it. "But I couldn't. The chores, the animals! How would you—"

"I'll manage," said Gwen firmly. "I'll give John Andersen a call. He'll be glad to send his boys over. You could leave first thing in the morning."

"Call them right now," said Lucy as she snatched up Mike's hat from the table. "I'll leave tonight." Suddenly adrenaline was coursing through her body. She paused in the doorway with the hat squashed to her chest, riled and breathless and primed for arguments. "There's no sense in waiting around. I'm not going to be able to sleep a wink anyway, so I might as well drive."

But Gwen just looked at her with her eyebrows arching and the smile brackets deepening in her cheeks and didn't say a word.

"A *reporter,*" Lucy exclaimed in a burst of laughter that was perilously close to tears.

She ran up the stairs, but barely felt the floor under her feet. *Mike is a reporter.* Not a crook or a gangster or a criminal—oh, well, she supposed he could still be a lawbreaker of some kind and certainly he could be a scoundrel. But somehow she knew he wasn't. Not the Mike she knew. Not the man she loved. She *knew* it. She knew *him.* With a sense of shock and joy she knew that it was true. In spite of the fact that he'd told her nothing at all about himself, she did know him. Without any knowledge at all of his background, what he did or where he'd come from, she'd fallen in love with him. How incredible. How amazing.

Now all she had to do was find Mike and let him know, and see if she was right about what he'd been trying to tell her with his body and hands in the silent, sultry nights.

An hour later she was on the interstate with the sunset filling up her rearview mirror. She drove all night with Mike's battered brown fedora on the seat beside her, where she could feel the brush of it against her thigh. She drove straight as an arrow toward morning and the sunrise-gilded towers of Chicago.

Lanagan sat in his car drinking black coffee out of a plastic cup and watching the sun come up out of the lake, just like old times. He thought it was weird that in some ways everything seemed exactly the same, and in others it seemed as if he'd been gone for years. As if he'd been whisked away by a spaceship or time machine to live a whole lifetime, growing older and more mature, and then put back in exactly the same place and time from which he'd departed. Everything *was* the same. It was he who'd changed.

He'd had plenty of time to think on the long drive back to Chicago. He didn't know how things were going to turn out, or what was going to happen to him after today, or if he was even going to have much of a future. But he had decided one thing—there wasn't going to be any more hiding. No witness protection program, no new identity, nothing like that. If he did that he wouldn't be able to take Lucy with him. To do that she'd have to give up her farm, and he'd promised himself he wasn't ever going to ask that of her. Never. And he'd definitely decided he wasn't interested in any kind of a future that didn't include Lucy in it. But he couldn't go back to her with this threat hanging over him and risk getting her involved in it—or worse, hurt—either. So there was only one thing to do. Tackle it head-on and see it through to the finish. And when the dust settled he'd either be dead, or... Either way, he'd be free.

He checked the time on the dashboard clock, then swallowed the last of his coffee and drove to a restaurant he knew fairly well, though not one of his favorite haunts. He ordered bacon and eggs and toast and oatmeal. He'd gotten used to a big breakfast; if he went back to a sedentary life-style, he supposed he'd have to make some adjustments in his eating habits. While he waited for the food to arrive he went out to the pay phone in the lobby and punched in his office number.

"Lemme talk to Bunny," he said to the person who answered.

It took some time to convince the suspicious staffer that senior writer Ralph Buncomb really would want to talk to a man who refused to give his name, but finally he heard the familiar early-morning snarl.

"Hi," he said. "It's me, Lanagan." Then he had to hold the receiver away from his ear for a while. "So much for secrecy," he said dryly when the Donald Duck squawks coming out of the phone had diminished somewhat.

"I'm in the fishbowl and the door's shut. Dammit, man, where the hell have you been? I thought you were dead. Hell, the whole world thinks you're dead!"

"I think I was supposed to be," said Lanagan. "I guess you heard."

"Yeah. Hey, I'm sorry about your house. That reminds me. Your insurance company has been trying to get ahold of you. What am I talking about? Don't you know everybody in the world's been trying to get ahold of you? The cops, the mayor's office, the FBI—where in the hell have you been? Are you all right? Where are you? Do you need anything? Shall I—"

"I'm fine. Never mind where, just now. I'm, uh, sort of sniffing the wind, if you know what I mean. You're the first one I've called."

"I see." There was silence on the line. Then, "You haven't seen this morning's edition, have you?"

"No, I haven't."

"Go get one," the reporter growled. "Check it out. Front page. Then call me back. I'll be waiting." The line went dead.

Lanagan hung up and went out to the sidewalk and fed quarters into a rack. *The Chicagoan's* main headline had to do with tornadoes in Mississippi. He took a copy, folded it in half and tucked it under his arm and went back inside, where his breakfast was waiting for him and getting cold in a hurry. He let it get a little colder while he scanned the front page for the article he wanted. Then he ate it while he was reading, and didn't taste a thing.

When he was finished with the article he pushed his plate away, tossed some money down on the table and went out to the lobby telephone. This time when he asked for Bunny he got through right away.

"Well?" Buncomb growled. "Is it true? Have you got 'em?"

"Yeah," said Lanagan. "In my briefcase."

"What're you going to do with 'em?"

"I've got some ideas. Listen, keep a lid on this, okay? I'll be in touch. You know you've got the exclusive."

"Yeah. I understand. Hey, Lanagan?"

"Yeah."

"Watch your step. I've got an idea there isn't much these guys wouldn't do to keep those papers out of the hands of the feds."

"Tell me about it." He hung up the telephone with a growing feeling of elation. For the first time in a long time he could see a way out.

Lucy had been to Chicago a couple of times, but she wasn't at all familiar with the downtown area or the Loop. It was late morning by the time she'd located the *Chicagoan* Tower and figured out where to park, and she'd been honked at quite a bit, so when she walked into the newspaper's main lobby she was in no mood to beat around the bush. She marched straight to the security desk and announced in a clear, carrying voice that she wished to speak to Mike Lanagan.

She didn't miss the little rustle of surprise that began with the guard at the desk and sort of rippled out from there. There were quite a few people in the lobby, tourists and visitors, she thought, strolling around looking into the display cases. Several of them glanced at her. One or two turned to stare.

"I'm sorry, miss," said the guard in a low, rumbling voice. "Mr. Lanagan isn't available at this time."

"I see," said Lucy. She took a deep breath. "When do you expect him?"

The guard cleared his throat and shifted uncomfortably. "Uh, miss, I guess you are not aware that, uh, Mr. Lanagan has been, uh, *away* for quite some time."

"Oh, I know." She brushed that aside impatiently. "But I believe he'll be returning very shortly. When he comes in, will you please tell him that Lucy is trying to get in touch with him?" The guard didn't reply; he appeared dumbstruck. She leaned across the desk and tapped the open register in front of him. "Sir? Did you get that? Please, it's very important. Just tell him *Lucy* was here. He'll know who it is. Tell him..." Oh, dear, what could she tell him? "Tell him he forgot his hat."

"Uh, miss..." The guard put his hands flat on his desk and started to rise. "Miss, wait! Is there a number...?" But Lucy had already turned and was pushing her way blindly through the crowd.

A man bumped into her as she was trying to get out the door. He murmured, "Excuse me," and stood back to let her go first, then followed her to the sidewalk. There she stood in the flowing crowd like a rock in a stream, hollow and trembling, trying to think what to do next.

Desperate impulse had brought her this far, but she'd driven all night and hadn't eaten much on the way, and her mind wasn't working very well. She didn't know what to do. She'd felt so certain she knew where to find Mike; she simply hadn't thought about what she'd do if he wasn't there.

People were bumping into her. The first thing she had to do was get out of the middle of the sidewalk and find someplace quiet where she could think. Yeah, that was it. And get something to eat, too. She looked around, got a good firm grip on her purse and began moving with purpose along with the flow of the crowd.

When she felt someone bump into her, then grab hold of her arms, she thought at first it was just some more of the same sort of jostling. Then she felt herself being propelled rapidly toward the curb, and not by her own will, and she opened her mouth to protest. But before she could get any sound out she was shoved roughly forward and at the same time a hand pushed her head down, and her scream came out in a breathy squawk of surprise that wasn't even heard above the noise of the traffic.

She put out her hands instinctively to break her anticipated fall, but other hands reached for her instead, and she found herself tumbling awkwardly, headfirst, into the back seat of a car. The same hands held her down while someone climbed in after her, breathing heavily. The door slammed. A voice rasped, "Come on, go, go, *go!*"

Good heavens, thought Lucy in utter astonishment. I'm being *kidnapped.*

From an interview on "The Today Show"
NBC news, June 8

Director of FBI operations in Chicago:

"I think people have to realize that these people are both desperate and dangerous. Maybe they wouldn't kill you for the money in your wallet, but let's face it, there's billions of dollars at stake here. So I don't think there's much these guys would stop at, do you?"

Chapter 13

Lanagan spent the morning faxing the contents of his briefcase all over the country—to the governor, the mayor, the D.A., the FBI and, just for good measure, to the newsrooms of the *Chicagoan,* the three major networks and CNN. By the time he was through it was nearly noon and he was hungry again and almost broke. He called the *Chicagoan* again from a pay phone and got Ralph Buncomb.

"Hi," he said, "it's me. I'm ready to come in out of the cold. I need you to work out some details for me."

There was an odd little silence. Then Bunny's voice, sounding even growlier than usual. "Uh, Lanagan. Listen, there's been a development."

"Yeah? What kind of development?"

"You know somebody named Lucy?"

"Lucy!" The name hit him like a fist in the gut. He huffed out air and said, "Yeah, but what—how did you—"

"A call came in for you a little while ago. Said to tell you they have Lucy. That's what he said. They want the papers, Mike. Mike? Are you there?"

The phone had slipped out of his hand. He grabbed for it, swearing, and tucked it in between his ear and shoulder while he wiped his hands on his pants and fought down an urge to throw up. He cleared his throat and said through a truckload of thick gravel, "That's impossible. She's—how—"

"According to the security guard downstairs she was in this morning asking for you. They must have had the place staked out, grabbed her when she left here. Look, Mike, I'm sorry. I told you there wasn't anything they wouldn't do to get their hands—"

"Where've they got her? Did they say? They want the damn papers, so what's the deal? They give you any kind of instructions?"

"Look, Lanagan, I know how you feel, but you can't handle this alone. The police—"

"Where is she, dammit?"

"Mike—"

"Where is she?"

Buncomb hesitated a moment longer but gave him the address, not sounding happy about it. Lanagan repeated it, then shook his head, trying hard to think clearly. "But that's... isn't that the high-rise office building—"

"The one Westside Development put up on the site of that neighborhood project. Right," said Buncomb. He sounded weary and resigned. "The one that got you into this whole mess in the first place. Ironic, huh?"

"Yeah. Geez, they just started that building. They can't have finished already."

"You've been gone quite a while, Mike. Structurally it's finished. They're still working on the inside."

"Where've they got her, Bunny?"

The reporter sighed. "They said to take the construction elevator to the top floor. Bring the papers, and no cops. But look, Lanagan, the FBI—"

"Screw the FBI," snarled Lanagan. "They've got Lucy."

He put the receiver in its cradle and leaned his cold, sweaty forehead against his arm for a moment. He wished to God he had a cigarette. He wished he had his hat. He could see it lying where he'd left it, on his bed, with the note to Lucy in it. *God.*

They had Lucy. And if they harmed one hair of her beautiful head he would kill them himself, with his bare hands. *Slowly.* You could count on it.

The bald-headed man was eating Oreos. He was heavyset and jowly, and his head was shaped like an egg, pointed end up. It looked very shiny, as if it had been polished. He ate the Oreos like a child, unscrewing them first and licking off all the frosting, then popping the cookie part into his mouth, one round half at a time. Lucy watched him, feeling slightly nauseated. She thought that was one good thing about adrenaline, at least; she wasn't hungry anymore. On the other hand she needed to keep her wits about her, and she had an idea it might help her to feel and think better if she had something in her stomach.

"Hey," she said to the bald man, "can I have some of those?"

He hesitated, then shrugged. "Sure, why not?" He leaned over and held out the package.

Lucy took four and said, "Thanks." He shrugged again. His eyes were small and cold. Indifferent.

The other man hung up the phone and leaned back in his chair, tapping his fingers on the table. He was very thin and had long, streaky-blond hair tied back in a ponytail and a whispy beard, and very pretty blue eyes, with long lashes. They reminded her a little bit of Mike's eyes. *Oh, God... Mike.*

"Well, did he bite?" the bald man asked.

The thin one shrugged, as if he didn't much care one way or the other. "I dunno. We'll see."

"So what do we do now?"

"We wait." He took a deck of cards out of the pocket of his shirt and slapped it down on the table.

"Wait for what?" asked Lucy.

The thin man swiveled his head around to look at her. Lucy decided his eyes weren't anything like Mike's, after all. Mike's eyes were interested, intelligent and kind. This man's eyes were flat and cold, like the bald man's. Indifferent.

"For your boyfriend to bring us what we want," he said in a slow, patient drawl.

"I see," said Lucy. "And when he does, you're going to let us both go, right?"

The bald man sort of froze, with an Oreo cookie halfway to his mouth. The thin one smiled and said, "Right."

Right, thought Lucy. When pigs fly. She wasn't stupid. Both of these guys were wearing shoulder holsters with guns in them, the kind of guns that are meant to kill people. She was quite certain they were meant to kill her. And Mike. *Oh, God—Mike.* If he did come with whatever it was he was supposed to bring in exchange for her, neither of them would leave this building alive. She knew it as well as she knew her own name.

Keep your wits about you, Lucinda.

The bald man jerked his head in her direction. "What should we do about her? Think we oughta tie her up?"

The thin one studied her with thoughtfully narrowed eyes. Lucy tried her best to look meek and insignificant; she really didn't care much for the idea of being tied up. "Naw," he said dismissively, "put 'er in the other room."

"You sure? I think we oughta tie her."

"Where's she gonna go? The roof? We're thirty-six floors up, for crissakes! Just lock 'er in. She'll be okay."

The bald guy got to his feet, still munching, and put the cookie package on the table. He took Lucy by the arm and led her over to a door, opened it and stuck his head inside to look around. The thin man picked up Lucy's purse.

"Here, don't forget this." He tossed it to the bald guy, who caught it and sort of shoved it into Lucy's chest, then pushed her through the door.

She didn't bother trying it to see if it was locked. It wouldn't make any difference, with those guys camped on the other side. She wondered if it locked both ways. Probably not.

The first thing she did was go to the window, to see if they'd been right about the thirty-six floors. The view made her a little woozy, so she thought they probably were. In any case, she was too high up for anybody to hear her if she yelled for help. She probably would have tried it anyway, if she could have figured out a way to open the window, but there didn't seem to be one. Plus, since she didn't have any way to bolt the door from the inside, she could count on both Baldy and Ponytail to come charging through it at the first peep out of her. She didn't seriously consider trying to break the window for the same reason. Besides, there wasn't anything to break it with. The room was pretty much bare, except for a few shreds of carpeting and some acoustical ceiling panels stacked against the wall.

She looked up at the ceiling. The metal grid was in place, awaiting the panels; beyond it she could see a shadowy cavern filled with vents and air ducts and electrical conduits. Her heart began to beat faster. She was small. If she could get into one of those ducts, maybe... Maybe she could get to the roof, or to another room, one that wasn't locked. Maybe she could find a way down to the street, where she could get to a phone and call the police. And maybe they'd get here in time to arrest the bad guys before Mike showed up. But what if they didn't? Mike would walk in and the bad guys would kill him and take whatever it was he had that they wanted, and after that it didn't matter what happened to her.

Oh, Mike...

She tilted her head back and closed her eyes, trying to control her runaway heartbeat, trying to quell a desire to curl herself into a terrified, whimpering ball.

Always keep your wits about you, Lucinda.

Okay, she thought, what do I do now? The Indians pretty much have me surrounded. *Grandma Rosewood, what would you do now?*

Great-great Grandmother Lucinda Rosewood... Lucy opened her eyes and stared hard into the ceiling cavern. What Grandma Rosewood had done was set her own barn and fields on fire, and then she'd climbed into the well and hidden there while the fire burned all the way to the river. Lucy raked her hair back with her fingers, then pressed them hard against her head, trying to keep her thoughts under control. *Her own fields...*

Fire. She snatched up her purse with shaking hands and dumped the contents onto the carpet. She needed something...matches. No matches. But, oh, God—*it was*—Mike's cigarette lighter! She remembered the day he'd given it to her. "You never know," he'd said to her then. She didn't remember putting it in her purse, but it didn't matter. Here it was. Now all she had to do was find something to burn. She picked up a scrap of carpeting and held the lighter flame to it, then watched in disgust as it melted and curled and stubbornly refused to ignite. *Damn.* Everything in the place was probably fireproof.

What now? Her thoughts were racing so fast she could hardly keep up with them, running into obstacles one after another, backing up and finding a way around them, like a mouse in a maze. She needed something to burn, something that would make smoke, preferably something that wasn't going to kill her with toxic fumes. Something like paper, or cloth.

Quickly she scooped everything back into her purse except the lighter, which she dropped into the pocket of her suit jacket. Then she marched to the door and knocked on it. The door opened, and Baldy was there glaring down at her.

"Yeah? Whaddaya want?"

"There's absolutely nothing to do in here," she said, trying her best to look sulky and bored. "I was wondering if you guys maybe had a newspaper, or some magazines or something? You know, to read?"

Baldy looked put-upon but turned to snarl over his shoulder at the man with the ponytail, "Hey, we got any magazines?"

Lucy could see him scowling at his cards. "Nah, nothing like that. Tell her to take a nap or something."

"It's chilly in here," she said plaintively. "Don't you have a blanket or a jacket or something?" Her eye fell on the package of Oreos. "And I'm hungry. I haven't had any breakfast or lunch. Can't you at least let me have some more of those cookies?"

The bald guy snorted. "What d'you think this is, day camp?"

"For crissakes, give her the damn cookies!" Ponytail picked up the package and threw it at Baldy, who caught it reflexively. He had his mouth open and looked as if he wanted to argue. Before he had a chance to, Lucy grabbed the cookies out of his hands, murmured a breathless "Thank you" and shut the door in his face. It wasn't much, but it was something.

Alone again in the empty room, she wolfed two more of the cookies and dumped the rest onto the floor. For a moment she held the wrapper in her hands as if it were diamonds. Then she set it carefully aside on the floor while she went through the contents of her purse again. A careful search yielded two tissues, a few gum wrappers, an old grocery list and a gasoline credit card receipt. She tore all the checks out of her checkbook, crumpled them up and added them to the pile. Then she stood up, stepped out of her shoes and began to unbutton her blouse.

She undressed in feverish haste, every nerve in her body quivering, expecting any moment to hear the door open and someone come to check on her. Or worse, sounds—gunshots!—from the other room that would mean Mike had come and it was all for nothing, anyway. But she couldn't think of that possibility. She had to keep her wits about her.

The sprinklers worried her. She knew there was a good chance they'd put out any fire she managed to start before it could produce enough smoke to be seen from outside, but there wasn't much she could do about that. She arranged her meager pile of clothing and paper scraps as far away from the sprinklers as she could, in a corner close to the walls, and propped a couple of the ceiling panels over it like a tent. Other than that, all she could do was hope they hadn't been connected yet.

The rest of the ceiling panels she piled up under the largest duct, except for one she'd saved to close off the opening from the smoke. She figured it was probably going to kill her eventually, but she meant to hold it off as long as possible. Wearing her underpants and bra, she climbed onto the panels and reached up as high as she could stretch. She was still going to have to jump, but she was sure she could make it.

She stepped down off the panels and looked around one last time. This was it. There was nothing more she could do. It might not work at all, this crazy thing she was doing, but what did she have to lose? The fire might actually catch, the smoke might be seen and reported. It might, at the very least, distract the bad guys and give Mike a chance when he walked into their trap. It might very well kill her, in any case. It seemed worth the risk.

She picked up Mike's lighter and felt it grow warm in her hand. Then she took a deep breath and knelt by the pile of odds and ends—her dressy Sunday suit, slip, panty hose, the Oreo cookie package, even her shoes. She flicked the lighter and watched the hungry little flame eat into the cotton fibers of her very best blouse.

Lanagan drove like a crazy man, drunk on adrenaline, breaking every traffic law in the book. When he finally got to the Westside Development Corporation's high rise he thought he was having an attack of déjà vu. Once again the streets were blocked off and filled with fire engines and pandemonium, except that this time it was happening in broad daylight, and police, fire and TV news helicopters were circling overhead like flies. He parked his car in a red zone and ran toward the barricades. People rushed to stop him.

"What happened? What's going on?" he demanded, grabbing at anyone he could reach. His heart was trying to beat a way out of his chest.

"Fire in the high rise," somebody finally told him. "Top floor. From the looks of the smoke they've about got it under control, though. Funny, I didn't even think anybody was in it yet. Hey! Wait, you can't go in there!"

"My God," Lanagan whispered. "Lucy..."

He pushed through the barricade and sprinted for the main entrance to the building, a broken-field run, dodging cops and fire fighters, hoses and equipment. The lobby was full of fire fighters, most of them too busy to pay much attention to him. A couple of them, loaded down with equipment, were just coming out of a door marked Stairs. He put on his very best of-course-I-belong-here look and held the door open for them, then slipped in behind them and loped up the stairs.

It was a long way to the top. If he hadn't had to keep stopping to get out of the way of fire fighters on their way down, and if he hadn't spent the past month getting into pretty fair shape physically, he figured he'd most likely have collapsed and died of a heart attack somewhere around the twenty-fifth floor. He kept expecting, and dreading, to meet EMTs bearing stretchers, but he didn't.

By the time he got to the thirty-sixth floor his chest felt as if it had steel bands wrapped around it. The smell of smoke there was strong and sickening, awakening all sorts of terrible memories. The sense of déjà vu grew more and more vivid as he made his way through a tangle of hoses and construction toward what was probably going to be a pretty classy suite of executive offices eventually, and where the center of greatest activity seemed to be. Cops were swarming all over the place, stepping around and over two guys who were lying facedown on the floor with their hands cuffed behind them. Both of them had on shoulder holsters—empty, of course. They looked disgusted.

Lanagan walked over to where a small knot of men were gathered near the door to an adjoining office. One of them, a plainclothes cop in a rumpled gray suit, seemed vaguely familiar, which he thought was all probably just due to his general sense of having experienced this before. Then the cop looked up and saw him, and his face lit with recognition, first startled, then pleased. He stuck the pen he'd been gesturing with back in his shirt pocket and held out his hand.

"Mike Lanagan. Hey, I thought you were dead."

As he shook hands Lanagan focused on the rawboned wrist extending from the cuff of a sleeve that wasn't quite long enough. He had a sudden flash of memory, of that same wrist and a pale strip of pajama sleeve. "You're the arson cop," he said, enlightened.

"Wilson," the cop confirmed with a grin. "Hey, you know, they've been making bets on you in the squad room."

"Bets?"

"Yeah, you know, which section of the new Beltway construction you'd become a permanent part of, that sort of thing."

"Naw," said Lanagan. "Just took some good advice, that's all. Got out of town for a while."

"Uh-huh." Wilson studied him with narrowed eyes while he got out his pack of cigarettes. He offered Lanagan one, which he had presence of mind enough to decline, then shook one out for himself and stuck it between his lips while he patted his pockets in search of a light. "Can't help wondering what you're doing here, though."

"Me? I was supposed to meet a friend here." Lanagan put his hands in his pockets and strolled casually into the next room. The arson cop followed. Lanagan looked at him. "What happened?" He felt hollow and suspenseful inside. The carpeting was sooty, and squelched underfoot. A fire scar gaped in one corner of the room, blackened and dripping, like an open maw.

"Funny you should ask." Wilson walked over to the charred wall, squatted down beside a little pile of rubble, balanced on the ball of one foot and took his pen out of his shirt pocket. "This friend of yours, the one you were supposed to meet?" He hooked the pen into something in the pile and held it up for Lanagan to see. "Wouldn't be a woman, would it? Wears about a...I'd say a size six-and-a-half shoe?"

Lanagan didn't answer. All his vital signs seemed to have been temporarily suspended while he stared at the shoe dangling from the end of the arson cop's ballpoint pen. It was a sturdy black pump, heat curled and scorched, but all he could see was a pair of red satin sling-backs with spike heels and open toes.

"Funny thing," Wilson was saying. "See, this building is pretty much state-of-the-art for high rises when it comes to fire safety. Sprinklers, fire retardant materials. But the most important thing is, the smoke detectors send an alarm directly to the nearest station. That happens to be right down the street. Now what happened is, with the ceiling open like this, see, the flames shot straight up to the roof and pretty much bypassed the sprinklers' heat sensors at first. But the smoke set off the alarm down at the fire station. So the first unit on the scene busts in here and finds those two guys in the next room, sitting there playing poker, wearing shoulder pieces. Didn't have a clue what was going on in here. Fortunately, since the place was supposed to be unoccupied, the fire department notified us before they came over. So they had uniforms for company. Good thing. Otherwise, I think we'd have some dead or injured firemen on our hands."

"So." Lanagan cleared his throat. He could feel the smoke and flames all the way to his lungs. "You're saying those guys didn't start this? Then who did?" *And where is she?*

"That's what's funny," said Wilson, shaking his head. He stubbed out his cigarette in the wet carpet. "Whoever set it did so and then vanished into thin air. Gone. Kaput." He fished something else out of the rubble and held it out on his palm for Lanagan to see. "Here's what she lit it with."

Air whooshed out of Lanagan's lungs. He reached for the lighter, swearing without any sound.

Wilson said softly, "Recognize it?"

Lanagan nodded. His mind and body had both gone numb. "It's mine." *Please, Lucy. Where are you?*

He couldn't feel his legs, but somehow he was moving, away from Wilson and the scorched wall and the pitiful pile of burned clothing, out into the middle of the room. His mind was racing ineffectively, like a motor in neutral. He saw the neat stack of ceiling panels, but it didn't seem significant to him at first. Just a tidy little anomaly in the midst of all that chaos. But he kept staring at it anyway, frowning, with the cigarette lighter growing warm in his hand. Something was tugging at his memory.

Great-grandmother Lucinda Rosewood... He could hear Lucy's voice, far-off and dreamy, as if she were reciting poetry from memory. *Set fire to her own barn and fields, and then....*

Climbed down the well.

Suddenly he knew. "Shut up," he said harshly, although Wilson hadn't said a word. *"Listen."*

He stared up into the ceiling cavern, listening with every nerve and cell in his body. All around him were the soft drips and snaps and cracklings of things cooling and settling. "Lucy," he called softly, and listened again. Once more his heart and breath seemed to cease. Oh, God, there'd been smoke, probably fumes. *What if—*

Then he heard it—the most beautiful sound, the faintest of scuffles. It seemed to be coming from the largest air duct. He stared at it in disbelief. She couldn't be. It seemed so *small.*

His heart began to beat again, faster and faster, stumbling and tripping like a child running down a hill. "Lucinda Rosewood Brown," he called loudly to the ceiling, with the beginnings of laughter, "you can come out now. The Indians have gone."

There was a suspenseful pause. The panel covering the air duct's opening quivered a little, then scraped open a bit...then farther. He saw Lucy's beautiful pointed chin and dust-streaked face, her beautiful Rosewood nose, wearing a smoky mustache.

"No, I can't," she said in her beautiful rusty-nail rasp of a voice.

"Why not?" asked Lanagan, shaken and husky.

"Make *him* go away first."

He glanced at Wilson, who had come unnoticed to his side. The arson cop cleared his throat and said gruffly, "Oh." He took off his jacket and handed it to Lanagan, jerking his head toward the pile of burned clothes in the corner. "Here, I think she's gonna need this."

He went out and the door closed gently after him, muting the voices of the cops and firemen, the sounds of mopping up. In the quiet, Lanagan looked up at the ceiling and said in a soft, wondering tone, "Lucy? Just tell me one thing. How in the world did you manage to get in there feetfirst?"

"You *would* ask that—you're a *man,*" said Lucy, grunting with effort. "I couldn't...pull myself up, so I...had to...swing my feet up and wiggle in...backward." Her arms and shoulders emerged from the hole. She glared down at him, resembling nothing so much as a singed owl. "I didn't stop to think about how I was going to get *out.*" She paused to survey the situation. "I think you're going to have to catch me."

"Don't worry, I'll catch you."

"Promise?" More of her body had come into view.

Lanagan caught his breath. "Always. You can count on it." A few thrilling, breathtaking moments later he had her in his arms. He wondered if he'd ever be able to let go of her again.

"Ouch, that hurt," she complained. "I had to use my bra to cover my nose, because of the smoke."

The image that remark evoked was finally too much for Lanagan. Holding her close, he smothered helpless laughter in her smoky hair, and after a moment she began to laugh, too. He thought of the other times they'd laughed together like that—the first day he'd met her, when the sow chased them over the fence; the first time they'd made love.

Dazed with emotion, he said, "Lucy, what in the world are you doing here? I thought I left you safe—"

"You *left* me," she said, suddenly fierce and pounding his chest with her fists. "I had something important to tell you, and you left before I got a chance. I mean, you can leave if you want to, but before you go I just thought you ought to know—"

"That you love me. I know," said Lanagan with a sigh. If he hadn't known it before, he certainly did now. When he thought how near she'd come to sacrificing her life for him...

"Well?" She pulled away from him, bristly and vulnerable. "That requires some sort of response. Either you do or you don't. Either way, I think you should at least tell—"

The response he gave her was wordless and unequivocal. After a long time he said brokenly, "I left for the same reason you did—because I wanted to tell you. And I couldn't until I'd...fixed some things."

Once again she drew back, but not too far, leaving her hands resting on his chest as if she needed the reassurance of touch, and studied him somberly. "Yeah, well, you'd better tell me about those things, I think. Those people out there were going to kill you."

"I think that's all over now," said Lanagan slowly, with growing wonder at the realization that it was true. The bad guys didn't want him, just the documents in his briefcase. And now that he'd made those very, very public, he couldn't think of any reason for anybody to want him dead, if you didn't count revenge. He didn't think he'd even have to testify. He simply didn't know anything that wasn't right there in black and white, in those papers. It really was over, at least for him.

"Then we can go home?"

There was so much in that question, so much meaning in those particular words, *we* and *home*. He studied her gravely, watching the rosy-pink wash under her skin, knowing it had very little to do with the fact that she was standing before him in nothing but her underpants.

"Yes," he said softly. "We'll go home. Soon." He tried to smile, but the tenderness inside him was too close to the surface; his crusty masculine exterior felt fragile as eggshells. So he coughed and touched her cheeks with his fingertips, frowning as he awkwardly rubbed at her smoky mustache with his thumb. "I, uh, have some things to tie up first. And in the meantime, you're going to see a doctor, just to be sure."

She protested that, as he'd known she would, insisting that she was perfectly fine, and that she hated doctors, and furthermore, if he thought she was going to let him out of her sight when there were people with guns out to kill him, he had another think coming. But there was a certain breathlessness in her voice and a shine in her eyes that told him she'd probably go to the moon on a dogsled if he asked her to. He felt awed and humbled by the miracle of it—the fact that she loved him—and silently vowed to spend the rest of his life trying to make himself worthy of her.

"I'm hungry," she said suddenly.

He laughed and murmured huskily, "I'll feed you."

But she went on standing there facing him with her palms melting into his shirtfront as if they'd become a part of him, as if she was afraid to move for fear of breaking that contact. He knew exactly how she felt.

"Are you really a reporter?" she whispered.

"Well, sort of." He sighed. "I have a lot to tell you."

She nodded. "Explanations."

"It'll take a while."

"Okay. Food first, then explanations."

"Aren't you forgetting something?" asked Lanagan with a smile. For a moment she looked puzzled. Then, following his gaze, she looked down at herself and he saw a lovely rose blush wash beneath her skin—the fairest parts, where the sun never touched her. She gave a soft gasp, and her nipples drew into buds as he watched. His body stirred and tightened. He ached with the urge to kiss them soft again. "I think I'd better get you some clothes," he said thickly, "or I won't be responsible for the consequences."

"I'm sure Grandma Rosewood never had this problem," Lucy said grumpily through chattering teeth as she stood docilely and let Mike pull the arson cop's jacket around her shoulders. "She had all her clothes on when they pulled her out of that well."

"Pity," he murmured absently, frowning down at his fingers, which were manipulating the buttons with unaccustomed clumsiness. "From that picture I saw of her, it's pretty hard to imagine her any other way."

Lucy smiled to herself, feeling the pulsing heat and tremors of repressed desire that were coursing through his body, and reveling in a new sense of power, one that was wholly and completely feminine.

"I wouldn't be too sure of that," she said demurely. "Don't forget, she also had a baby tied up in her apron."

She laughed out loud at the look on Mike's face.

"Promise me one thing, Cage," said Lucy as they were going down the stairs together, hand in hand.

"Anything," he said fervently.

"No red dresses."

He paused as if he was thinking it over. Just about the time Lucy was ready to punch him, he smiled and put his arm around her shoulders and drew her close against his side. "Actually," he said, "I was trying to think of a place that would sell overalls."

The Chicagoan, June 9 Front Page Missing Columnist Alive!
Police Arrest Two In WDC Scandal
by Ralph Buncomb, staff writer

CHICAGO—Two men were in custody Wednesday and warrants have been issued for an unspecified number of other suspects in what authorities are describing today as "a major break" in the Westside Development Corporation investigation.

The two men were arrested after police and fire fighters responded to an automatic alarm in the WDC building, which is still under construction. They found the two men, both of whom are known associates of a local crime syndicate, holding a hostage in an office on the top floor of the building, apparently in an attempt to force *Chicagoan* columnist Mike Lanagan to hand over certain incriminating documents believed to be in his possession.

In the meantime, however, in a bizarre conclusion to what has been a complex and puzzling case, copies of the missing documents had begun arriving yesterday afternoon at FBI headquarters in Chicago, the Chicago Police Department and the mayor's office, as well as the newsroom of *The Chicagoan.* Shortly thereafter, Lanagan himself contacted friends at *The Chicagoan* to report that he was alive and well, and that as soon as authorities had acted on the information recently made available to them, he would be ready to make his whereabouts known. (See related story.)

Details of the hostage situation and fire in the WDC building were not available at press time, but according to arson investigator Chuck Wilson, the hostage, who remains unidentified, evidently managed to elude her captors and set the fire which summoned help.

"I'll tell you this, though," said Wilson. "She's quite a lady. Not very many people would be able to keep their wits about them in a situation like that."

The two men arrested in the high rise are charged with kidnapping, extortion and conspiracy, and are being held without bail.

The Chicagoan, June 11

"This Is My Country" by Mike Lanagan

Hello, Chicago, I'm back.

A lot's happened since the last time my words of wisdom appeared in these pages.

I've been through some fire, and that's changed my perspective a bit, as I think a crucible is supposed to do.

First I lost everything I had in the world. Then I found it again. Or her, actually. Her name is Lucy.

Her full name is Lucinda Rosewood Brown. She's named after her great-great—I don't know how many greats—grandmother, who they say foiled a Sioux raiding party when she set fire to her own barn and fields, then tied up her baby in her apron and climbed down the well and hid there while the fire burned all the way to the river.

What Lucy did was set fire to a high rise and save my life. I intend to spend the rest of my life making sure she doesn't regret what she did.

You might have noticed that the title above this space is different. That's because I also found out there's a whole different world out there. From now on I'm going to be writing to you from and about that world from time to time, because we all need to believe in a place where the sky's still blue and the cornfields stretch all the way to the horizon and people aren't afraid to open their doors and hearts to a storm-tossed stranger.

Don't get me wrong, though. I still love Chicago. It's still my kind of town, and I've got a brand-new apartment right on the shore, where I can see the sun come up across the lake.

Oh, and one more thing. I'm still going to be going after the bullies whenever I see some little guy who needs my help.

You can count on it.

The Aftermath

Lucy stood at the window, hugging herself and watching lightning dance gleefully across the horizon.

Mike called to her softly. "Lucy, love, come to bed. Watching won't keep it away."

Tense and breathless, fluttery inside, she said, "I know. I was just . . . thinking about Gwen. Do you think she's—"

"She's fine. She knows better than to drive home in this. She'll probably just stay at the Andersens' until it's over."

She heard the bed creak, the soft pad of Mike's bare feet on the hardwood floor. She felt his solid presence behind her, his hands warm and heavy on her shoulders. Outside the thunder grumbled, and she shivered.

"Hey," he murmured, pulling her back against him, "it's a storm. You can't stop it or control it. Let it go." His strong arms crisscrossed her breasts. She sighed and closed her eyes, nestling her head beneath his chin. Her body felt tense and needy.

"Let it go." He turned her to face him, and she lifted her arms thankfully to his neck, breathing in his warm, musky

scent, trembling a little in anticipation of his body's sweet security. But instead he caught her wrists and held them, denying her the closeness she sought. "No," he said hoarsely. "Not tonight."

"I need you," she whispered, frightened and bewildered.

"Lucy, sweetheart . . ." His lips brushed the backs of her fingers. One hand lay warm along her jaw while his fingers stroked the hair behind her ear. "I don't ever want you to need me. Just want me, that's all." He kissed her then, his lips firm and gentle as always, his tongue a tender intrusion. She opened to him with a relieved, hungry chuckle, not really understanding.

His hands rested briefly on her hips, then swept upward under her T-shirt to cover her breasts. Nested in his warm palms her nipples grew tender and vulnerable. When he suddenly roughened his touch and chafed them instead, her nipples shivered to hard, tight buds. She uttered a small gasp of surprise.

His reply was a sound low in his throat, a sound she'd never heard from him before, a sound of pure masculine pleasure and triumph. It roused strange contradictory responses in her, both anticipation and apprehension. Excitement and fear.

He turned his head slightly; his mouth moved over hers, finding a new, more dominating angle. She rose instinctively to the challenge, thrusting upward against the hard, demanding pressure of his mouth, pushing her breasts into his hands with silent demands of her own. His tongue took possession of hers, probing deep and then deeper in primitive rhythms until she felt as if it must touch the very center of her being. Sensation crackled like lightning along every nerve in her body. Her knees buckled.

"Oh, boy," she gasped as she gripped his arms and pressed her forehead against his chest. "Okay, I want you.

Boy, *do* I!" His chuckle as he lifted her into his arms was deep-throated and pleased.

Lightning flashed and flickered through the darkened bedroom. A crack of thunder shook the house like a blow from a brutal fist, and Lucy cowered in instant response. But before she could utter so much as a whimper, Mike gave another primal growl and brought his mouth down on hers again, his tongue demanding, penetrating deeply as before, his body hot, his heartbeat rapid and urgent, as if he meant to drive the storm, and everything else in the world but him, from her mind.

She didn't know he was carrying her until she felt the mattress come up to meet her back. She reached blindly for him then, but again he captured her hands and held them, refusing to give her what she asked for.

"No," he said in a hoarse whisper. "Let it go. Understand? Let it all go. It's *all right* to let go."

The storm slammed into the house like cannon fire. Demon light flickered across the walls; thunder was continuous, a violent, deafening barrage; rain spattered like buckshot against the windowpanes. Lucy whimpered a little, but more in confusion and frustration than fear. She felt as if the storm had come inside her. She felt sultry and hot; electricity skated beneath her skin; her pulse pounded in her ears like thunder.

"I can't," she whimpered, shivering. "I don't want to. I'm afraid I'll—I'm afraid of losing—"

"You're...not...going...to lose anything." Mike's voice was a harsh rasp, his lips the softest brush across her skin. "I want you to relinquish it, sweetheart. Give it to me. Please, Lucy, love me enough, *trust* me enough to do that. Will you?"

She drew a long, trembling breath and held it. Unable to speak, she finally nodded. She felt his breath pour like melted honey over her throat, her breasts. But although she tried to make her body relax and go warm and pliant in his hands, she couldn't. She *couldn't.* I won't be able to stand it, she thought. It's too much. He doesn't know...

She's so intense, he thought. Everything she feels is so much *more.* He'd asked for her trust, but now that she'd given it to him he was afraid he wouldn't be able to hold himself together, much less her. "It's all right. Relax," he murmured, more for himself than for Lucy.

He lowered his mouth to the sensitive hollow where her neck and shoulder came together and laved the silky skin there with his tongue. He sucked gently at first, then more and more strongly, until she gasped, and he knew he'd marked her. Then he swept his hot, open mouth down across her chest and closed it over one tender, budded nipple and sucked that instead. Her captive hands jerked in his grasp. She arched slightly, beginning to squirm a little, and her legs drew together in instinctive defense of her body's most vulnerable places. But he swept his hand down over her taut belly and trembling thighs, then stroked up again along the inside of her legs, spreading them apart until that which she sought to protect lay all open to him. His callused fingertips pushed into her warm, damp hair in an invasion that was both tender and ruthless.

The sound she made when he touched her most sensitive place was indescribable, a raw, throat-rending cry of primal passion and need that exploded through his senses and threatened to shatter his own precarious self-control. He pulled his mouth from her breast and pressed his nose and lips softly against her heaving belly, breathing deeply of her sweet, sunshine scent, his neck and jaw muscles rigid with the effort it took to pull himself back from the edge. And then, holding her legs open and pinned beneath his, he began to stroke her, sometimes light and feathery, circling...now almost roughly, rubbing...penetrating her with one strong finger, then withdrawing...then again, deeper this time, and still deeper, while she panted and cried, and her body arched and quivered like a tightly drawn bowstring.

When he felt her legs open wider of their own volition he let go of her hands, knowing she was beyond fighting him. He moved his mouth lower on her belly, brushed his lips lightly over the fluttering muscles and silky curls, and finally, holding her fully open with both of his hands, closed his mouth over the sensitive, throbbing center of her femininity. He felt her hands in his hair, first pushing him frantically, then suddenly tangling, holding on with equal desperation. He began a hot, inexorable pressure, drawing her oh, so gently into his mouth, laving and probing her softness with his tongue...circling and suckling. Her pants became whimpers, then high, panic-stricken cries. He grabbed her buttocks and lifted her, sucking more strongly, probing more deeply. She clutched at his shoulders and arched backward, and her cry was swallowed up in the thunder.

He held her tightly, encouraging the spiraling spasms, nursing the terrible throbbing in the comforting heat of his mouth. But as soon as he felt the coils of tension in her muscles begin to ease, as soon as he felt the heat and pressure seep from her body like a slowly receding wave, he began it again—the sucking and stroking, the delicate probings and tender penetrations. At first she whimpered a protest and pushed ineffectively at his shoulders, but in seconds the whimpers had become pants, and her body was taut and her skin fiery to the touch.

This time, when he knew she was once more beyond fighting him, he suddenly, roughly turned her into the position he knew must be the ultimate in vulnerability for a woman. She settled onto her stomach with a sigh, liquid and pliant in his hands, and, turning her face into the pillows, raised her shoulders slightly so that her hair slithered forward and the vital nape of her neck was arched and exposed to him—the ultimate act of submission and trust. Tenderness flooded him.

There was so much love and gratitude for her inside him he thought he must explode. Outside the storm was raging in full fury, but it was nothing—*nothing*—to what was happening inside him.

Aching, bursting, he leaned over her and took what she gave him, closing his mouth over her sweet, fragile nape with exquisite and unwonted care. At the same time he reached under her and found her heated, sensitive, throbbing places. He penetrated her again with a fingertip, then two, deeper, deeper, searching for the very center of her being, while she panted and whimpered, and ground her buttocks against his belly. By the time he'd brought her once more to the brink he knew he'd reached the limits of his own control, so he turned her again and reached to open the nightstand drawer.

He felt Lucy's small, strong fingers close around his wrist. "No," she gasped, shaky but certain. "Not this time. I want you, just you. Please."

"Lucy, are you sure?" His voice was husky; he felt slightly dazed. His insides quivered with the full and complete awareness of what she was asking.

She nodded and lifted her arms around his neck, pulling him down to her as she raised herself to meet him. She gasped when he pushed into her swollen, sensitized body, but it was a gasp of pure pleasure. Joyously she wrapped her legs around him and held him close, refusing even to let him support a part of his weight on his elbows. "I *love* you," she whispered fiercely.

And on that pronouncement the storm within him finally broke. His body bucked and surged, and emptied. It was his turn to relinquish control at last. With a hoarse, guttural cry Lanagan gave it up into his wife's capable, loving hands.

"I don't think we'd better try that when Gwen's home," she mumbled, slurred and sleepy in the aftermath. Pure Lucy.

He laughed softly and cuddled her close, kissing the damp hair on her temple and listening to the grumble of dying thunder. He watched light play in changing patterns across the walls of their bedroom—warm, yellow light, car lights, not lightning.

"I think she's home," he whispered to the top of Lucy's head.

But she was already asleep, gently snoring, while the rain dripped softly from the eaves of the old farmhouse.

The Chicagoan, March 23

"This Is My Country" by Mike Lanagan

Open letter to a newcomer:

Hello, Rose. Welcome to the world.

You don't know me very well yet, but I know you. I've been talking to you for several months now—which Lucy, your mother, says is sure proof I'm crazy. That's okay. She's a very special lady, your mother. I'll tell you more about her someday. All about how she set fire to a high rise and saved your daddy's life, which of course also made it possible for you to be born.

I hope you take after your mother. I hope you have her beautiful pointy chin and sparkly brown eyes and a smile that splits your face in two. We already know you have her voice, and we're pretty sure you have her nose, the Rosewood nose. That's something else I'll tell you about someday. It's too soon to tell if you have her courage. I hope you have her orneriness and independent spirit—but not until you get to be about twenty-one.

Because, see, there's something you should know about me, right from the start. I'm your dad. And although this is a pretty wonderful world you've come to, it can be scary and dangerous, too, sometimes. My job is to do my very best to make this world a better, safer, happier place, so you, and all the other little ones like you, don't ever have to know what it is to be cold, or hungry, or scared. But sweetheart, I know that, no matter how hard I try to change things, the world is always going to have its thugs and bullies and bad guys.

That's why I'm making this promise to you, Rose Ellen Lanagan. For as long as I live I'll always be here for you, to protect and defend you from the bullies of this world. Even when you'd probably rather I didn't.

You can count on it.

* * * * *